T0207697

PRUETT'S SECRET

OTIS MORPHEW

Order this book online at www.trafford.com
or email orders@trafford.com

Most Trafford titles are also available at major online book retailers.

Print information available on the last page.

ISBN: 978-1-6987-0212-4 (sc)
ISBN: 978-1-6987-0211-7 (e)

Trafford rev. 06/29/2020

www.trafford.com

North America & international
toll-free: 1 888 232 4444 (USA & Canada)
fax: 812 355 4082

PROLOGUE

UFO, a natural phenomenon, some will explain. But if so, they have been seen by countless millions throughout history. Christopher Columbus logged one in 1492. Prehistory shows proof of alien visits in pictographs, stone carvings, statuettes and paintings depicting actual visitations by star-people, aliens that were believed to be responsible for modern technologies.

But, as it may be, In America in the late eighteen hundreds, unless one was a professor of science, renowned explorer or researcher, a UFO sighting in the night sky was not thought to be more than a shooting star or meteor, otherwise not thought about at all. In those times, those lucky enough to have attended school knew of the sun's orbiting planets, but none knew, or even thought there might actually be other worlds in space,...and most did not care, because surviving in a world of hardship and hard work took precedence over everything else. Thus, leaving the stars to be nothing but brilliant lights in the sky to be admired and wondered about.

Maxwell Pruett was one of these. A few dozen weeks of schooling taught him about the earth, stars, and its sister planets. But now, as an adult rancher with a family, only wanted to be left alone to raise that family and work his cattle. It was not meant to be, however, because the night he witnessed his phenomenon would change his life forever, and that of his family,...and would become the biggest secret a man was ever sworn to keep!

A newspaper in the Rocky Mountains of central Colorado, unless one lived in Golden, or in Denver, was a rarity,...and one that Max Pruett did not put much stock in anyway. Therefore, he would never have known of UFO sightings occurring anywhere in the country, would have thought them a tall tale if he had, not knowing the meaning of the word!

But all that was before, and now, Maxwell Pruett has a Secret, one so unbelievable that he was afraid to tell anyone about it,...would not have told anyone had he not made the promise. He had read the Bible, read it from cover to cover, mostly by candle and firelight. Although there were many passages in the good book he did not understand, passages that could have spoke of life elsewhere, he could not read between the lines. But in a whole, he could not believe that it did. All he did know, was that he had a secret, one that he must keep, and if he did not, one that could change the Bible from what it was, to just being another book,…and even he was educated enough to know what might happen if this sort of thing was known.

You be the judge, because this is Pruett's Secret!

CHAPTER ONE

Having finished range-branding the two calves, Lance Pruett loosed the last one back to the protection of it's mother while his father scattered the fire and poured water on the embers then coiled his rope to hang it back in place on his saddle.

"Got to be more calves out there, Pop. I spotted forty head or so up two mile canyon last week....Want a head over that way tomorrow?"

"Yeah, we can do that." Returned Pruett absently, then sighing. "Better bring 'em all in closer to th' barn, too,...be easier now, than when th' weather turns."

"Think it'll be early?" He asked, still watching his father.

"Thirty days, maybe....It'll get colder'n hell before it snows, though."

Nodding, Lance watched him hang the canteen back on the saddle-horn. "Is that it, Pop, ready to pack it in?"

"Good idea." He said, turning to look westward at the once tall, red and blue clay bluff that from there was almost hidden in the forest of giant, towering Sequoia Pines. "Put th' tools away, will ya, son?" He mounted his horse and crossed the running water of Carbon Creek then continued through the waist-high prairie grass toward the bluff, leaving young Lance shaking his head as he picked up the branding iron and stowed it away. He watched his father for a moment then sighing, mounted his horse and followed him, and looking at the sun as he crossed the creek, knew it would not be long until dusk and hoped that today his father would break tradition and they could make it home before midnight.

Max Pruett was already sitting his horse amid the tall grass of the rock-strewn meadow when his son walked his mount in beside him, and there to sit and watch the older Pruett as he sat his saddle and gazed at the once very tall bluff, seemingly unaware that a frustrated and highly curious Lance was there watching him,...and this time with more than a little concern on his face.

This was not the first time he had sat and watched his father's fascination with that area of the bluff, and though he didn't understand it, had never questioned it before. But he was older now, and after several dozen trips to the site without explanation, had slowly become concerned thinking that either his father was ill, or that something had happened here that his father wouldn't talk about,...and he wanted desperately to know what it was. He had wanted to ask him about it for a long time,...and all he needed was the nerve to do it!

Max grunted then as he shifted his weight in the saddle, and though he didn't show it, was seemingly surprised when he saw Lance beside him. "Hard to believe this old bluff used to be two hundred feet tall, son." He shifted his sore backside again and reached tobacco and paper from his shirt and with Lance watching, deftly rolled and lit his smoke. "You never seen this valley here ten years ago,...this old bluff really set it off."

"No sir, but it looked like this eight years ago, I saw it then...So why do you tell me that every time we come up here."

Max turned to peer at him. "Do I?...Sorry, son, I didn't realize that."

"Don't you think it's about time you told me about it, Pop?" There, he thought, his nerves suddenly overwhelming him. 'I finally did it!' He could see the surprise on his father's face at the question and decided to run with it. "I think you want to, Pop....I know that something happened up here,... so tell me what it was."

Pruett stared blankly at him for a few seconds before shaking his head. "First, you better tell me what you're talkin' about,...what do I want a tell ya?"

"This!" He gestured at the bluff as he spoke. "All this!...What's with you and this place, Daddy?" He breathed deeply of the crisp, pine-scented mountain air and watched his father's probing eyes and frowning expression. "Tell me, Daddy, did something happen up here that upset you?

"Boy, for th' life a me, I don't know what you're talkjin' about!"

"Awww, Pop!" He breathed deeply again. "Okay,...we been coming up here to this same spot for more times than I can remember,...and every time, we stop right here while you stare at that crumbling old bluff. I know that something happened up here that you won't talk about!...What was it, Daddy?...You keep it bottled up too long it's gonna make you sick or somethin'....I think Mama's a little worried about you, too, I see her watchin' you a lot."

Pruett turned to stare at the bluff again, and finally sighed loudly. "Okay, son,...since you're so sure somethin' happened up here, you tell me?"

"Come on, Daddy, you're beating around th' bush. I know you!...This is the only place on the ranch that effects you this way, and it's far from the prettiest spot on th' ranch,...and believe it or not, Daddy, I ain't stupid!"

"Now, what made you say that, Lance? I know very well you ain't stupid!"

"Okay, Pop,...you're tellin' me nothin' happened up here, right?"

Maxwell peered at him for a moment and then. "I think I said that, yeah."

"Then tell me who's buried over yonder?" And when the older man's eyes widened. "Yes sir, I know about that!...I work this ranch, too, a lot a times on my own,...and I've been up here on my own, and I know a grave when I see one!"

Max seemed to wilt some in the saddle, whether from relief or something else, Lance didn't know. He did know that he had hit on the truth, and was almost sorry that he had.

Max peered at him narrowly for a moment longer and then sighed heavily again before nodding his head in submission. "You're right, son, somethin' did happen here, a long time ago. I just don't know if I should tell you about it....I promised I wouldn't!"

"Promised who, Daddy?"

"The man in that grave yonder....I only knew 'im for a few days, Lance, but we was friends, I guess, best friends!" He dropped his head to his chest and sighed before looking up again. "I must a wondered a hundred times what might a come of it all if he hadn't died?...He would a taken to you right off, I'll tell ya that!...Aw, hell, I guess you're right, son. Truth is, I don't think I can keep it to myself any more. Ain't had a good night's sleep in ten years,...too many nightmares and monsters." He looked back at the bluff then and chuckled.

"I tried to tell your mother about it five or six years ago,...she thought I was spinnin' a yarn, so I never tried again....Thing is, I would a proved it to her if she'd only heard me out. I'll tell ya one thing though,...if that man over there had ever met you, or her, he'd never a made me keep a promise like that!" He looked around the area of the bluff again and gestured with his hand. "You ain't talked about none a this to any of your friends, have ya,...you know, about me and this place?"

"Pruett business, is Pruett business, Pop!"

"Yes it is!" He nodded. "Tell me somethin', Son....Do you believe that a man can fly?" He looked at Lance as he spoke. "I'm serious here,...in all your wildest dreams, did you ever think a man might be able to fly?"

"I've imagined it, Pop, yeah. Imagined myself flyin' like a bird. I even saw a picture once where several men was in a basket and was lifted in the air by a giant balloon of some kind."

"That ain't flyin', son."

"Like you always said, Pop,...if a man was meant to fly, God would have given us wings....Nope, a man can't fly."

"What about a machine, one a man could sit down in and fly away?"

"Far as I know, there ain't one a them been invented yet, either."

"Exactly my point!...I never thought it was possible neither, hell, I never thought about it at all!...Not till ten years ago." He shifted in the saddle again. "Man in that grave there could. His name was Korak, and he had a machine that could fly, rode in th' thing big as you please. I never heard tell a such! True though, I seen it." He shifted again in the squeaking leather and dismounted with a grunt to stand and peer up at the brilliant twinkling of the coming night.

Lance was still not convinced that his father was really himself, and quickly dismounted to come around Max's horse. "Are you really okay, Daddy?"

"You don't believe me either, do ya, son?"

"Course, I believe you, Pop, at least I want to!...It's just that, well, none a what you said could possibly happen. Nobody knows how to even build something like that, let alone make it fly!"

"It's okay,...your thinkin' now, was my thinkin' ten years ago. But I'm gonna tell you about it anyway, and when I'm done, you can come to your own conclusions. I'm gonna tell you because I'm tired a keepin' th' secret, that, and because it could be useful some day."

"Pop, whatever my way of thinkin' is, or might be,...I know you don't lie, so go ahead, tell me more about Korak, what was his last name?"

"Weren't none, just Korak,...and here I am, right here in front a th' all mighty Creator,...in the most natural Church there is!...And I'm tellin' you straight out, that what I'm gonna tell you tonight is the God-honest truth!... All true, Lance, all of it! I was here, I know,...and at times, I still can't believe it really happened! But, Son, it did!...That's why I come up here so much, to make sure I didn't dream it all. Now come on, let's make camp, it's a long story, and I told your mother we might stay out." He began gathering wood for the fire as he spoke.

"I have to warn you though," He said, straightening to look at him.... "You can never tell anybody about it."

"They likely wouldn't believe me anyway, Pop."

"All it would take is one, Lance. Start a rumor, true or not, and it'll spread. It could change everything, too!"

"I'm a Pruett, Pop, I'll never tell."

"I know you won't." He dropped the dead wood in a pile between some rocks. "Wouldn't tell ya, I thought otherwise."

"Way you're talkin', though,…it must a been pretty bad?"

"Not so bad now, as it was then. It's what happened that was bad, worse than bad,…fifty good people brutally lost their lives, and most was acquaintances of mine!...No tellin' how much livestock?"

Heyy!" Exclaimed Lance excitedly. "I remember all that now, you made me and mama stay in town for two weeks….Th' Werewolf, right?"

"You remember all that bullshit?"

"Sure I do!...It was a big uproar in town when everybody heard about th' murders, scared me and mama to death! Yeah, it was about a week after you left us to go help that lawman catch a killer! I remember because we were eatin' supper when we heard th' yelling…Wasn't long before somebody began yellin' werewolf! That's all anybody talked about after that." He grinned at the astonished look on his father's face. "It was even in the newspaper, Pop, mama saved it for ya, remember?"

"I remember." He chuckled, shaking his head.

"Come on, Daddy, I was seven!...It sure sounded like the work of a werewolf to me, especially after I heard tell what a werewolf was,…full moon, wolf-man. I couldn't even sleep, and I know mama didn't from worryin' about you!"

"I know, I could see it in her eyes and face when I came for ya. She never mentioned it though, relief at seein' me, I guess. She did ask me if we caught th' Killer though….Your mother is some kind a woman, son."

He smiled, and nodding,…"Yes'ir, I know."

"I sure never thought you knew, boy, you never said much, that I recall."

"Like I said, I was seven, Pop. Priorities, I guess."

"I never meant for either one of ya to know, not ever." He nodded and chuckled again. "I read that werewolf story….You do know there ain't no such thing, don't ya, never was, never will be….Myths and legends been a lot a folks downfall."

"It was true though, right, about those people bein' killed?...That was the fifty murders you referred to, right?"

"It was true all right, I still dream about it!...I wondered many times why Korak made me swear never to tell anybody about 'im. But I think it had somethin' to do with your werewolf, myths and legends and th' like."

"How?"

"Cause folks will believe th' worst about anything they don't understand, and when they don't understand somethin', they give it a name, like your werewolf. They talk it up long enough, they cause a panic and pretty soon you got neighbors accusin' neighbors….That's how a feud starts….If folks should ever find out th' truth of all this, the good book won't mean a thing anymore. It would turn religion up on its heels, pretty much make every word in it a lie."

"How, Pop?"

"Think about it!...Th' shape th' world's in now, war, famine, folks killin' each other in th' streets, distrust, hatred?...But through it all, the one thing, the only thing holdin' us all together in whatever balance there is left, is our book of moral rules, the Holy Bible!...Destroy that, we destroy ourselves!...We have laws now, and mostly good men to enforce 'em,…and it's a dangerous, hard row to hoe. We'll never put an end to it, as it is now,… but without religion?" He shook his head and shrugged.

"I get it, Daddy….But myth or not, it sure kept me close to home."

"Load off my mind, too, son."

He looked from his father's wrinkled face, to the clay mound again. "What did kill them folks, Daddy?"

"Most was killed by th' killer we was after. The rest, by somethin' a hundred times worse than any werewolf, worse than any stretch of a man's imagination,…and then some."

"It was an animal though, right?...What did it have to do with that killer anyway, were they connected?

"They was connected all right….But as far as that thing bein' an animal, it weren't one as we know it, I don't know what it was!...But thinkin' back, I guess animal is the only way to describe it, it and that killer both….Only difference between 'em was that th' animal had four legs, a four legged monster is what it was, and it weren't from this earth!"

"What do you mean?"

"Just what I said!...That thing could kill a man in a whisper then eat 'im on th' spot. I know, I seen what was left on th' ground. Hell, I even helped kill th' son of a bitch!"

"You actually killed it?"

"Not me, I blinded it when it charged us, stopped it in its tracks,… Korak killed it!" He squatted and grabbed a handful of dry grass, struck a match to it and stuffed it beneath the wood. He stepped back then to watch the licking flames grow, then looked back toward the bluff as the area lit up in the fire's flickering light.

"This is a haunted place, son….Too many secrets hidin' here." He stood, and turned away then to un-cinch his saddle and pull it from the horse's back, prompting Lance to do the same and at that point the conversation lulled while Max retrieved skillet, tin plates and cups from the sack of supplies, and seeing this, Lance grabbed canteen and coffee pot and put the brew on to boil while his father opened the canned beans and dumped them into the large pan, along with several small slabs of cooked pork and placed it on the fire to heat.

Once they were eating the meal, Lance, patience not being his best virtue, began thinking his father had changed his mind about telling him the story,…and unable to contain his curiosity any longer, quickly swallowed his food and cleared his throat. "Come on, Daddy, finish th' story."

"Plenty a time, boy, hold your horses!...A man's got a digest his food proper. We got all night." He grinned and slowly finished his plate of food then sighing, looked up at the brilliant, star-studded sky. "Look up there, Lance,…sure is pretty, ain't it? Hard to believe it would be anything other than peaceful….But to me, it sure ain't th' same when I look at it now!... Okay, pour th' coffee, son." He held his cup for Lance to fill it.

"Thinkin' back on it,…I guess that thing was an animal of some kind, but if it was?...Well, anyway,…Korak said it was a hunter! Damn thing was tall as a horse, twice as wide and twice as heavy,…quick as a cat, too! Could come up on a man and not make a sound,…claws and teeth like straight-razors."

"You said it didn't come from earth, Daddy,…then why was it here?"

"It was huntin' Korak,…and me!" He sighed then and shrugged. "And everything in between, that breathed!...We spent several days in these mountains lookin' for th' man Korak was after, comin' back here ever so often to see if maybe th' killer had found our camp while we was gone! Anyway, that last time we went lookin', we met a man and his wife leavin' th' mountains in fear for their lives, they told us about th' killings at the Preston homestead, so we went to see about it….I near-bout puked my guts up at th' sight of it,…blood and half eaten body parts everywhere. Lorne Preston had a wife and ten kids, and all of 'em was dead. Anyway, that farm bein' so close to our campsite here, we decided to come back and wait on th' thing. We both knew it was bound to find us!" He shook his head as he remembered that night.

"It found us all right, a whole day later, and by then we weren't expectin' it. Guess it was watchin' us check out th' farm and followed us, cause along about ten that second night, I had a good fire goin' and was makin' a pot a coffee when it jumped us." He took a deep breath of the crisp air then and pointed toward the thick stand of pines that surrounded the area.

"Came out a them trees yonder….Korak was out in th' rocks takin' a piss and didn't see it. I hadn't been lookin' that way, I would a missed it. Scariest lookin' son of a bitch you ever saw, right out a th' bowels a hell, Lance. Almost stopped my heart!...Anyway, I managed a hoarse yell at Korak and grabbed my rifle, that's when I noticed that Korak's gun was against a rock between me and him, twenty feet from both of us."

As Korak ran toward me, and his gun, I levered my Henry and began firing, and when I did, th' thing began shakin' its god-awful head and bellowing as it rushed us. I got lucky as hell then, I guess, cause th' bastard was within twenty yards of us when I fired my last shot and saw the blood and skin fly from it's right eye when it exploded....It faltered and almost went down, but then it went crazy, with screams so loud it rocked the ground up here,...whirling and thrashing about, from the pain, I guess.... But by then, Korak had his weapon and killed th' thing. A split second and it was gone, nothin' left but that burned ground over there....Not countin' my wet pants, which I had just pissed in!"

"Jesus, Pop, I wish I had seen that!"

"No, ya don't,...I had a lucky shot, that's all. Skin was too thick for a bullet to do it in,...weakest point was it's eyes....We was ten seconds from bein' eaten alive!"

"What kind of gun did Korak use?"

"A far cry from anything on this earth!...Had several of 'em, all different, burn't that thing to a memory, right on th' spot. It fired some kind a,...hell, I don't know what it was now, he told me but,..." He shrugged his shoulders. "It looked like a thin, red and orange streak of pure lightening bolt leavin' th' barrel a that rifle."

"Man!" Exclaimed Lance excitedly. "Who was he, Daddy, really,...I mean, were they all really not from earth?"

"That's what I said, son."

"Well where then, th' Moon, Jupiter, where?"

"You ain't too awful far from wrong." He chuckled and looked up at the sky.

"Where, then?"

"Somewhere the other side a th' Milky-way up there, Planet called Promas! Man we was huntin' was from somewhere even farther away, his animal, too!...I know it's a little hard to believe, couldn't believe it myself at th' time." He peered at the slack-jawed expression on his son's face and grinned even wider.

"What's wrong, boy, did ya think ours was the only world?...It's okay if ya did, I did, too! Fact is, Korak said there's a billion trillion planets in th' universe, and half of 'em got people a some kind on 'em, and that's just in the known universe, space goes on forever out there!...Unfortunately, not all th' people on some a them planets are human, not even close to bein' called human, just life forms, like that killer and his pet. There's more of 'em out there, too, and they ain't friendly!"

"And you and me are the only people on earth that knows about it, is that right, Pop?"

"Lots a folks know about th' stars and th' close-in planets, been lookin' at 'em for years with telescopes. But yeah, after tonight, we'll be the only two people on earth that knows th' truth."

"Tell me about th' killer, Pop, who was he?"

"Just an alien killer,...he walked like us, but that's all, more an animal than a man! Seven feet tall, clothes looked like a rattlesnake's skin, all scaly lookin'. Korak said it was armor a some kind, and I guess it was because a bullet couldn't dent it!...Bastard was big and clumsy, big feet and thick, muscled-up arms. Wore a helmet over his head with nothin' but his eyes showin'....that's how I killed im, by th' way."

"You killed 'im, Pop,...how?"

"Eyes, shot 'im in the eyes, same as that animal a his."

"And what was Korak doing?"

"He was already dead, son,...killer ambushed us right here, well, back over there in th' rocks."

"Why did he come to earth, Daddy, there had to be a reason?"

"There was a reason all right, he came to kill us!...Like I told ya, Korak said he was from one a them billions a worlds out there, said all they did was travel through space and destroy other worlds and th' people on 'em, leavin' th' planets dead. Korak was here because they invaded his world, which was a mistake. Promas had much better weapons and technology. They destroyed most of the alien ships and soldiers,...it took a few years!...The war was all but over when they detected the alien ship leavin' for earth....Korak was sent here to stop it."

"Oh, man! Sighed Lance. "Makes me wish I had known him."

"I wish you had, too. He was a good man.

"Is that all of it, that the whole story?"

"In a nutshell, yeah, but till I tell you th' whole story, you ain't gonna understand....Because deep down, I still see some doubts in your face, like you don't one hundred percent believe me! But you will, cause I'll show you proof when I'm done!"

"Okay, Daddy,...but I'd really like to hear about that flying machine first. Could it really fly?"

"See what I mean?" He chuckled. "You're a true skeptic, son."

"Sorry, Pop, I know you said it could. It just seems so impossible."

"It is, for us!...It was pretty damn big, too, made out a some kind a silver lookin' metal, and not a screw or bolt in it,...floated through the air like it was a glidin' bird. Had a motor in it that made it fly, Korak said it was a gravity engine, and don't ask me what that is, cause most everything he told me was above my head!"

"He said they been comin' to earth for millions a years, since th' time a th' Dinosaurs!...Said his people were the first people on earth, sort a makes us all related, I guess! Think a what that could do to our religious beliefs, Lance, Adam and Eve, th' whole thing!...Boggles th' mind, don't it?"

"It scares me, if that's what you mean!...I mean, it makes Church on Sunday a waste of time."

"No, no, that's never a waste a time, keeps our moral fabric intact." He reached to spoon more beans and pork into his plate then, as did Lance, and then poured more coffee for them both before gesturing at the bluff.

"That's why I come up here so much." He nodded. "Why I watch the skies, too!...We're not as safe here as we thought we was."

"You think they'll come back, don't ya, Pop?"

"Them,...or somebody else!...And that's what I'm afraid of, Lance, good or bad, sooner or later, somebody will. Could be here already, we just don't see 'em! But believe me, it'll be them, we do see, we'll have to worry about!"

"Them from Promas, too?"

"No, not them, son, they'll be our only hope if, and when it ever happens. It likely won't be in my lifetime, maybe not yours,...but someday!" He finished his plate of food as he talked and when done, placed the plate on the ground and rolled then lit his smoke before looking skyward again..

"Looks so peaceful there, don't it?...Son, I'm gonna tell you everything I can remember about Korak and what happened ten years ago and believe me, I tried to hang on to every word!...You'll understand when I'm done, might even know what to do if it happens again,...because I'm gonna show ya!" Sighing, he sipped at his coffee and continued to stare at the sky for a minute to finish his smoke.

"Okay," He said finally. "September, tenth, eighteen hundred and seventy one. That's th mornin' one a Ben Semple's hands rode up to th house to tell me a half-dozen of our steers was in one a Semple's holdin' pens on their south range, said I could go get 'em when I chose to. So I saddled up and went,...drove 'em back as far as Carbon Creek, down there. It was already late, so I decided to stay th' night, and made camp in th' trees." He looked up at the sky's brilliance again then.

"Full moon that night, be one tonight, too!...Almost bright as day, it was. I made coffee and ate my cold ham and biscuits, th' cows was grazin' all peaceful, and I was feelin' pretty good,...so I leaned back on my saddle to smoke and sip my coffee....Yeah, it was a great night, son,...for about an hour!"

"What happened?"

"Contain yourself, boy!...Th' cows started actin' up, movin' around all nervous-like, same with old Blue. He was snortin' and grunting, pawin' at the ground....I figured they had got 'em a good whiff of Puma or somethin', happens up here all th' time, as you know. Weren't no wolves around that I could hear!...Well, it weren't long till I started hearin' what sounded like a low hum, not loud, but steady, sort a unsettling. I still weren't too worried, thinkin' it was th' wind or somethin' at first, but I knew it couldn't be because th' animals was still actin' up pretty bad. But I had my rifle in case a real trouble, so I didn't bother to get up for a look around,...not till th' cattle suddenly broke and ran!"

"That's when I got up and walked out to th' creek. Cows were gone by then. Anyway,...and that's when I saw th' dark shadow comin' across th' grass toward me." He shook his head and grinned at Lance then. "When I looked up, I almost pissed my pants. There was this very large, metal-lookin' thing glidin' over my head, blocked out th' moonlight for twenty yards around me....I froze on th' spot, son, and watched th' thing. I could see that th' front of it was pointed, and the rear of it, sort a rounded, scared th' shit out a me! But I watched it float over me and all th' way up to this bluff here where it crashed,...nosed itself right into th' side of it over there, buried up about halfway in, and that's where it stayed."

"What did you do?"

"I saddled old blue and came to see about it, of course!"

"And that was Korak's flying machine?"

"He called it a Star-fighter, and yeah, that was his flyin' machine,... but I'll get to that!...When I got up here, right about where we are now." He gestured with his hands to indicate the campsite. "I was sittin' old Blue and starin' at th' thing when I saw th' side of it open up, and there stood Korak, staggerin' around like he was hurt or something, dazed, I guess. Anyway that machine was lodged in th' bluff about ten, twelve feet off th' ground.... Anyway, that's when he fell out a th' thing right on th' rocks below it, snapped his leg like a twig!"

"When I got up th' nerve, I got down and went to see about 'im. He was out cold, his leg bent all out a kilter, so I took his shoulders and drug 'im into some rocks over yonder away from th' ship and laid 'im down....I aint never seen nothin' like him before, son!"

"Different than us?"

"Oh, yeah. His clothes was all silver-lookin', not made a cloth that I could tell, cause when I tried to cut it away from his leg, I couldn't, knife was sharp, too!...His boots was made a th' same stuff, but I managed to get one off and roll up th' leg a th' pants enough to see th' break. But I needed more light than th' moon provided, so I built a good fire, hunted up some splint-wood and set his leg....After that, I got old Blue and went back for my gear. I reheated my coffee when I got back then sat down by th' fire, rifle in hand, and watched 'im!"

"What was he like, Daddy?"

"At th' time, I didn't know. He looked to be about your size, slender and muscular. His clothes was all in one piece, covered his whole body, had some kind a skin-tight mask over his head and face, with openings on the sides for ears, but there weren't none. Had what looked like eyeglasses across both eyes, just a long, narrow strip of colored glass. Mouth was covered, too, couldn't see it!...I sat there a while, and then noticed that the area around us began to smell, smelled a lot like swamp gas,...never did know what it was! Anyway, I started to get a mite more leery at that point, especially when I saw th' other one. He was a little fellow, tryin' to crawl out through th' door a that ship, but didn't make it,...he died there, half in and half out!...After a while, I climbed up on one a th' rocks and pulled 'im down to th' ground. He was a little one, totally different than Korak, short and stocky. He weren't no human, that's for sure! His head was larger than ours, bald, th' skin all gray-lookin'. He had a nose and mouth, but no ears,...and th' eyes were big as silver dollars, all black and shaped like a drop a rain....Creepy-lookin' little Bastard!...Korak told me later, he was his navigator, whatever that is?...I buried him over there, too!....Anyway, Korak didn't come around till noon th' next day."

"What happened to the other alien's space ship, Pop, the one the animal came in?"

"Oh, Korak destroyed that thing!...Took us two days to find where it went down. Couple a shots from that rifle a his, and the whole ship evaporated!"

"Must a been something to see....Was it bigger than Korak's ship?"

"Awww, I don't really know, Lance, we was a good half mile up th' side of a mountain!...Probably was though, the other one was."

"What other one, Pop, you saying there was two ships?"

"I am,...I'll get into that!" He laughed then. "Was all up to me, too, never so scared in my life....Anyway, like I said, Korak didn't wake up till the next day!"

CHAPTER TWO

Martin Maxwell Pruett was twenty-nine when he married the then nineteen year old, Helen Maybell Banks, and had she not met him, was well on her way to becoming a spinster, or as they called an unmarried woman past marrying age, an Old Maid.. But they did meet, and they did fall in love, and shortly after were married,...and shortly after that were disowned by the Banks once Max informed them of their plans to go West and settle.

They had been married only a few months, and had lived in the large Saratoga for half that time when they finally arrived at a roughly put-together log structure, in what was then a part of the Territory of Kansas, and later to be near the site of Denver, Colorado. It was mid July of1858 when he helped her down from the Saratoga's tall seat into the mud of a recent rain and ushered her into the make-shift store and Trading Post, with its many trappers and gold prospectors, intermingled amid the smell of rot-gut home made whiskey, tobacco smoke and the odor of puke and unwashed bodies.

Finding her a rickety, un-level table against an outer wall, he left her there and with help from a young Arapaho Indian girl acquired food and water for them both. Later, while purchasing several items of depleted supplies, he overheard and became acquainted with two prospectors, Green Russell, and Sam Bates. The two were about to prospect an area around Little Dry Creek, some twenty miles distance to the West. This presented Max with an idea that Gold might just bring their dream of owning their own land and cattle a little closer to reality a little quicker, so, he asked to go along, convincing them that his wife would do the cooking, and his large covered wagon could act as supply wagon and shelter when needed.

It took only a few weeks to find gold and though it was not in the quantity needed, nor anticipated, Max was able to pan several ounces of the precious metal. By then, however, another party of around twenty prospectors had converged on the scene and that, combined with the scarcity of the yellow metal, Max and Helen decided to try elsewhere and moved to the area of Clear Creek, just East of Table Mountain, and at the gateway into the heart of the vast expanse of Rocky Mountains.

Gold was found here as well, discovered by a man named Jackson on Chicago Creek, and the gold rush was in full bloom. Setting up his location, Max found traces of gold once again, adding several more ounces of wealth to his poke. But unfortunately this as well was beginning to disappear as the gold was depleted.

It was during this disappointment, however, that he met another out of luck prospector, who had arrived too late to pan any significant color, and by this time most were making ready to follow the water higher into the mountains, to find the source of the Placer Gold. Seeing this created a very dejected and depressed, Lucas Bell, who had readily accepted help from Max and Helen who provided him with food and a place beneath the wagon to sleep,...and they were all three sitting by the cooking fire at the Pruett wagon that day to watch as one by one, the miners packed up their mules and burros with their meager supplies and equipment and plodded off up-stream.

It was during this observation that Max learned that Mister Bell had a small ranch just North of there in the foothills of the mountains, several hundred acres of meadows, streams and timber, as well as a couple dozen head of long unattended cattle. At that instant, a light had been turned on again in Max's mind,...and when he learned that Bell's wife had died the year before and he no longer had a desire for ranch life, he quickly offered Bell close to fifteen ounces of gold, a little more than half of what he had panned, for his ranch and holdings. Max and Helen Pruett had purchased their dream.

Bell readily escorted them into the hills and a day later, all were seated at an oaken, meticulously hand-carved table inside the well made log house where they signed deed, and bill of sale for the now, Pruett Ranch,...they were home!

*   *   *

Max Pruett shifted the old Henry Rifle to the bend of his left arm and held it there, with the crackling of the fire being the only sound in the lighted area of the bluff. He was bone-tired and mind-weary from today's ordeal and still, his mind was flooded with questions and disbelief at what he had witnessed. But he dared not try to rest, and sleep was out of the question! His eyes hurt from staring at the prone body of the unconscious stranger, or whatever he was,...had even mulled over the idea of shooting him and burying the evidence, but another look at the suspended flying machine discarded the idea.

Besides, he thought, that was not who he was, he had never been a killer, hated it even when he had done so,...and that's why he had sat out the war, live and let live! Not to say he would not kill a man because he had when he was younger, and wilder,...before he met Helen.

"Damn it!" He muttered as he watched the steady rise and fall of the alien's breathing. "Who th' hell are you, man, where'd you come from?... Shit!" He looked across at the body of the smaller alien then and knew he would have to be buried soon, wouldn't take the sun long to do it's work come morning. With that thought, he looked up at the trillion or so flickering lights in the crisp, pre-dawn sky and was suddenly very tired and alone. The night sky would never again have the same effect on him as it once did. It was not the unknown anymore, the feeling of adventure he got when looking at it. Because he now knew what was likely out there,... because that's where these two had to have come from!

Sighing heavily, he grunted to his feet and plodded over to the dead alien, took it by the collar and dragged the body into an area of strewn rock past the suspended airship, and spent the next better part of an hour covering the small body with a mound of stones. A fitting memorial for an alien, he thought as he walked back beneath the ship and looked up at the hull. He was unable, however, to see the intricate design of the vessel, or its obvious markings in the half-light from the moon and fire and so, sighing once again, he looked the campsite over before walking back to the fire to make fresh coffee.

* * *

He awoke with a start to the shrill cawing of several large crows in the branches of the towering pines, automatically clutching the rifle and pointing it at the still unconscious man. He didn't even remember closing his eyes, but he had, remembering that it had to have been well after midnight when he made the coffee,...and at that moment considered himself lucky to still be armed and breathing. He shaded his eyes in the mid-morning sun to look the camp over and spying his hat, where he had obviously laid it, put it on and silently cursed himself for putting his own self in danger.

The fire had burned down to mere cinders, and the coffee he had poured for himself was still in the tin cup by the rock he had sat down against.

"That was a dumber than shit move, Mister Pruett!" He said aloud as he grunted to his knees to stoke up the fire with fresh wood, and when it was ablaze again, placed the blackened pot back in the flames and got to his feet. But as he stood up, the blinding reflection of sunlight on the alien ship's metal caught his attention and still curious, once again walked closer as he looked it over. Stopping to look up through the slanted opening in the fuselage, he could see what appeared to be small flashing lights against the upper inside roof of the craft, but nothing else. But it was when he began looking over the craft's slender shape and size, the half that still protruded out of the bluff, that he became impressed with the sleekness of it.

It was the metal, however, that amazed him. It was all perfectly smooth, and silver looking, no sign of any rust what so ever, not like the metals used on earth. The rear of the ship was rounded with wide, narrow openings set close together along the bottom. But for what purpose, he wondered? On top of the ship at the rear was also a fin that looked to be around four feet tall and to him, also had no logical purpose. He saw the strange markings on it then, figuring they had to be words or maybe just symbols of some kind.

Shaking his head again, he walked beneath the ship's belly to stare up at it, and to wonder how it had been built? There were no seams, no joining of the metal, only molded squares and rounded bulbs of metal. It appeared to be all one solid continuous formed piece of whatever metal it might be.

The ship had him so engrossed that he almost didn't feel the warning, and when he did, he turned to see the injured man sitting upright and intently watching him. At that moment, fear of the unknown once again took over and he clutched the Henry Rifle in readiness as he slowly walked back to look down at him. Breathing deeply, his legs like rubber, he sat down atop the large rock to watch the man, who only stared silently back at him.

"I don't know who th' hell you are, or where you come from, Mister,... or what th' hell that thing is you came out of!...But if you can understand what I'm sayin', you better know that I'm more afraid a you than any man I ever met, and Mister, that makes me dangerous!...You understand what I'm sayin'?" He was surprised to see the man nod his head.

"Then pull that mask off and let's talk!" Nodding again, the man raised his hands and touched both sides of the mask, which quickly receded from his face to disappear altogether into the collar of his clothing. Max, dumfounded by the feat, numbly studied the man's smooth features for a moment to at last decide that he was actually a human. He even had ears except they were flatter against his head than most men he had seen. However, it was the eyes that held his puzzled attention. They were not near as large as the smaller aliens', but still larger than an earth mans'. The pupils were dark and quite large as well.

"Who are you?" He finally asked again.

"My name is Korak." He returned with an almost husky voice, still watching Max intently.

"Where'd ya come from?"

Korak looked skyward for a moment, and then. "From beyond your Milky-Way, a planet called Promas."

"My God, man!" Breathed Max in disbelief. "Okay," He said breathlessly. "How far away is this, Promas,...and how do you know our language?"

"Promas," He nodded. "Is forty of your light years away from Earth, twenty light years beyond your Milky-way....And we have known your language for many generations."

Max stared at him for another minute before looking up at the suspended ship again. "That thing bring you here?"

"My Star-fighter, yes, it brought me."

"How does it fly?"

"By means of gravity engines, you would not understand the principle."

"You're damn sure right about that!" He cleared his throat then. "My name is Maxwell Pruett." He looked around at the trees. "You crashed on my land, here."

"Your land?" He asked, almost in disbelief. "All this," He asked, quickly looking around at the landscaping scenery. "How is that?"

"Bought and paid for." Nodded Pruett...."It's a cattle ranch!" He looked around again with pride. "Not very big yet, but I'm not much on big anyway....What's so strange about it bein' my land?"

Shrugging, Korak looked around the clearing again. "It is not strange, I think,...it was foolish of me to think we might have the same culture, forgive me....This world is so different,...so beautiful. The air is so sweet to the smell, how can anyone own such a place, it should be enjoyed by all. We have a chosen place in which to dwell, but all Promas belongs to its citizens."

"What do you use for money, how do you make a living?"

"I know nothing of money,...On Promas, everyone works for the good of all."

"Make like I didn't ask!" Breathed Pruett not fully understanding.... "Tell me what you meant by Light Years? What kind a distance we lookin' at?"

"A light year is the distance my Star-fighter can fly at the speed of light in one year's time."

"Forget I asked that one, too!" Sighing, he reached up to remove his hat and run his fingers through his hair, and then saw Korak reach down and touch his splinted leg.

"Does it hurt?"

"Yes, very much."

"You fell out a your machine and broke it, it's th' best I could do with what I had."

"Then I thank you, Mister Pruett,…I am in your debt."

"Nothin' I wouldn't do for any man!...You are a man, ain't ya, a human being?"

"Very much so. Although, the word human is only synonymous to the people of Earth."

"I'd be careful here, Mister Korak, you're already ruinin' my day!" He looked back at the ship then. "You said that thing had a engine, would it be like one a them Motor Cars, I read about?"

"A gravity engine, Mister Pruett….It manipulates gravity….In this case, Earth's gravitational field causes it to work against its own principles and by doing so, provides my Star-fighter with lift and propulsion. It also provides many other duties to sustain life."

"That explains that, I guess." Sighed Pruett, reaching up to scratch his head.

"Mister Pruett, I can sense that you are a good man, and a confused one,…and I am very much saddened to have put you in this very awkward position. It was never meant for anyone from Earth to ever witness my presence here….But you are here, and I am here, and the damage is done, so I must confide in you and answer your questions truthfully." He gestured outward with his hands. "I am at an unfortunate disadvantage, therefore at your disposal. But I can assure you that my being here at all, is for the good of your world, and mine."

More confused than ever, Max stared at him as he relived the scene from last night again, the ship floating above his head, the crash, everything.,… and it made him shudder. How could it all be real, he wondered,…and deep down, he knew that it couldn't be. Because if it was, it would rock the foundation of everything he had ever believed in. He looked at the ship again, yet, there it was, big as life and hanging there in the side of the bluff,…it was real!

"You're right about one thing, Mister Korak, I am confused." He took a deep breath then and let it out. "I don't know about th' rest a th' world, neither,…but this is my world, and I can't see any good comin' from you bein' here!...You ain't near as saddened about it as I am, neither! So tell me, do I look as strange to you, as you do to me?"

"No."

"Why not?"

"Because we are the same."

"Now that, Mister Korak, sends a chill up my spine!" Laying the rifle down, he moved forward, reached for the pot and poured the scalding coffee into his tin cup. "You drink coffee where you come from?" He asked then leaned to give him the cup. "Careful, that cup's hot." He watched as Korak took the cup and smelled it before tasting it and giving it back.

"Well,…it is an acquired taste, a habit once ya get used to it." He moved back against the rock again. "Best drank in th' mornin', when ya first get up, opens your eyes, gets you ready for a day's work." He drank a mouthful of the hot brew and continued to watch Korak. "Me, though," He continued. "I like it any time, mornin', noon, or night….Keeps me alert. Best served with food, though, you hungry, Mister Korak? I am,…thinkin' I'll heat up some ham and biscuits!...You do eat where you come from, don't ya?"

"May I, Mister Pruett?" He slowly reached to open a flap on the utility belt around his waist to remove two, almost large wafers, placing one in his own mouth to eat as he held the other out to Max.

"What is that?" He asked, getting up to accept it.

"It is condensed food." Nodded Korak. "It has many flavors, complete with all your bodily needs, as well as antidotes for many accrued illnesses….. Chew and swallow it, it will expand into one full meal, and you will no longer be hungry."

Curious, he ate the wafer and to his surprise, experienced no less than a dozen noticeable flavors before swallowing,…and was surprised again when he suddenly felt as if he had just pushed his plate away after a large Sunday dinner.

"Unbelievable!" He exclaimed, and then saw Korak looking toward the ship and shook his head, because he knew why. "Your little friend didn't make it, I'm sorry….I buried 'im in th' rocks over yonder."

"You have my gratitude, again!" He nodded. "He was a good friend, and soldier."

"Well, he weren't nothin' like you,…who was he?"

"An ally,…he was my navigator, and weapons specialist."

"He live on your world, too?"

Korak nodded. "Until his duty was fulfilled, yes….His name was Idak. He was of a race of very wise and mentally empowered people from the world of Cryor, another large planet in our solar system….Each Star-fighter employs a Cryoran. They are called Space Benders!...You would not understand that, either."

"Try me."

"I do not understand it myself. But aboard the Star-fighter is a machine capable of creating a hole in space. It will bend the very fabric of space in on its self, folding it, and then creating a hole through the folds. It will turn a light year into a few hours."

"You're right, I don't understand!...I don't understand nothin' about any a this....I don't even know if you're real?...For all I know, I'm still asleep by that creek down there havin' th' damndest nightmare I ever had! Right now, I don't know whether to believe all this shit you been feedin' me, or just shoot ya!...Naw, just forget I said that, man!"

"I understand." Nodded Korak. "My presence here should not have been detected."

"How th' hell did you find us anyway, by accident, or what?"

"It was no accident, Mister Pruett. We have been coming here for thousands of your years without being seen, rather our emissaries have. You see them as a moving star in the night sky and thought nothing of it."

"For thousands a years,...how many, two thousand, three, four?"

"Many more than that."

"Why not?" He sighed heavily then and drained the cup. "Well, If I'm dreamin' all this, th' coffee should taste a lot better'n it does, but it don't!... Settles that shit!" He stared at Korak then, and finally took another deep breath and let it out.

"You ain't goin' anywhere for a spell, Mister Korak, so why not tell me th' whole thing?...At th' beginnin', all of it!"

Korak studied him for a moment longer and then nodded. "I agree that you should know, Mister Pruett, at least as much as I know. But I must warn you, you will not understand most of what I tell you."

"Again, try me!"

"Eighty million Earth years ago, our home planet, as it was then, died. We could no longer sustain life because the atmosphere became poisoned by gasses from one of our exploding moons....We left our world in search of a new one. It took many years of wandering before we found Promas, but we knew the search was over once we did." He looked around at the hills then. "It was much like Earth here, trees, lakes of water, large mountains.... Once my ancestors arrived there, they discovered yet another problem, it was already inhabited by a race of animal-like creatures that, according to our archives, were very tall, covered in fur and very strong as well as aggressive. They tried to communicate with them at first, but the creatures lived underground, and in caves making them hard to find, and once they did, were met with aggression. The creatures had no language, none that we could ascertain, only grunts and growls and at times, howling, which could have been some form of communication, but if it was, only they knew the language."

We knew that if we were to live there, the creatures would have to be moved, or destroyed,...and we were not destroyers....We hunted them down, and our weapons rendered them unconscious, and once we had them all, they were loaded into starships and sent in search of another planet to release them on.....The Elders already knew where, because they came to Earth before moving on to find Promas, and it was ideal here, but was also inhabited by very large carnivores, animals much the size of this clay embankment, so they passed it by."

"They brought them things here?"

"The creatures, yes....They are called many things now, Yeti, in your Himalayas, wild man in Europe, and I believe here, it is called Sasquatch."

"Big foot!...We call it Big foot. Never seen one though, always thought it to be a myth, or a fairy tale. But there has been those who swear they seen one."

"They are as elusive as ever, but very much alive on Earth."

"Mister Korak,...from what I learned in school, th' Dinosaurs died out millions of years ago,...you sayin' Big foot's been here that long?"

"More than seventy million of your years, yes,...a year on Promas is much longer....My ancestors at the time realized these creatures might not survive in such a hostile environment, so they injected them with a monitoring chip. Their existence was recorded for more than a century, until the signals stopped coming. The Elders thought they must have all perished, perhaps becoming a food source for Earth's giant animals, and they thought them dead for sure when the giants were all destroyed some millennia later....But they did survive, the Cryorans have seen them. And yes, the Cryorans are the emissaries I spoke of,...they are explorers of the stars....As for me, Mister Pruett, this is my first visit to Earth, and it has been more than two thousand years since any Promasian has been here."

"In other words, that movin' star in the sky at night is most likely gonna be one a them little gray fellas spyin' on us!"

"Or a moving star....Mister Pruett, a Cryoran would never intentionally allow themselves to be seen, nor their presence known. They do not interfere in any way, they only observe, they are not spies."

"Okay!...Go ahead, man, what's th' rest of it?...And I got a tell ya, you already changed my whole outlook on life here. It suddenly don't feel as good as it did!...Hell, I wish I'd never laid eyes on ya!"

"Me as well." Nodded Korak. "But it would have been far worse if you had not!"

"I needed to hear that, too, man....I already don't feel safe on my own land anymore, and it weren't all that safe to begin with. But till I met you, I had faith in my own ability to protect what's mine!...If ya know what I mean?"

"Yes, very much so....You were never meant to know!...My ancestors went to great measures to destroy all traces of our presence on Earth.

You see, a few thousand years ago, the Elders sent another expedition to Earth. They were to only explore the planet's surface in search of life and/or resources not available on Promas, but while here, many of them chose to stay. They formed colonies and for generations, used our technologies to build things that would aid them in a new world's population, to help them grow, and prosper. Which was good, Our Elders approved wholeheartedly.... But then, much, much later, there were some who would set themselves up as kings, and insisted on building monuments to honor themselves instead of prosperity....That's when we came to take back that technology, our starships, our machines, everything, and allowed the world to grow at its own pace. You see, Mister Pruett, we all have our faults."

"What brings you back then,...why now?"

"Since you are now my only ally, Mister Pruett, and I am forced to enlist your help, I will tell you....Many years ago, beings from a Rogue Planet, located almost a hundred light years away on the far side of the known universe, began an all-out war on any, and all inhabited planets they would find. They are a race of warriors of the most ruthless sort, leaving those planets in total devastation, devoid of all life. Ten of your years ago, they found Promas!...But this time they will not succeed. We have proven to have more powerful weapons than they, more technology and of course, we have the Cryorans. When I began this journey, the invaders had all but depleted their cruisers and warships. Their invading horde of foot soldiers are amassed aboard the mother ship in space with no ships left to bring them to Promas,...and we are there, too, waiting to see that they do not attempt to do so."

"Then I'll ask again, why are you here?"

"The invaders intercepted a centuries old signal from our colony here, and we do not know how this happened....But we picked up the same signal. That's when Idak detected one of their last remaining warship's warp-signature as it left our stratosphere. It was one day later when the Elders ordered me to go in pursuit, wanting me to find and destroy him before he could locate the source of the signal. We were hoping to either get here before him, or to at least find him before he knew I was here and hopefully, before he made it to Earth."

"And you didn't." Sighed Max heavily.

"No....We underestimated the speed of his warship, and even though we traveled the worm-hole, and was here in a matter of hours, he was waiting in ambush as we exited the space warp. Idak sensed his presence and fired on his ship. But he had also fired, and both our ships were damaged. Neither of us had a choice but to enter Earth's atmosphere. Him to survive and carry out his objective, and me to try and stop him."

"Where is he now?"

"In these very mountains somewhere. Idak followed his signature all the way down….We were about to locate him when the gravity engines failed…. You are lucky it was me you found, if it was him, you would be dead!"

"Then I want a thank God for that one!...But my wife and seven year old son is at home, some ten miles from here,…if that son of a bitch finds them?"

"Then please, go on home, Mister Pruett, protect your family….When I can walk, I will find him!"

"No, ya won't!" Breathed Max loudly. "It'll be weeks before that bone heals enough to stand on it, let alone walk on. By then everybody in these mountains could be dead!"

"I am sorry, Mister Ptuett."

"Yeah,…me, too!...Guess I got no choice now, but to believe you're who you are,…and after what you told me, to help you find this,…whatever th' hell it is?"

"There is something else, Mister Pruett….This warrior has a pet, a beast of great size and deadly tendencies. It is a hunter, and it knows my scent."

"Well, ain't that damn good news!" He got up and quickly brought his horse in to be saddled. "Can you ride a horse, Mister Korak?...Beats hell out a walkin'!"

"I have never ridden one,…but I will, yes."

"Good, I'll bring ya one,…just as soon as I get my family out a these mountains!...Hope your guns are in workin' order?"

"Yes, they are, if I can get to them….They are still in the Star fighter."

Max looked up at the ship's doorway then tightened the saddle's cinches. "Where do ya keep 'em, I'll get 'em for ya?"

"On a rack inside the doorway there, touch the light on the side, the panel will open, bring the long one, and the shorter one."

He dropped the stirrup in place and shoved the rifle in the boot. "Horse ought a be tall enough, if I stand on it,…I'll get in there all right."

"Once you are inside, place your hand on the blue light beside the portal, a stairway will extend downward."

"Yeah, I wouldn't a thought." He shook his head and led the horse around the large rocks below the suspended ship, and then looked back at Korak.

"How much damage can this other man do,…what kind a weapon's he got?"

"No one on Earth can defeat him, Mister Pruett, because he is not human. He is much larger than you and I. He wears armored clothing and his weapons fire blasts of pure energy. He can burn one of your villages to the ground in seconds, and destroy everyone in it….As can I with Mine."

"That's comforting as hell, too!...Can you kill I'm?"

"Yes!"

"What about his pet?"

Yes,...but I must find them first."

Nodding, and with a sigh, he pulled himself into the saddle then boosted himself up to stand on it and pull himself up, and then in through the open hatch of the Star fighter before leaning out to shoo the horse away.

* * *

Urgency caused him to push the horse extra hard over the heavily timbered and rocky terrain, and he rode with expectations like he had never before experienced in all his thirty-five years. Visions of an alien killer waiting in ambush behind every tree and rock pushed him to recklessness, and he did not breathe with any relief at all until he finally rode through the double gates of home and saw it still intact.

Sliding the hard breathing animal to a stop in front of the house, he dropped the reins and ran for the barn and horse corral where he wasted no time in hitching a nervous team to the spring wagon. Once done, he led the team and wagon back to the house where Helen and young Lance were waiting on the porch watching him. Without a word, he climbed the steps, took their arms and ushered them both back into the house.

"Maxwell?" She stammered, pulling her arm from his grasp. "What's wr,..."

"Listen to me, Helen." He said, interrupting her. "I want you to get clothes together for you and Lance, enough for a week or so, pack everything you might need, food for the trip, everything, only hurry!"

"No, Maxwell, not until you tell me what's going on!"

"There's no time, Helen, we have to hur,..."

"Then take the time!" She interrupted. "And tell me what's wrong?"

Raising his arms in surrender, he nodded. "I met a man in the mountains last night, down on Carbon Creek. He was wounded, so I set his leg for 'im....God damn it, Helen, there's a crazy killer loose in these mountains somewhere and I'm takin' you and Lance down to Golden City till we can catch 'im, now come on!"

"Catch him, what do you mean,...are you going to catch him?"

"I'm gonna help catch 'im, Helen."

"Who is this man you met, some sort of a lawman?"

"You could say that, yeah,...and he can't very well track 'im down with a broke leg."

She gazed into his troubled eyes foe a moment. "I understand!" She said suddenly, and quickly set about preparing to leave.

With a sigh of relief, Max opened the bureau drawer and removed the last box of cartridges, stuffing them into his jacket pocket before going back out to lead his winded horse to the barn. Removing the saddle and bridal, he opened the gate and let the animal into the corral, and with saddle and bridal went into the barn where he saddled another horse, then led Helen's horse out of the stall and saddled it before leading them both back and tying them to the rear of the buckboard.

Helen and Lance were loading their things in the wagon as he tied the animals, and he noticed the look on her face at seeing her horse.

"Th' man lost his horse, I'm loanin' 'im yours. You got everything?"

"I suppose."

"Then climb in, come on." He went around to help her to the seat, and as Lance climbed into the back, climbed to the seat himself. Using the crop, he whipped the animals to a gallop out through the gates and onto the worn, rutted road out of the mountains.

Holding on to the cast-iron armrest with one hand and the backrest with the other, she watched the strained profile of her husband's face as he urged the team to an even faster pace along the rutted, brush and tree lined roadway, having to grip tightly her hold on the seat for fear of being thrown out. "What aren't you telling me, Maxwell, what's wrong?"

"Nothin' more to tell!" He yelled back at her. "I just don't want you hurt!"

"What about you, you could be hurt, even killed?"

"I'll do my best not to be!"

"That's not good enough, not for me!"

He reached across and squeezed her hand. "Just trust me, honey, I have to know you and Lance are safe. I can't do this if you're not!"

"Must be pretty bad!"

"Believe me, it is!"

"Well, you'd better slow down. You kill the horses, you'll never get us there."

He reluctantly slowed the team to a walk. "You're right, honey....It's just that time is not on my side in this, that lawman is waitin' up there at th' clay bluff with a broke leg.!...Th' man we're after is a killer of th' worst kind, and he has to be caught!"

"I bet it's a monster, huh, Pop?" Yelled Lance.

"You could say that, son, but it's nothin' for you to worry about!"

"Gosh!"

"Where will we stay in town?" Asked Helen, still watching him.

"Th' hotel, you can have your meals there, I don't want you on th' streets a town." With that, he clucked the horses into a mile-consuming trot again.

CHAPTER THREE

He awoke to the sounds of his wife's voice calling his name, and as reality slowly put its wheels into motion, suddenly sat upright in the bed to stare wild-eyed at her for a moment before swinging his legs off to the floor. His sudden reaction caused Helen to gasp and back away to watch him.

"What time is it, Helen, how long was I asleep?" He bent and quickly pulled on his boots. "How long, Helen?"

"Three hours, you fell asleep about four this morning….You needed the sleep, honey."

"No time to sleep!" He got up to pull on his shirt then saw the hurt and fear in her eyes as she watched him.. "I'm sorry, Helen, there's just no way I can tell you how important it is that we find this killer and stop 'im!...I have to go now."

She grabbed him and hugged him tightly as she sobbed. "Whatever you do, take care of yourself!...I love you so much!"

"And I love you both more than life." He kissed her, grabbed his rifle and coat and left, saying that he would come for them when it was safe.

*　　　*　　　*

In all his life, good times and bad, Max Pruett had never experienced an urgency such as he was feeling now, and that was what pushed him to hold the animals to a steady gallop as often as he could during the rest of the day. But because the winding old road was so steep as it twisted its was back into the rugged foothills, the horses seemed to tire at a faster rate forcing him to constantly have to walk them to cool them down.

It was during this time that his mind kept going over the events at the bluff, and what Korak had told him, thinking about every word of their conversations, and it still seemed too fantastic to be true. He knew Korak was who he claimed to be, and he knew that ship could fly, he saw it!....But what if it was all a lie, what if Korak himself was the killer from space, and the other man, th' good guy?

Before that night, he had never dreamed there could be life on other planets, never thought about it one way or another. He did know that the night stars had always excited him, presented a mystery of the unknown,... had even sparked his exploring instincts. But that was all gone now, and what a disappointment it was. He now knew, and believed that space was a hostile place to be. The romance was gone now, and if Korak proved to be other than who he otherwise said he was, he could very well be riding back into a trap,...and with vastly inferior weapons with which to defend himself.

Korak was now armed and dangerous if it was true, with weapons of unheard of proportion,...and he was the one who armed him! He also knew that none of it mattered, the threat was real and good or bad, it had to end. Earth might well depend on it.

He saw a familiar break in the trees then, recognizing it as a shortcut back to the ranch and slowed the animals to a walk again before urging them up the steep embankment and into the trees. It was much rougher country away from the road, and he could seldom hold the horses to anything other than a walk through the dead, fallen timber, thick brush and ancient pines. But even so, would still save valuable time, cutting the distance back to Carbon Creek by at most, five miles.

He just hoped that Korak was who he said he was, because he liked the man, even though he had yet to see him smile or show any sort of emotion. He wanted desperately to help destroy the threat that lurked over his way of life, wanted things back the way they were,...or at least a facsimile! Before a few days ago, he would have been on his knees praying for guidance, but now it was questionable as to who the Good Lord was,...or even if he was? The only thing he could actually believe at this point was that it was eminently probable that people were going to die up here if he couldn't kill the threat.

He thought then of Korak's description of the killer's pet. If that beast was set loose in these mountains, he thought grimly, there would be a bloodbath! The thing could be on the prowl even now, he thought as he reined the animals up through some rocks and onto level ground.

He stopped the horses there for a rest while he studied the darkening tree-line, and knew that he was still almost ten miles from the bluff, and with the worst of the country still ahead of him,...it would take most of the night to get there.

Breathing deeply of the crisp, slightly chilled September mountain air, he looked toward the star-studded sky,...and with a shake of his head reined the horses back into the trees and briars, keeping them at a fast walk through the thick, brush infested maze of Towering Sequoias. He found himself having to work the animals into, and around littered fields of dead timber and fallen branches. Not counting giant boulders and the ever pricking briars,...and patience had already become a stranger to him.

A few days ago, he loved the wild beauty of all this, he thought sadly, but not now! "Come on, horse!" He said roughly, reining the animal higher through the large rocks, and it was at that moment, the horse squealed and tried to shy away from the surrounding trees, almost unseating him before he controlled it again. Wrapping the reins of Helen's horse tighter around the saddle-horn, he pulled the Henry from its boot and sat silently to study the dark of the trees,...and was there for several minutes before hearing the animal's grunts. He saw the black bear then as it lumbered out of the trees some twenty yards away, and slowly released his grip on the rifle.

"Come on, horse, let's go!" He prodded it into motion again as he rebooted the rifle, thinking that he was allowing his nerves to get the better of him. But he also knew that it had been two whole days since both of those flying machines were forced down, plenty of time for that beast to be roaming around.

*   *   *

The sun was still hidden behind the mountains and trees, but already bathing the morning with pre-dawn light of a new day by the time he urged the horses in toward the campsite. Expecting to see Korak still on the ground where he left him, he stopped the horses several yards away from the fire's remains when he did not! Sitting the saddle, he strained sleep-starved eyes at the camp and could see nothing out of the ordinary, other than there was no Korak,...and fearing the worst, loosed the rifle from its boot, and was pulling it free when Korak appeared in the star-fighter's open hatch,...and he was standing on his busted leg.

Surprised, he clucked the horses forward, seeing Korak wave in greeting then step onto the escalating steps to descend to the ground as he was reining the horses into the campsite.

""You're walkin', I see." Remarking this as he peered at the thin, cast-like boot around Korak's leg.

"Yes,...not well, but I am walking." He said as he entered the rocks and looked down at himself. "We, too have our survival methods, Mister Pruett."

"I see that!" He dismounted and dropped the horse's reins. "What else do you have there?" He asked, peering at the odd-looking, handheld object he was carrying.

"This will lead us to the invader's damaged warship." He opened it then turned it so that Max could see the screen, and the flickering blip in the corner. "It is there." He said, indicating the blip.

"Exactly where is, there?...No way I can read them wavy lines and symbols."

"The uneven lines represent terrain, the symbols, distance and direction. We were following this signature when our engines failed....The ship is there." He said pointing westward. "Eleven kilometers away."

"Kilometers,...What th' hell is that?...Can't it give distance in miles?"

"I am afraid that is another word synonymous to Earth....It obviously has the same meaning in reference to distance, however."

"Yeah,...well, only thing in that direction is more mountains, so I brought our transportation

"Yes," He nodded. "I can see that."

"My wife's horse." He grinned as he said it. "Well,...you got everything you need for this hunt?"

"I have the locator and weapons, yes, I am ready."

"What's that you got on your belt there?"

Korak removed the almost small, L-shaped, tubular device from his utility belt and held it up. "I decided on this lighter weapon than the smaller one you brought down....You have your sidearm, I have mine now!" He looked past Max at a grouping of stones some fifty yards distant. "See the larger stone there in front of the trees?" And when Max nodded, he pointed the weapon and fired. The sound it made was nothing more than a sudden burst of whistling wind as the fleetingly visible streak of orange shot from the weapon's muzzle, followed by a zapping pop as the large boulder disintegrated.

Max's eyes widened at the sight of it, not believing how fast the rock disappeared, and with no debris, or fallout. He looked back at Korak then and cleared his throat. "I'd say we're ready....Can that thing kill this guy, or his pet?"

"Yes, nothing can withstand it!...But it is only for close encounters, the energy fades at distances much beyond the stone." He replaced it then removed the larger, and much longer weapon from across his back. "This, however, is much different. Aside from our star-burst cannons on Promas, and the weapons aboard the Star fighter, there is nothing in the galaxy more powerful." He touched the weapon and a small screen emerged.

Once I locate the target on the screen here." He showed him the small screen then. "I will destroy it!...We will use this one to destroy the invader's ship, and the invader,...if he is there!"

"What does it fire?"

"It fires a burst of condensed energy plasma, a star-burst torpedo.... Destruction is eminent."

"Shit, man!...I can't believe all this!"

"Why not, Mister Pruett, you had your cannons in all your past wars, with their exploding shells. Nothing in its path could withstand it. My cannon is smaller, and easier to carry."

"Yeah, but ours didn't shoot lightenin' bolts!...Why do ya want a destroy that guy's ship, ain't it useless?"

"Yes, unless he repairs it, but should it be seen, it will be proof of our being here." He shrugged then as he shouldered the weapon again. "It is also sending a weak beacon toward space as we speak. That is what we see blinking on the locator,... otherwise the signal would not blink. It is not yet powerful enough to reach the atmosphere on Promas, therefore, the invaders have not received it,...and will not, once it is destroyed."

"What'll happen if they do?...Never mind!...Will I have time to make coffee before we go, I've been ridin' since yesterday mornin'?"

"Yes, of course." They both went to the campfire's remains once Max retrieved his canteen, and while he poured water and grounds into the pot, Korak put fresh wood in the ashes, took out his sidearm, adjusted it and fired down at the wood, causing Max to jump when the wood burst into flames.

"You never cease to amaze me!" He placed the pot in the open flames and moved back to sit against the rock. "You think this killer knows you're here?"

"No,...our monitors did not indicate a probe from his ship as we crashed. His ship's sensors must have been damaged....He does know that we sustained damage, and that we followed him down,...but he may not know of our engine failure, or that we crashed."

"Maybe not,...but I'm willin' to bet he's lookin' for ya!...He has to know you could a crashed, else he'd a seen your ship lookin' for 'im."

"Yes, he would know that!...He would also know that I must be killed.... But he will send his pet first, I think! I think also that he will attempt repairs to his warship before he himself comes....If the beast does not interfere, we will have the time to destroy the ship,...if it does, we will need to destroy it first."

"Sounds easy when you say it!"

"Easy?...No, Mister Pruett, this beast lives only to kill. It is swift, silent and very deadly....Hundreds of them were set loose on Promas at the war's onset, and before we realized they were there, had murdered as many Promasians before our foot-soldiers defeated them. That is when we detected the invader's warships as they were descending....As our star-burst cannons fired into space, we manned the star fighters and carried the war to them.

No enemy fire touched our world....This beast is only one of a very few the invaders have left,...and I will kill it as well."

"But how many people will it kill first?"

"I grieve for them even now, Mister Pruett,...but it is inevitable."

"I figured as much!" He breathed deeply then. "By th' way, Korak,...my friends call me Max."

"Thank you, Max, I am honored."

Max nodded and cleared his throat. "What about your ship there,... think somebody might find it, th' killer, maybe?"

Nodding, Korak took a small, flat narrow unit from his belt, pointed it at the ship and rubbed across it with his thumb. The entire ship faded away until only the twenty-foot hole in the bluff was visible.

"What th' hell just happened?" He asked incredulously.

"It is only one of the many gifts from the Cryorans,...it helped to defeat the invaders in deep space, before they could come within firing distance to Promas."

"If you defeated them, why are they still there?"

"Only the mother ship is there. But it is the size of a small planet, and a very strong force field protects it....Our star fighter's weapons could possibly break through it's defenses, only we would need to be very close and the large ship's weapons are too powerful for that, so they sit there in the stratosphere and wait. They have only a small force of warships left, and they have retreated back inside the mother....They are too far out in space to reach us before being destroyed, even the mother ship dares not venture within range of our ground cannons,...and they wait there, unwilling to leave, or admit defeat....When this warship fails to return, they will know all is lost to them. They will leave soon, unless they are planning some other means of attack."

"What about these allies of yours, Idak's people,...think they might be close enough to help us out?"

"While you were gone, I monitored my ship's sensors and to now, I have not detected their presence in Earth's atmosphere. They are not here.... Besides, Max, they are observers, not warriors."

"Okay, what about Promas, wouldn't they send help?"

"Yes, of course, but the invaders will be listening for any signal from earth, asking for help could bring more warships here. Should that happen, more star fighters would come,...and the war would be fought on earth."

"Then our job's cut out for us!"

"Cut out?"

"Just a saying, Korak....Means we're on our own." He looked back at the bluff then. "How long will that ship a yours stay hid like that?"

"As long as the crystals remain charged, but then, I have no way of knowing the extent of the damage, so I do not know."

"You really depended on that little fella, didn't ya?"

"Yes,...I am a warrior, Max, I can make a star fighter perform any and every fighting maneuver in space. I am considered one of the elite on Promas. But I can not repair the damage to my own ship,...I know nothing of the inner workings of the vessel....The Elders insisted we fighters had no need to know, because we had the Cryorans to do it for us....Yes, I will miss him."

Nodding, Max studied Korak's expressionless face, thinking he could actually see the pain and regret in the alien's eyes,...and thought he knew why? Clearing his throat, he grabbed the boiling pot from the fire and poured his coffee before looking up at him again.

"Ya know,...I ain't th' smartest man on Earth, Korak, but I get th' feelin' you don't think you'll live through this!...I say that because either way it turns out, until that threat is gone at home, you ain't goin' home....You got no ship, ya can't ask for help,...you're on your own on a strange world with a mad killer huntin' ya....Are you sure we can kill this guy?"

"Max,...every man dies....When I followed the invader here, yes, I knew I might not return home. But this is what I was trained to do....and it is only strange because I am not a foot soldier, and now I must fight as one....I will kill this being, because if I do not, Earth will suffer for it!"

"It's that last part that worries me."

"I am sorry, Max, if not for my war, this would not have happened."

"Don't know about that, not with all them other worlds you say is out there. Seems to me it was only a matter a time anyway."

"Perhaps,...but each of those worlds live with that same possibility, even Promas....Max, if you do not wish to help, I will find him."

"Oh, no,...I have to see that Bastard dead! Besides, you don't know these mountains like I do." He drained the cup and put it aside before taking the pot and pouring it on the fire. Getting up then, he used his foot to scatter the unburned wood and embers.

"Okay, I'm ready, you sure ya got everything?"

"Weapons, food-stock, water,...yes, I am prepared."

Got any horses on Promas?"

"No,...we do not use animals for transportation. We use anti-gravity vehicles, small ones for single unit travel, larger ones for those with families. To explain,...observe the dark birds in the sky there, the way they glide through the air, now imagine hundreds more being there and next, imagine each one of them being an anti-gravity vehicle moving in every direction.... That is the skies of Promas." He looked around at the ageless pines and tall mountains. "I very much prefer this, Max,...and if I am destined to remain here, I do not think I will mind!...And you are wrong, Max, I have no thought in my mind of dying here. I do not intend to die here."

"That's good, because I wouldn't mind you stayin' here, neither!...Okay then, just watch th' way I mount my horse, and do it th' same way, It's easy. Once you're on, balance'll do th' rest." He mounted his horse then sat to watch as Korak pulled himself aboard Helen's pony and swung his injured leg over its rump and sat down.

"How's it feel?"

"Strange." He nodded as he adjusted the plasma rifle across his back.

"Just keep your feet in the stirrups, helps keep your balance....Stay loose, let your body adjust to th' movements of th' horse. You want it to go left, pull the left rein slightly, right, same thing. Straight ahead relax 'em."

"It is simple when you say it, Max." He nodded, and gingerly picked up the reins. "I am ready."

"You want it to go forward, just touch its sides with your heels." Grinning, Max led the way out of camp and through the rocks where the alien lay buried, then down the sloping hillside to the entrance to a deep ravine, that nature had carved into the harsh landscape and once on it's rocky floor, followed the winding path westward as he periodically cast furtive glances over his shoulder at Korak.

The large crows seemed to be excessively loud and active, he thought as he looked up at the circling black birds. Always before, he would watch the immaculate creatures with envy at their ability to fly. But it was not the same anymore, because now, all he could picture when he watched them was flying airships and their unearthly weapons destroying all life on earth! He knew that if that happened, that if they failed to kill this alien and his pet, it could very well be the end of everything. No army on earth could stop it! He twisted in the saddle again to check on Korak and as he watched him, knew that this strange, alien relative of his was the only chance in hell his beloved earth had to keep that nightmare from becoming reality.

He sighed then as he allowed his horse to pick its way through the debris of rocks and dead timber strewn across the gully's sandy floor. This killer they were after must be a scary bastard, he thought, and likely much worse than Korak's short description of him, his pet, too,...and his best effort to try and visualize the pair was a failure. In all truth, his own weapons would have no effect on them, just an irritation,...and in all likelihood, he was only tying the knot in his own hangman's noose by helping him....Can't be sure though, he grinned. Never want to underestimate the power of a Henry Rifle!...Besides, can't hide from the war forever.

It was late when the winding ravine began to change course, and that was where he stopped to rein his horse around to face Korak.

"How ya makin, it, Man?"

"Max," He shifted his body around in the saddle. "My physical condition was said to be the best in the fleet,...but I have never experienced muscle ache such as this before. My legs pain me here." He touched his upper, inner thighs and crotch area. "And my back aches,...so much for physical condition."

"It'll take a few days." He looked up at the tree-lined crest of the gully then back at Korak. "That screen a yours still show th' location a that ship?"

Korak opened the thin case and studied it for a moment. "It still lies in our direction of travel. It appears to be along the base of a very tall mountain, in a cover of trees....The signal remains weak, however."

"That's good news, ain't it?"

"Yes, he has not yet repaired the damage."

"Well here's where we leave th' ravine, it's turnin' South on us. We'll have to climb out and go overland from here, and this is th' best likely place to do it, th' sides are caved in....Your horse will climb out, just show 'im where to go and grab th' saddle-horn....Better yet, I'll lead 'im up behind me." He reached and took the horse's reins from Korak.

"When it starts to climb, lean forward and hold on."

Leaving the twisting gully, they were in some of the roughest terrain of the Rocky Mountain foothills, confronted by ageless pines, Fir and Spruce Trees. Rocks and boulders of enormous size, spreading Oak, Wild Pecan and Dogwood Trees,...and an almost impassable route through a maze of fallen, rotting timber, the up-thrusting branches of which grabbed and gouged at them and the animals relentlessly. Dozens of times, they found themselves having to detour around massive growths of briars with their dagger-like thistles.

Then, there were the snakes, the buzzing of their rattles constantly working to un-nerve the horses. Combining all that with their efforts to work the animals through the most dense forests of Sequoia Pines in the Rockies, they were ready for a rest when Max finally found a wind-blown section of mountainside and held up his hand.

"Be dark in half an hour, Korak,...suicide to travel up here at night." He hesitated then when he noticed the mask back in place over his eyes. "When did you put on th' mask?"

Korak touched his face to retract it. "Some time ago."

"What's with that colored glass, an eye-shade?"

"Yes, but it is also a sensor....It shows me terrain elevations, distance and also the heat signature of living entities, the same as my larger one. However, this one will only record for a few hundred yards."

"Heat signature?...I meant to ask you about that?"

"Yes, before retraction, I had seen three animals in the valley below us, another on the mountainside across from us, and a bear, I think. It was one half kilometer away. Heat signature is body heat, Max, the screen shows it as yellow, or sometimes orange figures, and their shape is fairly accurate."

Thinking about that, Max dismounted and went to lend Korak a hand, who stiffly managed to slide from the saddle. "How's th' leg?'

"It is well,...and a minor thing compared to the pain here." He massaged his inner thighs as he spoke.

"Helps to walk around a bit, you do that while I make camp."

*　　　*　　　*

A cold camp was never one to his liking, but he knew that a fire's light would be seen for miles by anything that might be hunting them. However, after another one of Korak's food pills, he was pleasantly full and quite satisfied, except for the absence of coffee. They were leaning against the large rocks, both watching the sun's red glow as it slowly dipped out of sight behind the mountains,...and almost immediately, the air began to cool.

"We have no sunsets on Promas." Remarked Korak with regret. "Our days fade into night slowly, then back to day. No sunrise....Because we are so far away from your sun, it only provides us a little light, but combined with what we call solar light, it gives us a quite comfortable environment."

"Can I ask ya about that suit you're wearin'?"

"Yes, of course. I believe it is what you would call a uniform, all Star Pilots wear them."

"You ever take it off, you been wearin' it for a week now?...You do pee, don't you?"

"Yes, my functions are the same as yours. I have a magnetic seam under my utility belt, when in need, I can pull the trousers down."

"Other than that, do you wear it all th' time?"

"Until I return from a mission, yes. There is no need to remove it, it's components are of such that it keeps my body at a controlled temperature, it moisturizes my skin, aerates it, and kills all bacterium that might do me harm....I do not perspire as you do, and I do not feel heat, nor extreme cold. It is a clean-suit, Max,...I am free of odor, and of being unclean."

"Holy shit, man!" He exclaimed, and shivered from the cooler air on his own sweat-soaked skin. "That's some suit all right." He cleared his throat then. "As long as we're baring it all, what about your eyes, nobody I ever seen has eyes like that?"

"Everything and everyone evolves, Max, most out of necessity. They evolve to survive, or they die....Not every world out there is environment friendly, and no other place in the universe has an atmosphere like earth. Most are harsh, a struggle to live in, so life is forced to evolve. It may take a thousand years, but eventually they will grow new organs with which to compensate, that or rearranging existing ones to change their shapes. Once evolution is complete, they become as one with their environment. It is the way of life."

"It's crazy, Korak, but I almost understand,…I think!"

"Do not feel bad, Max,…you and everyone on earth are us, tens of millions of years ago and now, you are the descendants from our first earth colony. You, Max, are an Earthling, and a Promasian, both at the same time….You are a primitive people, but one day your descendants, your yet unborn ones, will travel to the stars as we did, and maybe they'll even discover Promas. It will be a monumental meeting."

"But you asked about my eyes…..Millions of years ago, the environment on our home planet became very bad, and according to our book of ancient recorded history, it was subtle, but noticeable….It began to affect our eyes, nothing else. Some were going blind while others only experienced failing sight. But eventually our scientists developed eye-covers that at the time seemed to solve the problem. Even though no more blindness occurred, the entire population had been infected with whatever caused the problem…. It took most of a thousand years before our eyes evolved, now they are larger!...I have no iris, or pupil, none that you can see, yet I see everything with more concentrated clarity that you, or anyone could ever imagine. Which is essential to a star-pilot. I am able to focus my every thought and instinct on what I am doing."

"More I learn about you, th' more it scares me."

"I understand." He looked at the grazing horses then. "I think I like these horses of yours, Max, riding on them gives you time to explore earth's primitive beauty….They would provide a wonderful recreation on Promas."

"Like I told ya, it beats walkin'." He reached down and pulled his bedroll blanket up to his waist. "How far away is this alien ship now?"

"More than eight kilometers."

"Can I take a look at that thing again?" And when Korak opened it and turned the screen toward him. "Them wavy lines, they show terrain, right?"

"Yes, the low and high points in the landscape."

"Point it west for me,…yeah, I can see now! Everywhere th' larger line dips down, it's a canyon, and up, that's th' shape of a mountain, correct?"

"Yes."

"Then I think I know where your airship is….That there is Table Mountain, top's almost flat, see it?...That ship is right below it!...That tall spike behind it is Pike's Peak. That ship's close to five miles away from us,

Korak, another couple a days at th' speed we can travel, and it's damn rough country!...If I remember right, there's several homesteads in th' area of Table Mountain, and if our killer's pet ain't found 'em yet, it will."

"Is your family in a safe place, Max?"

"If we can keep these monsters in th' mountains, they are. I took 'em down to Golden, a town about thirty miles South a here,...but Safe?" He sighed heavily and shrugged. "They are for now!...But there's another settlement southwest of us yonder, a gold camp,...two, three hundred miners livin' there, and they ain't safe!...Ain't there any way for you to see that thing, if it's out there?"

"Only my scanner, Max, but it will register any life form's heat signature. But only if it is in our search scan."

"How far?"

"A kilometer."

"Why is it registerin' that ship, it's five miles away?"

"The ship's signal is ten thousand times stronger, the same with my Star fighter, see." He turned the scanner back the way they had come, and there it was.

"Can he see it, too?"

"No, we did not detect a scan as we crashed, in fact, we did not detect one since we fired on his ship. His damage must be severe."

"When it shows a life form, will it tell ya what it is?"

"It will clearly show the shape for identification, yes.....Besides, I will know the invader's signature."

"You can't see everywhere at one time, though."

"No,...that's why we must destroy the ship first, to stop the beacon."

"Well, one thing's for sure, once that ship's gone, he's gonna come lookin'!"

"Yes, but we will be waiting."

"Ain't you afraid of anything, man?"

"I doubt things, but then I make adjustments,...but I do not fear, no!... My training disallows it."

"Well I ain't that brave!" He grunted then. "Thirty-five years old and afraid a th' dark!"

"It is not the dark you fear, Max, but of what is in the dark. Fear is a good thing, it will eliminate carelessness,...you must try and rest now." He picked another wafer from his belt and passed it to him. "Your night's meal." He nodded when Max took it and ate it then reached for a smaller one. "Swallow this now, my friend, it will clear your mind and let you rest."

CHAPTER FOUR

He opened his eyes to the heavy cone-laden pine branches above him, and lay there at peace with himself until reality returned and he remembered where he was. Raising himself to his elbows, he saw Korak standing amid the rocks with his detector screen pointed in a westerly direction and sitting up, moved the blanket aside, yawned, and got up to quickly move back into the trees to relieve himself.

Korak was watching as he returned, and as he entered the rocks, gave him another food-wafer. "How do you feel, Max?"

"I'll do, man, thanks! And thanks for these things, too, you're a damn good cook!...You sure you brought enough for both of us?"

"If I did not, then you may cook."

"If I do, you might not make it home!...Sorry, man, bad timin' for a joke like that." He shook his head and ate his meal then turned to look west also "Our man still there?"

"Nothing has changed....But I am pleasantly surprised at the quantity of wildlife on earth, it exceeds my expectations. There are hundreds of species, and as many different birds....I am truly envious, Max, your world is beautiful!"

"And I sure would like to keep it that way!" He squatted and rolled up the bedroll. "You sleep any?"

"I had rest, yes. But mostly, the night sounds held my fascination. Nothing on Promas compares to what you have here. Earth has no equal."

"Appears I might have to add an extra bedroom to my house, you keep thinkin' that way."

"I must say something, Max." He said, turning to look westward again. "You asked If I can kill this invader and his pet,...yes, I can!...But he can also kill me, as well as every living thing on Earth!...All he will need is time. It is also true that I have no fear of this being, but being without fear does not save a life....If I fail, you must take my weapons and kill him,...and then you must remove any evidence of our being here!"

"Will I have a choice, Korak?...I don't think so, if he gets you, he'll likely get me at th' same time.....But If I'm alive, you got my word, man! As long as there's a breath in me, I'll try to kill that son of a bitch!" He blinked then and stared at Korak's profile, and as if really seeing him for the first time, and hearing the sincerity and feeling in his voice, at that moment knew that he was human after all. "But right now," He said with a sigh. "We have a job to do. Come on, man, let's saddle up!"

They were once again working the animals through a dense maze of trees, and mid-morning found them on a treacherous descent along the downside of the mountain, which slowed their rate of travel to a snail's pace. But eventually, they had just made the floor of a small box canyon when Max caught movement in the trees some fifty yards away and stopped the horse.

Korak opened the locator screen and scanned the area in question.

"What do ya see? He asked in a low voice, and he could suddenly feel his heart beating faster in his chest.

"It appears to be a group of animals,...and they are feeding on another animal, whose heat signature is rapidly fading....Do you know them?" He turned the screen toward him, and he could see the fiery-red images as they moved about their prey.

"Wolves." He said with a sigh of relief. "Killed themselves a deer."

"These wolves, they are carnivores?"

"Meat eaters, yeah, and mean when cornered. Come on, man, we got another mountain to climb." He led the way through the underbrush, and they were quickly traversing up the side of yet another sloping mountainside,...and the animals were having to make several attempts at times to maintain a footing, and if not for the hill's massive growth of trees that footing would have been impossible,...but by mid-afternoon, they were on another sidelong descent down the other side, only this time they were able to continue westward along an animal-trail that wound its way along the side of the mountain.

By late afternoon, both were tired, and the horses worn out, when suddenly the stillness was shattered by rifle-fire. Instantly alerted to a possible danger, or of someone in trouble, they stopped their horses to listen. They heard the muffled screams of terror then, and then several more gunshots before it became silent again.

Korak had turned the sensor toward the sounds when they heard the shooting, and when Max turned to look at him. "We have found the beast, Max." He said grimly. "I also show that it is retreating back up the mountain."

"What about th' shooting, th' screams?"

"I show two life-forms still at the scene."

"Then let's see about it." He led the way off the beaten trail and down the hillside into the valley below them before continuing on toward where the sounds had originated.

He recognized the squatting Indians right away, but then spotted their ponies some distance away in the trees behind them, counting four animals in all,...and immediately knew that at least two of the party had been slain by the beast. It was not until the Indians heard their approach and got to their feet that he saw the dark, widespread stain on the ground at their feet.

The two Arapaho Indians held their rifles on them as they watched them approach, waiting patiently until they stopped in front of them,...and Max could see the terror still on their faces and in the way their weapons wavered in trembling hands as they stared at him.

"What happened here?" He asked, looking past them at the bloodiest scene he had ever encountered. What appeared to be a woman's leg, complete with moccasin lay in the giant pool of blood, along with other assorted, unrecognizable body parts. The remains of a gutted pony's mutilated torso lay nearby.

"What happened?" He asked again hoarsely.

"Diablo!" Returned one of them, lowering his weapon to step forward. "A mountro!" He said, raising a hand in front of him and looking back at the death scene.

"A monster?" Asked Max in a trembling voice.

"Yes," Returned the Indian. "A monster,...Bestia!" He stared at the scene again. "My woman, my brother, my mother, all gone!" He looked back at them with tears on his leather-like face. "It ate them,...it tore them apart and ate them....My woman's horse as well." He gestured hopelessly with his hands. "We shoot it, but it does no good, so we run and shoot some more.... It was Diablo!"

Max looked at Korak and shuddered. "Diablo means Devil, Bestia, th' beast!"

"Yes." He nodded, once again scanning the area. "I understand, but it is gone now."

"Wonder why it left them alive?"

"Noise from the weapons, perhaps,...it would not be something it would have heard before,...it was startled."

"Makes sense, I guess." He got the Indian's attention again.

"Your people are dead now, old man,…leave them and go home, you can't help them!...If the beast comes back, you'll be dead, too, so go home!...Warn your people, and those from other tribes to stay out of these mountains till we can kill it."

"You hunt Diablo?"

"Yeah,' He nodded. "We hunt Diablo."

"Then we will go….But if Arapaho bullets do not kill him, your bullets will not kill him….You will be killed, too!"

He watched them both turn and go for their ponies, which had scattered into the trees some forty yards away then sighing, looked back at Korak. "That thing tell ya where it went?"

"Only that it is gone."

"If it knows your scent, why did it stop to do this?...It must a known we was here someplace."

"Hunger, maybe, maybe wind prevented detection. It is a beast, Max, and like any animal, is driven by hunger. It is no longer a threat."

"Works for me, my friend." He sighed then. "Now we know he's huntin' us already, we can't waste any more time. Come on, we got us another hill to climb, and I'd guess, another two miles or so of mountains before we find that ship." He nodded farewell to the Arapaho and led the way back toward the hillside.

It was almost dark once again by the time they made the top of the tall mountain, and he had no choice but to call a halt for the night again. He reined around to face Korak.

"We can camp here for th' night." He looked up at the already darkening sky. "After what I saw back there, I'm sort a anxious to keep goin' and get this over with….But if somethin' happens to one a these horses, we'll be afoot, easy pickin' for that thing if it's followin' us."

"Yes, I agree." Nodded Korak.

"It ain't all that far now anyway," He said gesturing to the West with a nod of his head. "That's Table Mountain off yonder. "How close you got a be to blow up that thing?"

"No more than one kilometer, but less is better. My weapon fires a star-burst of pure, highly electrified energy plasma….Once the target is calibrated and I fire the weapon, nothing can stop it, the ship will be destroyed!...I will fire two missiles in case of error,…and to insure complete destruction."

"I hope that bastard is in his ship when it goes!"

"As I do, but we can not rely on that, Max."

"That's true." He sighed. "Anyway, th' other side a that smaller peak there, between us and Table Mountain, ought a be close enough if th' ship is visible....Shouldn't be more than a mile away, you sure that, uh, missile thing will hold up that far?"

"Hopefully it will, yes!...I do not know the calculations for your mile but, yes, we shall see."

"Then let's unsaddle these horses and let 'em graze. You might want a scan th' area too, I can do without any surprises."

"As can I." They unsaddled and placed the saddles and bedrolls on the ground, and after accepting his evening wafer, Max ate it and sat down while the area of mountain-top was being scanned.

"The beast is not within a kilometer of our location." Said Korak as he closed the sensor and sat down. "We are safe for now."

"For now?...I don't like th' sound a that!"

"Not to worry, Max, the sensor is scanning as we speak, should an animal larger than our horses come near, it will warn me."

"Elk up here's bigger than a horse!"

"Are you feeling ill, Max?"

"No,...no, I just can't get th' sight a them dead Arapaho out a my mind."

"Yes,...that was the sight on Promas before the war, only many times worse."

"I didn't realize that, sorry, Korak....I'll tell ya somethin' though, I might be getting' hooked on them cookies a yours, I feel stuffed!"

"There are more in the ship."

"Okay, now that I'm feelin' better. Where, exactly is this Milky-way you talked about?"

"It is there," He said, looking northward in the starlit sky. "More than a billion stars make up the Milky-way, all clustered together in such a way that it appears all white in color."

Damn, I never knew that's what it was called. I've seen that a thousand times and never gave it a thought!...Guess I took it all for granted, same as everythin' in my life. If I live through this, that's all gonna change, too!... And you say Promas is on th' other side?"

"Straight up from there, yes."

"If we're alive when this is over, maybe you could contact one a them little gray friends a yours and fix your machine....Maybe give me a ride up to that milky-way? Must be awful pretty up there."

"Perhaps I can, Max....It would be my honor to do so."

"Then would you say we got a fifty-fifty chance a pullin' this off?"

"At least that, yes."

"Works for me!...I'll take them odds any day."

"Do not worry, my friend, we will succeed!...So now,…I would like to know about your family."

"You would?...Okay….But first, I got a question!...I them Aliens took a notion to send another one to mop up after this one,…would that scanner there tell you it was comin'?"

"Yes," He said, opening the cover once again. "My ship's sensors recorded the alien ship's heat signature….If another ship enters Earth's atmosphere, the warning will be sent to me here….It will appear as a blinking white dot in the upper right corner." He pointed at the spot with his finger.

"My wife's name is Helen," He nodded. "And I might add, th' handsomest woman in all these Rocky Mountains, been married for ten years now! Got a great son, too, name's Lance. He's seven now and th' light of our lives." He sighed then and cleared his throat. "We came here in fifty-eight, hadn't been married all that long,…anyway, I teamed up with a couple prospectors and went lookin' for gold, found some, too! Didn't get rich, but we had us a good stake….A while later, we met another down-and-outer, who just happened to own title to my ranch here at th' time, so I bought th' place from 'im,…and that's my whole story in a nut-shell!...And after tomorrow, could very well be my entire life's story!

"It would be good to meet your family, Max, but it is best I do not….It is also best that you never tell them of this,…or have you?"

"No,…they think you're a lawman that broke a leg,…I'm helpin' you track down a killer."

"Thank you,…you must be the only one to know."

"Gonna be a hard secret to keep, Korak,…but ya got my word." He pulled the blanket over his legs then. "Gonna be another cold night,… we'll have snow in another thirty days, maybe sooner. You get snow on Promas, man?"

"Yes, our winters are very long, and quite frigid!...We have no direct sunlight, as you do here and the planet is slow to thaw….Snow is very beautiful!"

"Yes it is….When winter sets in, these mountains'll be a snow-covered paradise, and to me, a good time to stay in next to th' fire!"

"What about your cattle, Max,…I saw the animals grazing by the stream while you were gone?"

"We'll round 'em all up and keep 'em in close to th barn area. We don't, they'll wander off someplace and freeze to death….Chickens got more sense than a cow!"

"Chicken?"

"Yeah, a chicken is a large bird,...but it ain't a bird, exactly....Anyway, we raise 'em for th' eggs they lay, makes for a good breakfast....We also eat them, you should taste Helen's fried chicken. You'd stay here for sure then!" He became silent then and cleared his throat of the sudden lump in it. "Gonna be hard on them if I die up here!"

"I am sorry, Max."

"For what, if I hadn't come along, who would a fixed your leg, you'd a never made it to your ship alone?...Some things are just meant to be, man!"

"And I am grateful."

"No need for that, neither....I'm here by choice, my decision all th' way! Helen's tough as nails, too,...they'll be okay."

"As you will, my friend."

"Well, I don't plan on dyin', if that's what ya mean?...But tell me, man,...how do ya survive weapons like yours, guns that shoot explodin' fireballs, and lightenin' bolts, nothin' can survive fire power like that!...And it's hard to believe that we will if that Bastard ever shoots at us!"

"There is always a chance to survive, Max. His is a pulse cannon, it fires in bursts of energy, much like mine....We will see it coming, and because of that, there is a chance to avoid the impact,...a small one, but it is there. However, we must move quickly."

"What about a sidearm, he has one, don't he?"

"Yes, a disintegrator such as my own. But like my own, it's power fades with distance....We survive by destroying him first, Max,...and neither him, nor his pet can come near us without detection."

"This scares th' shit out a me, Korak, I want ya to know that!"

"Yes."

"I just hope like hell, he's in that ship when you blow it up!...If he's workin' on it, there's a good chance he will be.""Perhaps,...but if his ship's sensors detect my weapon's signature as it fires, he will have time to escape destruction. You must not depend on that. First, we destroy his ship's beacon and then we find and destroy him, and his pet."

"Wish I was as sure of all this, as you are."

"I am not sure, Max, no one can be sure of victory. But as you said before, we have a fifty-fifty chance of survival,...as does he!...If it is to be, with your help, I will complete this mission....It is what I do as a soldier." He looked around at the rocks and trees then.

"I have never fought a war on an alien world before now....I have spent half my life in a star-fighter patrolling our galaxy,...and when on the ground, my time was spent in a simulator preparing for war. I have been in training my entire life, Max,...and I have also been prepared to accept defeat, and death should I fail a mission!...I have never failed a mission, and I will not fail this one."

"And I'm gonna hold ya to it!...How many wars you been in?"

"Only this one, but I have been fighting it for more than ten years."

"Tell me about that, ah, th' mother ship that's still there, you really think it's pride keepin' 'em from leavin'?...Hell, they lost th' war already!"

"You are a wise man, Max, yes, we also believe that!...The Cryorans have succeeded in attaching listening devices to the hull of the mother ship."

"Thought you said they had a,…what is it, a force-field around it,… how'd they manage that?"

"It was an experimental project to test the shield's fabric, and it worked. Even now, they are using that technology to build a larger, more powerful cannon, one that can penetrate, and destroy the ship….But, out of curiosity, Max, why would you think they are still there?"

"It's obvious to me, they're plannin' somethin'!...I think they got a plan, and they think it'll work."

"We think that as well. Even though we have not been able to fully understand their speech, the Elders, as well as the Cryorans believe they are building a weapon of massive proportion, one that in all possibility could destroy Promas. That is why the Cryorans are working with our scientists to perfect one of our own….But should ours not be completed in time, we have a thousand star-fighters waiting in space. The one thing the invaders cannot do, is fire their ship's weapons without first dropping the shields. The shields take most all the ship's power to maintain its stability."

"Once they drop the shields to fire their weapon, one thousand star-fighters will fire on them!...Our technology is more than sufficient."

"That where you was when they sent ya here?"

"I was there, yes….It was Idak that detected the lone warship as it left our solar system and reported it. I received my orders several hours later."

"It's damn sure hard to imagine all that."

"It was hard for me to imagine this, Max….It's a wondrous planet, beautiful in its primitive state. Promas is nothing like this, not now….It was similar, so I read in the archives, but civilization tends to erase beauty. When we return to my ship, I will show you a bit of recorded history on Promas. You will see what a billion years of habitation does to a once beautiful world."

"Show me,…how?"

"From videos recorded on the ship's memory banks. I have logged much of it, including our war in space. We will use the videos later for training exercises."

"Videos?...Explain that."

"Moving pictures, Max,...do you have cameras here?"

"A black box that takes pictures, yeah, I've seen 'em."

"A moving picture camera takes pictures at a much faster speed, and on a continuous roll of film. The video is when we play it back on a screen to watch it."

"And the pictures move?"

"You might say that, things in the picture do....It is much like seeing something with your eyes, as if you are there watching it. That is called a video,.mine, however, utilizes a much more sophisticated method of doing the same thing. It's called electronics, It does the same thing, but without the film,...you'll see."

"I can't wait!"

"It is well after dark, Max, do you wish another pill to rest."

"I don't think so, not tonight!...I don't think that pill could make me sleep anyway!...Our war starts tomorrow, and I want a know I'm alive, not sleepin' part a my life away....You go ahead though."

* * *

He had unwillingly fallen asleep several times as he gazed at the night sky's brilliance, but each time, visions of a monstrous wild beast as it ripped and tore at its helpless victims awakened him with their screams of terror echoing in his mind. This time, however, he awoke with a mixture of fear and hatred in his heart and disgustedly threw the blanket aside and got to his feet. The moon was full and quite low in the western sky, and was lighting up the cold campsite with a bright, yet pale yellow glow,...and as he exhaled a cloud of steamy breath into the cold mountain air, was startled when Korak spoke to him.

"You were having dreams, my friend."

"No, no,...I was havin' nightmares!"

"The Arapaho?"

"I'd as soon not talk about it."

"Then I have two questions, the first is,...what exactly is an Arapaho? I know I saw them, but they are so different than you, or I, and their speech is different."

"They're Indians,...Native Americans. They was here first!...The Arapaho's only one of a thousand different tribes in this country, one of about thirty livin' in these mountains,...Arapaho, Ute, Apache, Cherokee and others. And at one time or another, we was at war with all of 'em....If what you told me was th' truth, they're descendants of your first colony as well."

"Of that, I am sure, Max, and it is interesting. These thousand tribes are all of the same skin tone and characteristics, is that correct?"

"They are all of the same race, yeah, different languages and all. Just like the blacks."

"There are black men as well?"

"Yes,...this country used them as slaves once....That's what our stupid war was all about!"

"Environmental evolution!" He muttered. "Max, that means that as my people spread across the earth those many eons ago, the environment in different parts of the world must have forced them to evolve differently in order to survive!...I do not quite understand the language difference, but it does show the resilience of your ancestors."

"You're talkin' over my head about all that," Chuckled Max...." So, what was your second question?"

"Oh, yes....I have been sitting here while you slept, and wondering about the red glow in the clouds over the mountains there....Is it the moon's reflection, or a normal occurrence?"

Max quickly looked and could see the orange glow, and as he watched it, a chill ran up his spine. "That ain't no cloud, Korak, it's smoke from that gold camp, I told you about. Looks like it's on fire, th' whole settlement from th' looks of it!...Damn it, those poor people!" He turned then to find Korak beside him. "You think he done that?"

"It's more than probable, Max, and I am sorry."

"For what?...We couldn't a stopped it!...But we can make th' bastard pay for it, and by God, we will!"

"Of that, I am sure, Max."

He watched the red-orange hue as it played against the smoke then took a deep breath. "Be daylight in a couple a hours, none too soon for me!...Will that magic screen a yours tell us if he's in his ship tomorrow?"

"If he is inside, no. But if he is nearby, and we are close enough, yes!... You are feeling anger as well as sadness now, my friend, and you must control both emotions. Because they will breed carelessness....Once the ship is destroyed, he will be angry,...and there will be more death until we find him."

"Then we'll have to try and warn folks, get 'em to leave th' mountains till it's over!...There's got a be six or seven homesteads scattered about out there, some I don't even know about!"

"That would not be wise, Max, this alien is a soldier. He will know we do this, and he can kill from a great distance!"

"We have to try, Korak, they'll be helpless if him, or that animal a his attacks. I know it's too dangerous, man, but we don't know where this bastard is and so far, he don't know where you are! At least not till we blow up his ship, he won't!...What I'm sayin' is this,...once we blow that ship, we go back a different way and warn a few a these farmers along th' way. If he finds out, maybe he'll follow us back and we can be waitin' for 'im!...Fight on our terms, not his."

"All right, my friend." Said Korak. "I understand, and I agree." He stared at the now fading orange glow as the distant smoke began to dissipate some. "I am not trained to fight a war on the ground, so I will bow to your knowledge of such things."

"I could get us killed."

"As could I, Max, but there is no dishonor to die while saving a life. If by warning these farmers, we help them to survive, then so be it!...But there is one important thing to remember,...this being is a raider, and unpredictable! He does not use a plan for war. Should we be seen, he will attack without warning!...If he should detect our presence, he will call his pet to find us first,...and he will find pleasure in watching the beast murder us!" He stared at the fading, orange glow for a few seconds before placing a hand on Max's shoulder.

"We must be prepared, Max. Because if we should kill his pet, he will not be far behind....He will know our location."

"Sounds hopeless when you say it."

"War is hopeless, my friend. There is only destruction in its wake!"

"Yeah, well, I know all about that sort a thing!"

"As do I!...My Mother and Father perished when these pets were released on Promas!"

"What?...Damn it, man, I didn't know, I'm sorry!"

"It was a long time ago, Max, but thank you."

"How did they put them things on th' planet without somebody knowing it?"

Korak thought about it for a moment. "A few thousand years of serenity, is my best answer, Max!...Our security forces were lax. The sensors warned us of a presence in space, but only those watching failed to see it as a warning, mistaking the blips on the screens as meteor showers, not alien warships!... Even the ship that released the beasts was thought to be a meteor striking the planet in one of its remote areas."

"It was not until the Cryorans warned us that the Elders took action!... Luckily, we were never lax in our training, we were ready when our star fighters took to space!...However,...hundreds of Promasians died and were eaten by the alien creatures by the time our ground troops destroyed them.... Now, our Councel of Elders consists of Promasians, and Cryorans."

"But you won, and that's a good thing."

"Yes, but only after losing half of our fleet of star fighters....The invaders sent most of ten thousand warships out to meet us. They were like a swarm of insects, all firing laser cannons and torpedoes in all directions!...Even though we were all cloaked, the weapons took their toll....They finally retreated, as did we to regroup and rearm....We battled them for years before defeating them!...The few remaining warships retreated back to the mother, and remained there."

"You didn't chase 'em, they were on th' run?"

"Yes,...but our weapons failed to penetrate the large ship's force-field, and that ship's primary weapons were much too powerful!...So we backed our fleet off until we were out of range,...and we wait for their shields to drop."

"All I can say is, I'm damn glad you saw this bastard leave!"

"As will I be glad,...when he is dead!"

Nodding, Max sighed as he looked at the predawn sky. "What say we saddle up and go take care a business?" And together they turned to retrieve saddle and bedrolls and walked off into the trees.

* * *

They were on the down-slope of the tree-studded hill when Max stopped them and pointed toward the valley below them. "See th' smoke, Korak, that's from one a th' homesteads....Another one off yonder in th' distance,... prob'ly sittin' down to breakfast, getting' ready for a day's work....They don't know they could be dead in a few hours!" He watched the drifting smoke for a moment longer then clucked his horse on down through the tangle of brush and trees,...and for the next several hours battled the rocky, broken terrain,...their horses at times having to fight for their footing on the sliding shale and debris.

It was mid-afternoon when they stopped the animals and peered up through the trees at the low hill.

"We're here, man." He remarked as he looked up. "Table Mountain's right on th' other side a this hill....Th' Bastard's ship is in th' valley under it....So, what do ya think, go up and shoot down at it, or go around to th' valley?"

"We could be seen in the valley....It is better to fire from above, I think.""Then let's leave th' horses here and go up on foot!...Think you can make it with that leg?"

"It will be difficult, Max, but yes, I will make it!"

They dismounted and once ready, Max led the way up the hill's rocky ascent, careful to keep the Henry Rifle from being entangled in the brush, or maybe cause him to lose his footing. They climbed steadily upward for another hour until he spotted another worn animal trail and decided to follow it around to the other side of the low mountain, following it for yet another hour until they could look down into the canyon-like valley below.

Dropping to their knees behind a large outcropping of rocks, Korak opened the sensors screen to scan the valley's forested floor.

"What do ya see?" Breathed Max, nervous anticipation like a half aired up balloon in his chest to make it harder to breathe than just the altitude itself.

"No life forms in the valley at all!" Responded Korak as he closed the sensor and removed the star-burst rifle from his back. "The ship is there, in the mountain's shadow." He touched his face then, and the mask suddenly appeared out of his suit and wrapped around his face, as did the colored glass-looking strip across his eyes. He stared down at the canyon's floor for a moment before lifting the weapon and flipping up a small screen that had been folded against it.

"You gonna be able to see, man?" Asked Max urgently, his nerves fast becoming on edge. "I mean, that sun's right in your face here?...Here!" He took off his hat and placed it on Korak's head. "How's that?...You can see better with a little shade."

"Very good,…thank you, Max!" He raised the rifle, and himself slightly above the rocks, and while watching the small screen, was startled when Max spoke again.

"You sure it's there, man,…I don't see a damn thing down there?"

"You will see it very soon, my friend, be patient." He aimed the weapon downward as Max watched, then suddenly there were two distinct, yet subtle sounds, like sudden puffs of wind as he fired twice.

Two brilliant balls of pure electrified energy could be seen flying toward the trees below them. Then it was as if all the oxygen had been momentarily sucked from the air around them as the fiery missiles hit, and as Korak pulled him down behind the rocks, there was a blinding flash of light, followed by what sounded like lightening strikes of pure energy whipping at the air around them, electrified energy that caused the hair on his head to stand to attention,…and then there was nothing!

Max raised up for a look and could not believe his eyes. There was a large area of charred, still smoking ground there, and nothing else! Burnt earth, for what looked to be a hundred yards around, even up the side of Table Mountain.

"My God, Korak!" He breathed, reaching up to smooth his hair down. "That's some kind a gun, man!...Took ship, trees and all!...That's gonna piss th' Bastard off for sure!"

Korak gave him his hat and as he put it on, retracted the mask. "He now knows the ship has been destroyed, Max, his sensor will tell him so.... He also will know that I am here." He shouldered the rifle as he spoke. "We must leave before he returns, should he fire at this location while we are here, we will die here!"

Nodding, Max quickly led the way back along the treacherous path, taking more than an hour to half-run and half-slide their way back down to the horses where they quickly mounted and worked the animals down through the valley's lush meadows of fresh-cut hayfields toward another of the several homesteads in the area. Keeping the horses at a fast trot across the field, his heart was pounding, both in fear of being followed, and of not being able to convince the farmer to leave their home and go down the mountain.

"How does it look?" He asked, stopping his horse to watch as Korak scanned the farmhouse and outbuildings.

"It shows four life-forms together, but not in the larger structure.... No others on the sensor at all! I think something is not right here, Max." He pulled the smaller sidearm from his belt, and after adjusting its power setting, nodded at Max.

"There should be animal-life near the structures, on the hillsides, and birds in the air,...and there is nothing!...They were all frightened away."

"Th' pet, ya think?"

"Since the structures are still intact, yes, I believe the beast was here....I will go first, Max." Korak led the way to within fifty feet of the large, old log house, and could see the deep, sweeping claw marks on the logs and door of the house.

"Look at that, man!" Breathed Max in almost a whisper. "Bastard was here all right....Don't see any blood on th' porch anywhere, so maybe they were gone."

"No." Returned Korak, still watching the scanner's screen. "They are still here, somewhere behind the structure....Again,...let me go first, my friend." With weapon ready, he urged the highly nervous animal along the long porch and around the side of the house, and was just as quickly confronted with what remained of the farmer's livestock. Remains of the mutilated animals lay scattered in wide pools of blood and waste all over the barnyard.

"Appears it got 'em all." Gasped Max as he gagged from the sight. "Cows, horses, hogs, there's nothin' left!" Looking over the yard, he spotted the crude, half-excavated hole in the side of an odd-looking earthen mound of heavy logs and dirt, and getting Korak's attention, urged his horse toward it.

"That's a root-cellar, is that where they are?"

"They are there, yes." Stopping his horse in front of the almost flat, heavy log door of the cellar, they could clearly see the deep slashes again and at one point, almost cutting through the large logs.

"Looks like it gave up on it and left." Said Max as he dismounted and walked to the damaged door to kick it a couple of times.

"HELLO, TH" ROOT CELLAR!" He yelled. "YOU CAN COME OUT NOW, IT'S GONE!" He kicked the door again. "Come on out a there, Shelby, it's Max Pruett!" He saw the heavy door move then and reached down to grab it, helping the two very scared and haggard-looking boys lift the heavy door and swing it open.

"My God!" Breathed Max as he stared into the dark hole at the dirty faces staring up at him. "Where's your daddy, boys?" And when they moved aside, a wide-eyed, badly trembling Leon Shelby came to the steps to grab one of his sons for support as he stared blankly up at them.

"Bring your family out a there, Leon, th' beast is gone." He reached down to take Shelby's trembling hand and help him up the steps into the yard where he went to his knees and cried brokenly at sight of the gruesome scene. Shaking his head, Max then helped Korak, and between them managed to get the wife and two boys up the steps and on solid ground,… and while the woman clung to the two boys and wailed, he went to help Shelby to his feet.

"You got no time for this, Leon, get yourself together!...Ya hear me, man,…ya got a get your family out a here!"

"Wha,…what?" Gasped Shelby as he turned terrified eyes to stare at him. "It,…it killed everythin',…never seen nothin' like it!...Never in my life seen nothin' like it!...I seen it comin', right down th' road yonder, I seen it!...I never want a see nothing; like that again." He grabbed Max's arm then and looked toward the front of the house.

"Ma, my hounds, th, they took off after th' thing, and it ate 'em, stood up on two legs and ate 'em!...It come straight from hell, it did,.,..straight from hell."

Holding back his tears as he listened to Shelby, he finally took the man's shoulders and shook him. "Get hold of yourself, Leon!" He looked back at the woman then and called her to come take care of him, and as she held her husband's wracking body, Max turned to see the two mules as they wandered back toward the barn.

"Hey, you boys!" He said quickly. "Catch up them mules and hitch up th' wagon yonder.…Do it now, damn it!" He watched them run toward the animals then turned back to the still sobbing farmer, pulled him from his wife's grasp and shook him again. "Stop blubberin', man!...You ain't dead yet!"

"Don't shake my husband like that!" Screamed the woman as she put herself between them, and as it seemed to Max, she saw the bloody yard for the first time then, because she screamed shrilly. "Oh, my God!" She yelled. "Oh my dear God!"

Max turned her around. "Maam,...Maam, listen to me!...If you don't get him and your boys away from here, you're all gonna die!...That thing could come back and look for ya!...You understand me, Maam?" And when she nodded. "When th' boys get that wagon hitched up, you all get out a here."

"Wha,..where'll we go?...Oh my God!"

"Just get out a these hills, go down to Golden, anywhere, only go!"

Nodding, she urged her husband around the root cellar and across the yard, where the boys had just finished harnessing the skittish mules to the light wagon,...and with their help managed to get Shelby into the carriage's bed. She scrambled up to the seat as the two boys jumped aboard and whipped the mules into a run toward the rutted old road.

"That poor bastard looked th' Devil in th' face, man,...and he might never get over it."

"Yes." Nodded Korak. "The mind is a fragile thing."

"Ya think it might come back?" He asked, grabbing the horse's dangling reins and mounting, to watch as Korak pulled himself into the saddle.'

"It is hunting me, Max....It is aimlessly roaming the mountains in search of my scent. I believe it only came here in passing, and as was its nature, when it saw the animals, killed them and feasted....If it should sense that I was here, yes, it will return."

"Maybe not, too." Sighed Max. "We seem to be followin' it, not th' other way around....Any way to tell where it went?"

"Only that it is gone."

"Then it could a gone down th road there, same as th' Shelbys."

"Perhaps not, Max. It is a stalker, it will hunt where it cannot be seen."

"I hope so....There's another homestead a couple a miles southeast a here, we'll warn 'em, if we can, then work our way back to th' ship." He gigged the horse back to the road and then to a gallop in wake of the Shelby's wagon. But as he twisted around to look back, could see that Korak was having to work hard at staying in the saddle and slowed the animal back to a walk while Korak righted himself and came alongside.

"Sorry, man,...th' urge to hurry got to me."

"I also feel the need to hurry, Max. But I am afraid my horsemanship disagrees."

"It's better this way, you'll have time to watch that sensor a yours....Sure wish we knew where that thing went?...Cause I don't mind tellin' ya, I'm scared to death!"

"I am sorry, Max."

"For what, you didn't bring th' thing here!"

"Because they are here!" He sighed. "This should never have occurred, Max....But they will both be terminated, of that I am sure!"

"I know that, man, I do!...But it would help if we knew where that alien killer is!...We know it was likely him done in th' gold camp last night, but where did he go?...If he went back to his ship, he's madder'n hell right now!"

"Yes, I am sure of that!" Nodded Korak. "But he will not rush blindly into battle, angry or not, he will follow his pet's signal....He will allow the beast to find us before he comes, and if it has not yet killed us, he is confident, that he will!"

"Well if he's followin' that monster, he'll come this way."

"Perhaps, perhaps not!....Over the years, we have tried to profile the invaders, as have the Cryorans, and we still do not know who, or what they are,...or what drives them to do what they do?...They are not human, yet they are not animals, they are something in between,...maybe reptile, or something akin to it. They are beings, seemingly without conscience, or moral code. Yet, they are capable of building highly technical starships and weapons....That tells us they are also highly skilled and intelligent!...We do not know what they are, except that they are relentlessly aggressive, and quite cruel!"

"Maybe they stole th' technology, you think a that?...Maybe even their starships....Ain't that what they do, kill planets and steal resources?"

"You are highly intelligent yourself, Max. We think alike, you and I."

"Well, hell, we're relatives, what would ya expect?" They both chuckled at that, causing Max to peer at him. "Hey, man, that's th' first time I got a laugh out a you, I was beginnin' to think you couldn't!...You don't get scared, you don't get mad, and that, right there, makes us different."

"My training did not allow for emotions, Max, and I have mused about it!...It felt strange to laugh,...perhaps I am becoming an Earthling!"

"I'll go along with that!...Hell, you're home now, emotions are allowed." He grinned then looked the terrain over again. "Wish it would rain, though, we could track that bastard a lot better,...and I'd feel better if I knew for sure it weren't layin' in wait for th' Shelby's somewhere along that road."

"As would I, my friend....But it is out of our control now. You did the right thing."

"I guess,...at any rate, we might ought a leave th' road ourselves, that other homestead's in a valley th' other side a this mountain, maybe we can get there ahead a that thing." With that, he reined the horse up the embankment and into the forest of trees to begin the arduous climb along the heavily foliaged side of the tall hill, and immediately found themselves in thick tangles of thorn-briars and fallen, dead limbs of which gouged and tore at both them and the animals.

Urgency was like one of the long briar-thorns stabbing at Max's gut as they climbed, and the memory of the scene at the Shelby homestead was like a sharp knife in his heart and mind. How could a good and just God of all creation, one whose very son gave his life for the good of mankind, also create a world of beings like the alien invaders?...Life has no meaning to them!

He had never hated anyone, or anything so severely before, and he wanted to see this alien dead, and the beast he brought with him!...How could this happen, he wondered? Had God finally forsaken the very world he created?...Maybe it was all just a myth to begin with, God, Adam and Eve, the Bible, all of it! It made sense, he thought sadly. Maybe they were all descendents of those first colonies on earth, making everyone on earth blood relatives, and the Bible a book of lies!...That, he thought then, would be the saddest thing of all!

What if Korak's theory of environmental evolution was true, maybe skin color and language was the only difference separating them all?... No, he thought, he would never be able to believe it was all true, part of it, maybe, maybe most of it, but not all,…and even if it was, the world needed its belief in God,…and what if the Bible was only a book of rules to live by?...There would be hell to pay without it!

It was late afternoon when they topped the forested hill, and that's where he stopped again to allow Korak to come in beside him. "Well,…I can hear birds in th' trees, and see Crows in th' air. Guess that thing ain't been here yet!"

"There is also wild-life on the sensor again.…Where is this farm structure you spoke of?"

"That canyon below us,…I can smell bread baking from here." He grimaced from pain at several places on his legs then, and leaned to check out the dozen or so blood-stained holes and small tears in his pant-legs,… and then noticed there were none at all on Korak. "That's one good suit a clothes, man, not a scratch on 'em.…I tried cuttin' 'em away from your leg th' other day and couldn't, never seen cloth like that before."

"That is because it is not cloth, Max, it is Valirium, a manipulative metal of great strength and durable flexibility. Your knife point will penetrate it by using some force, as will your weapon's projectiles.…It is a resource of Promas, and is also used as the outer skin of my star fighter."

"And not found on Earth, I guess.…You got gold on Promas?"

"We have gold stored in our vaults, yes. But the metal, you call gold can only be found here on earth."

"You got th' gold from here?" He asked, almost in disbelief.... "When?"

"According to the archives, our last mining expedition left earth more than two thousand years ago, Max."

"Where did you mine it?"

"Several places....In what you call, Europe, and Asia, the Continent of Africa."

"If you don't use money, what's it used for?"

"A great many things, circuitry in our Science labs, power chips, this sensor, even our weapons use gold as a power conductor....My star fighter has more than six kilometers of gold wire in the instrument panels alone,... and that is only a fraction if it's uses."

"Th' more I talk to you, th' more I feel like a bug in a sea of giants!"

"Yes, but I harbor no secrets from you, Max, nor will I...When my mission is complete, I will provide you with proof of my visit, and you will see Promas. It will be my gift to you, but only you!...You must not tell anyone."

"I know!" He clucked the horse into motion and began the descent toward the canyon floor. Coming through the trees, they descended the slight embankment and onto another rutted old wagon road and stopped again to study the old log house and outbuildings.

"Well, that's a relief." Grinned Max. "I see cows in the barn lot, horses in th' corral, goats, hogs and chickens! Appears we are in th' clear,...you pickin' up anything yet?"

"Nothing has disturbed the wildlife here." He returned, closing the sensor.

"That's good,...maybe we can get 'em to leave before somethin' does happen.." He clucked his horse along the road until turning off into the farmhouse, and then on to stop at the steps to the long porch.

"Hello, th' house!" He said loudly. "Alexander Webb, it's Max Pruett!" They waited then until the heavy door was slowly swung inward, and a shotgun wielding Alexander Webb stepped out onto the groaning planks of the porch.

"What's th' scattergun for, Alex?"

"For you, you come blamin' me for stealin' another cow!" Webb eyed him narrowly for a minute then frowned with distrust as he stared at Korak. "Who's this peckerwood, Max,...and what th' hell is he wearin?"

Max twisted to grin at Korak before looking back. "This is Mister Korak, Alex, he's, ah,...he's from Washington, works for th' Government.... That's his uniform, ah,...somethin' new they wear, so a hunter won't mistake 'em for a deer and shoot 'em."

"It's stupid-lookin', if it is!...Well, are ye?"

"Am I what?"

"Here accusin' me a stealin' again?"

"Alex, that was more'n a year ago, and I apologized for th' mistake."

"What do ye want then?"

"I'd like ya to hitch up your team and wagon and get your family outa th' mountains for a few days."

"Are ye teched, Pruett,...I ain't goin' nowheres!"

"Look, Alex." He said, crossing both arms on the saddle-horn and leaning forward. "Mister Korak here is lookin' for a killer that's loose in these mountains. He's a real mean one!...Leon Shelby's place was attacked today, killed his livestock and would a killed them, they hadn't locked themselves in th' root cellar....And he could be comin' here next!"

Webb stared at him for a moment longer. "Well, I say let th' Bastard come, I got buckshot waitin' for his ass....No man's gonna run me off my place, Pruett!...Now, I know you, don't like ya much, but I know ye....But I don't know this Government turd from Adam! So I'm askin' ye both to leave my property,...Go on, git!"

"Alex, don't let your stubbornness get your wife and kids killed?...That scattergun won't stop this lunatic, he'll hack ya to pieces!...Please, get 'em out a here, go to town for a few days, go anywhere, just get th' hell out a these mountains!"

"I ain't heard nothin' about no killer loose up here!"

"I just told ya, man, who else would a told ya?...We was at Shelby's place, we seen what he done! Son of a bitch burned th' gold camp down yesterday, too, don't know how many he killed....Alex, get your family out a here, please?"

CHAPTER FIVE

"Think of your family, Alex, Im tellin' you th' truth, man, come on!…I'm tellin' you, man, that scatter gun won't stop this thing, hell, a buffalo gun won't stop it."

"Ill study on it." Said webb, squinting hard at them both.

"Study on it?…Alex, there just ain't time enough to do that." He glared at Webb for a few seconds then nodded. "Okay, you do that, Alex,…but if you contemplate too damn long, you'll find yourself shit creek without a paddle."

"I'll study on it, Pruett, ain't sayin' I will, or won't,…now git!"

"Okay, Alex, we'll go. But don't be a fool, man, take your family down to Golden for a week, till we catch this Maniac."

"We?...You helpin' 'im?" He nodded at Korak as he spoke.

"That's right, we been huntin' 'im for three days now, he's close, too!"

"Like I said, I'll study on it!"

"Don't study too long!...Let's go, Korak!" He reined his horse around, and with a last look back at Webb, rode out of the yard to the road and headed back into the mountains.

"That's one hard-headed bastard!" He said as Korak pulled alongside. "Damn it!"

"Why did you not tell him of the beast?"

"Th' same reason you don't want me tellin' folks about you."

"I understand."

"Anyway, he sure wouldn't a believed me then!...He's shot and killed most every kind a animal in these hills."

"I understand." He said again.

"Yeah, well that ain't hard." He sighed. "He was me, till I found you!...I hadn't a seen you and that ship a yours,…well, I did!...We did all we could back there, Korak."

"I agree, Max.…Where to now?"

"There's a couple more farms along this road....Two or three back south a Table Mountain, but chances are, they're not there anymore. We'll warn these two and go back to your ship,...I need some coffee bad!" He looked at the ageless trees along both sides of them as they walked the horses, gazing at the dark beneath them and shuddered inwardly as he thought again of the fire-reflected clouds of smoke they had seen. He could almost picture the fear and panic of the men, women and children as they awoke to find themselves under attack.

He had looked down on the camp once while he and Lance were hunting Elk, and knew that the weathered tents and hastily-built log and lumber structures there would have burned quickly,...hopefully, he thought, most of them managed to get away.

"What are you thinking, Max?" Urged Korak as he studied Max's slumped shoulders. "You are feeling responsible for the lives of these farmers, are you not?"

"Yeah,...I guess I am, some."

"You did not bring the invader here, my friend, nor his pet,...nor myself!...No one on earth could have prevented it!"

"I know,...but I was thinkin' a th' gold camp....Do you think th' killer could a seen th' camp, and thought it was your colony?"

"No,...It was there, and he destroyed it! He is a destroyer, a murderer! Killing is what he does. Besides, our Archives told of a place devoid of trees and mountains, a place almost devoid of water as the original site of the colony,...and it was also the source of the ancient signal....Egypt, I believe was the site....No, this invader kills for the pleasure of killing!"

"Egypt?...Never heard a th' place!...But I can't imagine a place with no water. Had to be hot, too!...Wonder why it took so long fot th' signals to reach you?

"There was no mention in the archives as to their decision for the site, but they would have no choice but to adapt to the harsh climate!...As for the signals, we have known for centuries that a sound, once made, whether it be speech, or noise, never dies. Once made, it will travel through time and space, sometimes to be heard thousands of years later on some distant receiver's accidental frequency, whether radio receivers, or the human ear, of which is only a receiver,...and will hear things in a certain frequency....It is a phenomenon that our scientists continue to study. It was just unfortunate that it occurred when it did."

"Man!" Muttered Max, and shook his head. "We go through life here, believing we know all there is to know about th' world we live in,...turns out, we don't know shit about it!...I'll tell ya one thing, Korak, I'll never take it for granted again!"

"No, you will not!...But soon, you will understand much, much more."

"What about th' rest of earth, will they ever know, or understand?"

"Of course, in another few hundred years. When they do, time and space will no longer be a mystery, only a place for exploration."

"How do you know all this?"

"Because you are us, eighty million years ago!...Evolution is inevitable, Max, so is technology."

"You're givin' me a headache, man."

"Yet your need to know makes you ask the questions. Evolution in progress my friend. The more your mind knows and understands, the more it wants to know!...A time will come when the horses you depend on now, will no longer be your primary transportation, wagons, such as these farmers use, will be obsolete, given up for something more comfortable, and faster."

"Like th' Motor Car?" I doubt that, Korak, something like that'll never catch on. In fact, we already have some, I saw th' picture a one in a newspaper once, and ya know what, a horse can walk faster....They called th' thing a horseless carriage."

"If this, Motor car is to be your future primary transportation, I am sure that science will learn to build them better, and faster. If not, it will be in the form of something else entirely....But whatever it may be, it, too will evolve,...It's,..."

"Inevitable," He interrupted. "I know, you told me already."

"So I did. But if it is meant to be, I think you will live to see it."

"Don't know if I like that idea, be a rough ride on roads like these, and it'll never go where this horse will."

"You will adapt Max."

"What about diseases, dysentery, pneumonia and such?"

"We have no disease on Promas, not for several thousand years now. Once a cure is found, the antibodies are added to our food supply to prevent recurrence. Our immunities protect us from the most dreaded of human ailments. Cancer and diabetes are only memories in our archives. The food supplements protect us from all others."

"Damn!" He grinned. "I'll say it again, man....You never cease to amaze me."

"I try, Max....The wafers you have been eating contain the antidote for many of these as well."

"That's good to know, now I won't give that monster a bellyache when it eats me!"

"I am glad you are so lighthearted, my friend. But I assure you, this beast will never harm you....I will destroy it!"

"I hope so, Korak,...you don't how bad, I hope so!"

"I see livestock ahead of us." He said as he pointed the sensor at the road ahead. "Several of your cattle, and horses, several smaller images as well."

"That's th' Yohanson Farm, how does th' rest a th' area look?"

"I see wildlife as well, what you call Elk, with six smaller images." He turned the scanner for Max to see.

"That's got a be wolves, after th' Elk, I guess....That's good news anyway, it didn't come this way. There's th' house, too. Let's hope he has better sense than Webb does."

Earnest Yohanson was waiting for them on his porch as they rode in and stopped their horses. "Max." He nodded. "What brings you out this way?"

"I'm here with a warnin', Ernie, and to ask you a favor."

Yohanson stuck the pipe in his mouth and peered up at him before looking Korak up and down in the fading light. "Who might your friend be, Max?"

"That's Mister Korak, he's a government agent from Washington, Ernie. I'm helping 'im track down a killer in th' mountains here."

"Lawman, huh?...Funny lookin' get-up he's wearin'. What kind a clothes is that?"

"It's a uniform, somethin' new they wear, regulations, ya know....Ernie, about this killer, he's a bad one, a maniac. Killed a couple a Arapaho in th' hills two days back, attacked th' Shelby farm today, killed all their livestock out a meanness, would a killed them, they hadn't been locked in th' root cellar."

"My God, Max, you talkin' truth?"

"As God is my witness, Ernie!...He could be anywhere, and attack anytime. So far, we always seem to be behind 'im, havin' no luck at trackin' 'im, neither....Th' favor I'd like, is for you to take Maudie and th' girls and leave th' mountains till we can catch 'im.. Go down to Golden for a week or so, Lance and Helen are there at th' hotel."

"Lord God, Max, what kind a time we lookin' at here?"

"A day, hours, we got no way a knowin'. He might by-pass your place altogether, but again, he might not."

"I understand that, Max. How much time we got right now?"

"Don't know, but we'll wait till you get hitched up, if ya want?"

Nodding, Yohanson turned toward the door. "Maudie, come out here a minute!" And when she came out to exchange hellos with Max. "We're goin' down to Golden for a few days, pack some things for you and the girls, a clean shirt for me."

"When are we going, Earnest?"

"I'll be hitchin' the wagon in a minute, now go ahead." Without a word, she turned and re-entered the house. "I'm beholden to ya, Max."

"I hope I'm wrong, Ernie. If you see Helen, tell her I'm okay."

"I'll do it!...You watch your ass out there, ya hear?"

"I will do that....You need us to hang around?"

"Nope."

He tipped his hat and led the way back to the road. "I hope th' good Reverend Holt will be that easy."

"Reverend?...I do not understand."

"Preacher, holy man. Don't you have Churches on Promas?"

"No, we do not."

"We do....We go to Church on Sunday, and th' Preacher recites scriptures from the Bible. We call it religion, a belief in God, the all mighty."

"What is a Bible?"

"The Holy Bible tells us how the world was created, about how man was created. It gives us rules to live by,...although not all of us do."

"I would like to see this Bible."

"Don't you believe in God on Promas?"

"The definition of a God would be supreme-being, we have no supreme-being. Our archival records do not speak of God."

"Imagine that." He grinned. "If we live through this, I'll let you read my Bible."

"Thank you....It is getting late, are we to camp again tonight?"

"Your ship is only about three miles from here, as soon as I talk with th' good Reverend, we'll go back....I need some coffee."

"I have been thinking about this bitter brew of yours, Max. It seems to me that it is a, I believe the earth word for it is, drug,...am I correct?"

"Oh no!...Coffee comes from a bean, Korak, they grow it, pick it like fruit, dry it, grind it up real fine,...and then we boil th' grounds in water and drink it....It's a relaxant, like tobacco, quiets th' nerves....Opium's a drug, Laudanum's a drug, but coffee?"

"Sounds addictive, Max." Interrupted Korak. "Much like a drug!"

Max peered at him in the darkness. "Maybe you're right! Get down to it,...it does taste bad, till ya add cream and sugar. Takes some getting' used to. But if it is a drug, I ain't givin' it up!...I'm used to it, might say it's a tradition, a human one, cause everybody drinks it!"

"Forgive me, Max, I am not criticizing you. There is so much I would like to know about my Earth descendents. It is so primitive here, as yet untouched by technology. I am privileged to be witness to it, and honored to be in your company."

"Yeah, me, too, Korak....But I got a tell ya, man, in these last few days, I've learned things I wish I hadn't. My life'll be different from now on."

"I am sorry, Max, it was never intended to be."

"I know, I know." He sighed and then looked beside him at the now pitch-black trees and shrubbery, and it was the same on the other, making him feel very uneasy. "Are we still in th' clear here, feels sort a spooky?"

"The sensor shows only wild animals."

"Nothin' else,...like a blinkin' light up in th' corner there?"

"You are worried about another alien, aren't you?"

"Want th' truth?...Yeah!...I don't know why, but I think they're sendin' help for th' son of a bitch!...A gut feelin', I guess. Th' Wife calls it a premonition....Funny ain't it? I want a see that bastard in front of us so we can kill him, and his creature....But at th' same time, I'm afraid help'll come before we can do it!"

"I understand your fear, Max....You will never again see a predator such as this, and when we do kill them, they will have never faced a braver man than you!...I am honored to fight beside you, my friend....And do not worry, if they were sending him help, we would have been warned before now."

"You're th' brave man here, Korak, but thanks anyway....And I hope you're right!" He cleared his throat then. "Reverend Holt's place ought a be just ahead there."

"Yes, I see images of livestock."

Some twenty minutes later, they were reading a handwritten note by match-light attached to the door of the main house.

"Gone to Golden for a shipment of Bibles, back in a week!...I call that good news, Korak.....Let's go get my coffee."

* * *

The moon was high, and its pale, yellow glow was caressing the tall, waving grass in front of the bluff by the time they stopped in the trees to scan the area and sighing, Max shifted his weight in the groaning saddle and watched the sensor's screen as Korak slowly scanned the terrain again.

"Appears my cows are happy." He commented, seeing their heat images displayed there.

"It is safe for now."

Riding out of the tree line, they walked the animals the last fifty yards to the campsite and dismounted in relief. Max quickly gathered several sticks of dry wood and placed them in the ashes of the previous fire where Korak once again used his sidearm to ignite the flames.

"I like that pistol a yours, man!" He remarked as Korak returned it to his belt.

"Pistol?...I do not know the word."

"You know, gun, sidearm." He said this as he pulled his Colt Peacemaker from the holster. "This is a pistol, a Colts Peacemaker, fires six rounds as fast as you can cock th' hammer back."

"I have been observing your weapons. They fire a metal projectile, do they not?"

"A lead cartridge, yeah. Here, Take a look!" He gave the gun to him and went about putting his coffee on to boil, watching while Korak closely examined the primitive weapon. "What do ya think?" He asked, getting to his feet again.

"I think you will need to be precisely on target to destroy your prey."

"Yeah, and I'm real good at doin' that, too!...I'd show ya how it shoots, but th' noise might bring us an unwanted guest for supper."

"Speaking of which." Said Korak, retrieving two wafers from his belt. "We have not eaten since morning." He gave Max the gun and wafer, and once they had eaten, both sat down to lean against one of the large rocks while the coffee boiled.

"What did ya think a my gun, man?"

"It fits my hand very well, I like the feel of it, Max....So much that I think I will suggest to the council that we build our side-arms in its image....I do not, however, like that it will only destroy one target at a time, With only one firing of the star-burst, I will destroy many targets at once, it will vaporize them."

Max nodded. "Yeah, I sort a noticed that about it!"

"And the projectile will never penetrate the invader's armor, nor the skin of the beast that hunts us."

"I sort a had that feelin', too!...Ain't got an extra one, have ya?"

"Yes, but the star-burst is far too dangerous for you to fire. The wrong setting and it could vaporize you. It is designed to destroy the enemy should he take the weapon from me. ...I am sorry, Max, given the time needed, I would instruct you in its use, maybe, once the enemy is destroyed."

"No hurry, man, knowin' me, you're prob'ly doin' me a favor!...So tell me how that beast is trackin' you, what's its tactics,...it destroys everything in one place, and nothing in another?"

"It has no tactics, Max, it will wander the hills and kill until it crosses my scent, and then it will follow me. It seems that we have been behind it today, but should it double back, it will surely detect our passing, and then it will come!...But now, the invader has no ship in which to await his pet's signal, so he has become a bigger threat now because he is a soldier, he will use a tactical choice when hunting us!...And I would also think that he would have a heat sensor to guide him."

"Man, you don't know how much I want this over and done with!"

"Me as well, but not to worry, should one of them come near, my sensor will warn us in time."

The coffee boiled over at that point, and Max leaned to remove the pot from the fire to allow the grounds to settle. "Think it might be okay if I see th' inside a your ship tomorrow, I didn't really see it th' first time?"

"You can see it now, if you like?"

"But won't th' lights be seen?"

"No,...there is no danger within a kilometer of us, come." He removed the thin control from his belt and pointed it at the invisible ship, and the star fighter slowly materialized." "Damnedest thing I ever seen!" He said as they stood and walked to the extended stairway where Korak touched the control again and the hatch quickly slid open above them.

Korak stepped on the bottom step and was raised up to the door, and breathing deeply, he cautiously stepped on the lift, caught his balance, and then was lifted to step inside the most unbelievable room he could ever imagine,...much different, he thought, than when he had brought Korak his weapons. Of course then, he had been too worried about Helen, and Lance to really look at it.

The vessel's roof area was covered with multi-colored lights and switches, as was the entire front of the ship. Sensor screens, dials, and gauges of all sizes,...and in the mix of them was a chair nestled between even more stands of lights, buttons and switches. Directly in front of him, Korak was flipping switches beside the arm of a larger chair, and when he looked up at Max, nodded and began speaking.

"Unit rx-nine, activate archives for star-fighter x-three thousand.... Transfer video records to unit rx-three, activation code, zero." He nodded at Max again and gestured at the chair with his hand. "Come in, Max, sit in my chair. Come on, it's okay."

He swallowed hard then stepped all the way inside the ship before moving forward to ease himself into the soft, comfortable seat. The velvety fabric began to quickly conform to the shape of his lower body, and as he turned his head to grin up at Korak, the chair quickly whirled around to face him.

"Jesus, man!" He gasped with surprise, and as he tried to shift his body, felt the chair's up and down movement. "Man!" He said again.

"It will detect your slightest movement." Said Korak. "And in space allows you to follow an enemy vessel, and maneuver the ship accordingly, without having to twist your body and neck uncomfortably. I can control the ship's every function and maneuver with a hand-grip." He flipped a switch on the chair's control panel, causing a small portion of the panel to open and a small lever to pop up.

"How do you see anything with no windows?"

Korak reached to move another switch and suddenly a three-foot wide section of the entire ship instantly turned into one continuous, wrap-around panel of smoky-gray windowpane. He could see everything with unbelievable clarity, the campsite below them, the trees and valley,…and it should be impossible, he thought, because it was totally dark outside. He looked back at Korak, and was about to speak when Korak nodded.

"The view-port conforms to the conditions surrounding the ship, dark to light, brilliant light to one easier to see. It is complicated. From the outside, all you will see is the vessel's metal hull."

"How does it do that?"

"It is a one-way panel of Cryoran glass, made transparent by an electro-magnetized natural resource of Cryor. The glass is only two millimeters thick, same as the ship's hull, yet will withstand the pressures of space many times over, as well as bombarding space-rocks and dust. The panel along the wall there is the light-bender,…it provides the cloak of invisibility. The large, covered section behind us contains the gravity engines, and the covered sections along the bottom sides there aim and fire the ship's weapons when activated….The entire front section of panels contain the means to manipulate the space surrounding the ship,…in short, the Space-bender!…. That was Idak's responsibility as well."

"That's his chair in front there?"

"Yes,…he could also control the ship's every function from there. His reaction time to any circumstance was many times greater than my own. His, as well as the chair here will lie back flat, and foot rests will appear when there is need for sleep." He looked up at the ship's roof then and gestured. "The panels along the upper side there are the ship's sensors. They are always vigilant, and always recording, as they are now….You have seen the entire ship now, Max. Of course there are many more functions that you would not understand, and truthfully, neither do I. Idak was the ship's brains."

"You're right, man." Sighed Max. "I'll never understand any of it,…I'll never in my lifetime forget it, neither!...Thanks, Korak."

"It was my pleasure, Max….Shall we return to the fire, and your coffee?"

"Oh, yeah,…I need it more than ever now!...All this is unbelievable, man." He said, getting out of the chair to look it over again. "Unbelievable!" He followed Korak back down the escalating steps and back to the fire, and as Korak remotely closed the hatch and activated the cloak again,…shook his head in wonder one more time and knelt to pour his coffee before sitting down to lean against the large rock.

Korak picked up the sensor case and came to sit down beside him, opened it and touched several of the lights along its side, and then turned the screen so that Max could see it. "This was our war with the invaders, Max."

"My God!" He exclaimed as he watched the battle among the stars, seeing the unbelievable quickness of the warships, the blinding explosions as the ships were destroyed only to be replaced by another warship,...and then displaying the destruction all over again. It was like he was sitting in Korak's chair and manning the weapons himself, able to see the starbursts of energy fired from the star fighter, and the missiles flight path as the enemy ship was destroyed. Streaks of laser-fire literally filled the screen, starburst torpedoes and explosions were constant."

Korak touched the screen again. "This is Promas before the war." The picture changed then to show hundreds of tall, shining buildings, some taller than others, but all looked to be touching the clouds,...and around them all, the sky above, and between them was filled with the floating airships, appearing like flocks of birds in places, and all moving in different directions at the same time.

"How do they keep from hittin' each other?"

"Sensors will sense when another transporter is too close, or when in danger of colliding, and react accordingly. They are quite safe....And these buildings are dwelling places." He said, touching another light. These buildings were not tall at all, but square-shaped with all-glass fronts.

"They house as many as one hundred tenants each. My dwelling is on the lower corner of the center building,...and this," He said as he touched another light. "Is the Council room of the Elders, you can see them all at work alongside their Cryoran counterparts....And here is the archival room of records." The room was very large, and long, and filled with metal chests with drawers, row after row of them. At the end of each row stood a panel with a large screen and a chair.

"This is mind-bogglin', man!" Exclaimed Max.

"And here, Max, is the creature that is hunting us." Another touch of the lights and the beasts could be seen as they ripped and tore the poor Promasians apart, devouring parts of some as they overtook others, their sharp teeth and claws cutting their victims in half,...and then suddenly he could see the Promasian foot-soldiers as they fought back, their weapons firing long streaks of laser beams to vaporize the monsters.

"Is that sufficient, my friend?" Asked Korak. "That is what we are faced with here."

"More than enough, yeah." He nodded, taking a large swallow of hot coffee. "That's one scary son of a bitch, man!"

Korak touched another light to clear the screen and closed the sensor before sitting down. "I have shown you only a small part of what is here, but it is the proof I promised you."

"It's all I needed, too!...I still don't understand how th' pictures move, it's like bein' there and seein' it happen, in color, ta-boot."

"It is a continuous picture, as I explained, much like your camera. Except ours takes photographs at a very fast speed and the pictures are stored inside very small electronic chips to be played back on a screen like this one,....and it will show them back to you at such a fast speed that they appear to be moving pictures."

Max stared at him narrowly for a few seconds then shook his head and turned to look back at the deep impression in the bluff. "I don't recall seein' any gun-barrels on that flying machine?"

"Weapon ports open as the weapons are activated, Max, and there are ports surrounding the vessel. It is capable of firing in any direction, at any angle,...one at a time, or all at once."

Max stared at him with awed disbelief then shook his head again. "I might need one of your sleepin' pills tonight, man."

"Yes, Max, when you are ready, and I did not mean to confuse you.."

"That's okay, I've been confused for days now. You got any plans on how we might find our killer tomorrow?"

"No, I have not....But we must try! Our problem will be, that should my sensor detect his presence, he will also detect ours....I thought perhaps you might have a plan, he will not be prepared for human tactics?"

"Well,...hell, I guess we could use a duck-blind!" He chuckled at the ridiculous implication.

"A Duck-blind?...This is an earth thing, right, Max?"

"Don't tell me there's no ducks on Promas, either?"

"We have no birds at all,...that's why they are so fascinating."

"Man,...I couldn't imagine not havin' any birds!...Okay, a duck is a water-bird, they can fly like any of 'em, but they nest in, or around water. They eat insects and I guess, tiny fish,...I don't really know what they eat?... But we hunt 'em, makes a good meal, too!...Anyway, huntin' 'em ain't easy, they see ya near th' water, they won't light there. So we hide and wait, and sometimes put out a decoy while we wait....But hidin' ain't easy, neither, so we use the tall grass all tied up like hay-stacks and hide in 'em, and sometimes in a blind that we build from grass and wood....A Duck-blind!"

"What is this Decoy you spoke of?"

"Usually just a piece a wood whittled out to look like a duck, we place it in th' water and let it float around, they see it, they think everything's okay and here they come!"

"I see,...all right,...how will we use this against the invader?"

"Well,...that sensor a his sees what yours does, heat images. Now, he has been here a few days so he has seen images of horses, cows, deer and such, and knows they are animals. So he pays no attention when he sees 'em!...So, what we do when your sensor detects him, is quickly slide off our horses and dig ourselves into th' foliage on the ground, with nothing but your big gun pointin' in his direction....He sees the horses and thinks nothin' of it, they ain't no threat to 'im!...And when he shows his self, adios amigo!"

"And what does that mean?"

"Good bye, you Bastard!...That's what it means."

Korak looked at him for several long moments before nodding his head. "I like your idea, Max, should we find him, we will try it!...A Duck-blind,...I like it very much."

"Well, don't like it too much. If it don't work, we'll have to get on our horses fast and run like hell!"

"Perhaps not,...If I should miss him, it will also mean that he is running away. We will have time to leave....However, if he should see the starburst in flight, he could be quick enough to escape it. That is why I will use the laser, I think."

"It's settled then....Anyway, there's still more farms out there I want a warn. We can do that while we hunt, if you're agreeable?"

"The saving of human life is always agreeable."

CHAPTER SIX

Lance Pruett had been listening to his father relate the incredible story with wide-eyed intensity, and felt overwhelming disappointment when Max suddenly grew quiet to roll and light his smoke,...and when he leaned back against his saddle to stare up at the stars and smoke, it was almost too much to take.

"That can't be all of it, Daddy." He blurted. "Is it?"

"What,...that ain't enough?" He chuckled then. "Be patient, son, I'll get to it. I been talkin' for more'n a hour already, let me rest th' vocal cords a minute....Cup a coffee might help, too."

"What?...Oh, yeah, Pop." He quickly reached and grabbed the almost empty pot and shook it. "No more coffee, Pop,...I'll have to make some."

"I'd appreciate that, son." He leaned his head back on the saddle and smoked while Lance hastily made more coffee, and grinning, looked up at the trillions of lights in the night sky with an involuntary shudder.

"I'd sure like to have seen inside that spaceship, Pop. Way you described it, it must a been something,...all them lights and switches."

"It was, for a fact, made it's own electricity, ran th' whole ship on it."

"They got electric lights all over Golden now, Pop. Lights on poles along the street....Wonder when we'll be able to get some?"

"Nothin' wrong with what we got."

"No sir, but it's hardly enough light to read by,...and with electric lights, we wouldn't need to go for coal-oil anymore. Coal-oil lamps are almost obsolete now."

"You're wrong there, Lance....They'll be around for another thirty, forty years. Besides, ya got a have a power plant to have electricity, I been readin' up on that stuff. For us to get it, th' power plant would have to be in Golden where there's water then they'd have to string wire all th' way up here to carry th' current. Wire's got a have poles to hold it off th' ground, too, men to put up th' poles and string th' wire....The only power plant's in

Denver right now,…be years before they string wire into th' mountains, here, expensive, too, to them, and us!"

"I know, Daddy." Sighing, he closed the lid on the pot and placed it in the fire. "If we knew how that ship did it, we could make our own!"

"That mean you believe what I'm tellin' ya?"

"I always believe you, Pop, you don't lie."

"I sometimes spin a yarn, though."

"Nobody could make up a story like this, Daddy. It's fantastic th' way you can remember all of it, even th' conversations you had!"

"Like I said, I was too scared not to remember. I knew that what he said might just help me save our lives some day!...That's why I'm tellin' you about this now, cause my memory won't be this good always,…and you'd best remember it, too!"

"I will, Daddy.…But I think you ought a try tellin' mama again. She can't think we're both spinnin' yarns."

"No, I'm sure she wouldn't. I'll think about it!"

"Then again, she might not want a know, Pop. She scares easy, ya know."

"Yes she does.…Just seein' that creature put Leon Shelby in th' crazy-house, poor Bastard lost his mind completely."

"Where is he, Pop, you never mentioned that?"

"Hospital over in Denver, accordin' to Reverend Holt. Th' boys got jobs over there, I hear, to pay th' bills. Maudie spends most a her time sittin' and talkin' to 'im.…He'll never get out a there."

"What about his farm?"

"Gone to ruin. She tried to sell it, but after what happened, nobody wants it. In th' backs of everybody's minds, I think they still believe his werewolf story!...Place has been jinxed."

"I remember when they got to town that night, it took three men to get 'im out a that wagon, he was th' one yellin' werewolf. I heard 'im plain as day, me, and mama had the window open. Watched them take 'im to Doctor McCoy's house.…Funny how certain things somebody says can jog a memory."

"You was seven, remember?"

"I was so scared, guess I pushed that part from my mind. To me, that's what it was, and that's all that mattered."

"Well, I ain't so lucky." Sighed Max. "When I ain't thinkin' about it, I'm dreamin' about it!...Fact is, I'm still as scared now, as I was then, Lance.… And I think I always will be.…Coffee's boilin' over, son.…I was scared that next mornin', too,…scared that if we found th' son of a bitch, my Duck-blind wouldn't work!"

* * *

He opened his eyes to find Korak sitting on one of the smaller rocks beside him. "Mornin'." He said, raising himself to sit and look around the campsite, and at the fire's flickering flames. "Don't you ever sleep, man?"

"I do not require much sleep, only a few hours rest." He gave Max his usual food wafer as he spoke. "I have made your coffee for you, it should be ready to drink."

"Thanks, Korak." He said, and then ate the wafer before reaching to pour his coffee. "Didn't know you could make coffee?"

"I observed your method of doing so, it was not hard."

"I don't think anything's too hard for you, man." He grinned and drank a swallow of the hot brew before nodding and holding up the cup. "Just right, too!...Want a thank ya for that sleepin' pill last night, too, not a bad dream, one."

"It was my pleasure, Max."

"Anything on that scanner this mornin'?"

"Wildlife, yes,...and your cattle below us there."

Max drained his cup and used water from his canteen to rinse it out before drinking some of it. "Guess we better saddle up then." He said and got to his feet. "Got a question for ya though, didn't think about it when we was buildin' our Duck-blind....Can that sensor a yours see under th' ground, through leaves and brush, and stuff?"

"Yes, of course, but only after I make the adjustment....But no need for that, we are looking for the invader and his pet, and his sensor will be hunting us."

"So that sensor a his works th' same way?"

"I do not know this for sure, Max, but I would think so....Why is this important?"

"If we see 'im, and we hit th' ground, it'll be good to know he can't see us!"

"If we are not on our feet, he can make no identification, Max. To a heat-sensor, we will appear as only a yellow spot on his screen. But, I do not believe his sensor will penetrate below the leaves and soil, as there would be no presence of a heat signature."

"Good enough....Okay, I'll saddle th' horses so we can be ready come daylight. You watch th' scanner,...and don't pour out my coffee, it'll be good later." He got up to leave then looked back. "And watch for that blinkin' light in th' corner there!"

* * *

It was mid-day when they rode down off the heavily timbered hillside and onto a crudely-graded road leading up to the Johnson homestead.

"Are we still safe, I hope?" He asked, nervously looking both ways along the narrow road.

"Yes,…I see wildlife, and that way, I can see animals grouped together, maybe in an enclosure."

"That's Johnson's place, come on." He led the way up the narrow lane and when the cabin came into view, they approached slowly as the large dog got to its feet to watch them, and then it began barking.

"Better hold up here, Korak." He said as he stopped his horse, and then cupped his hands to his mouth. "ELI JOHNSON!" He yelled. "IT'S MAX PRUETT, YOU HOME?" The dog was really making a noise at this point, but when the door was swung open and Johnson stepped out on the porch, it became quiet.

"What brings you so far from home, Max, lose another cow?"

"Nothin' like that, Eli."

"Well step on down from there and come in, coffee's hot?"

"Nothin' I'd like better, Eli, I mean it!...But we just stopped by to tell ya there's a killer loose in th' mountains, and we're here to ask you and your wife to go down to Golden for a few days till we can catch 'im?"

"Who is he?"

"We, ah, don't really know his true name, Eli, he's a fugitive!...This man here works for th' Government, been after 'im for weeks now….Anyway, he's here to catch 'im, and I'm his guide. So, how about it, will ya go,…it's for your own safety?"

"I don't think so!...How do ya know he's here, anyway?"

"Cause when he escaped, they lost 'im up here! He's a mad-dog killer, Eli, he already attacked th' Shelby farm yesterday, killed all their livestock, them that was in th' barnyard, Shelby seen 'im and got his family to th' root cellar….It's all that saved their lives!"

Johnson looked up at Korak then. "He talkin' gospel?"

"Gospel?"

"Th' truth, Korak." Said Max, turning to look at him.

"Yes, he speaks the truth." Nodded Korak.

"Th' Webbs already left, Eli, so did Reverend Holt….Will ya go, man?"

"If I believed ya, I would, Max Pruett….But I can't believe ya."

"Then I hope ya don't live to regret it, Eli….Just remember that I warned ya." He turned his horse around and led the way back to the road.

"This one makes two farmers that refused to leave, Max, why is that?"

"Mountain folks, Korak,...uneducated, hard workin' mountain folk!... They don't trust anybody, believe nothin' they hear, and only half a what they see."

"Interesting....Where to now?"

"Well, there's th' Preston farm, three miles or so to th' West. But ya know what, Korak?...With his ship gone, you said th' killer would be following; his pet, so let's just go ahead with our plan of action....Ain't that what ya said, he'd be followin'?"

"That is my belief, yes,...but where do we erect our Duck-blind?"

"That's easy, we don't know where that creature is, but we know where its been."

"Shelby's farm?"

"Shelby's farm!...I think we ought a find us a good spot on that hillside in front and wait for that bastard to show his self."

"If he has not passed already?"

"Maybe not, he would a spent most a th' day lookin' for you on that mountain, or one a th' others thereabout....He knows you were there cause his ship's gone, and he's one mad son of a bitch now, cause he can't find ya!... We can go look for him, or wait for 'im,...your call, man."

"You are the foot soldier, my friend, I am not!"

"Oh, no,...I ain't never been a soldier of any kind. There's just a lot a mountains here, is all."

"Then,...it is your Duck-blind."

"Thanks!...Okay, it's two miles back to Shelby's homestead. We ought a make it before dark. We'll go over th' mountain, just like when you destroyed his ship,...we'll dig in about halfway down the other side, in full view a th' road."

"Then we erect the Duck-blind, yes?"

Max chuckled. "Yeah, but we are th' duck blind, Korak, it was just a figure a speech!...let's just hope he's as easy fooled as a duck!....Okay, we have to go due North from here and a little West. Ready to climb another mountain?" They left the road to climb an overgrown, grass-covered embankment, and were once again on an uphill climb through a wilderness of trees.

Two hours of fighting briars and Pine Trees found them descending down the other side into a rich meadow of waving grassland and were able to cross the narrow valley at a fast walk. Smoke from the Webb farmhouse could be seen in the lower side of the valley, a mile away, and he wanted to cross his land without being seen. But finally, they were climbing again, and the rock-infested terrain was littered with cracks and crevices that in some cases looked as if they could swallow both man and horse, but they finally were over the top, only to find that the descent was no less difficult.

But by late afternoon, max stopped amid the tall grass and loose shale amid two very old, and tall Sequoia Pines and turned to look back at Korak. "I think we ought a leave th' horses here and go down on foot. If he sees 'em and decides to fire on 'em, we won't be caught in th' blast." Seeing Korak nod, they dismounted, and dropping the reins, Max took his canteen and began the descent over the flat, moving stones that covered the hillside. "Watch your step, Man." He said over his shoulder. "You slip, grab a branch, anything to stop your fall."

They were a good fifty yards downhill from the horses when Max stopped again beside two large boulders. Brush, leaves and assorted debris lay against the rocks and trees and to Max, would present them a clear view of the bloody yard.

"Why are the birds in the yard?" Inquired Korak as he removed the rifle from his back.

"Vultures." He breathed. "They eat dead things....Damn sure found a yard full down there!...Disgusting creatures!"

"But necessary, I think." Returned Korak with interest.. "Nature's way of cleaning the land, it is unique."

"Never thought of it that way!" He looked down at the debris and then at Korak. "We in range from here?"

"Yes, we can see the house and yard through the trees there, as well as the road and hillside through the trees over there."

"Let's dig in here then, but first!" He began kicking at the debris with his foot and then, taking one of the dead branches began punching and displacing it until he heard the familiar, telltale warning.

"I thought so." He breathed, and then gently moved another branch aside with the end of the stick until he revealed the coiled snake.

"You got snakes on Promas, man?"

"No,...we do not!...Explain it to me, Max."

"Timber rattler!...Big one, too....That is a Diamond-backed Rattle snake, and there's millions of 'em in these hills....And where there's one, there's usually another one." He worked the dead stick slowly beneath the reptile, lifted its writhing length and then tossed it farther down the slope,...and as he did, he heard the second one and after more searching around the rock, eliminated it in the same way.

"One bite from that thing is a death warrant!"

"Interesting creature." He commented. "I have not seen one before."

"A deadly creature, Korak, carries enough venom in one bite to kill three or four men!...Okay,...pick your spot, man, and dig in."

And as Korak moved the debris around enough to lie down comfortably, he looked back at the yard full of vultures and almost gagged again,…but was damn glad it was not human remains the giant birds were feeding on, then sighing heavily began preparing his own bed to lie on,…and hoped it would not be his last as he laid down beside Korak.

"Got your sensor on, Man?"

"It is always on, Max, not to worry!"

"Yeah, right!...Hope th' bastard don't suspect somethin'."

"He is a warrior, he suspects everything."

"That makes me feel better!...I just hope he ain't already been here."

"I think not.…He would have found pleasure in destroying the,… Vultures."

"I'm gonna take pleasure in seein' that son of a bitch destroyed!"

"As will I, Max." Returned Korak as he placed the starburst rifle alongside the boulder, brought up the small screen and then pointed the gun down toward the farmhouse first, and then at the road and along the opposite hillside.

"Wish we knew th' direction he'll be comin' from?"

"He will be coming from there." Said Korak, still scanning the old road's northward route. "He will be coming from his ship's location, I think."

"What if he don't?...Right down to it, he could be anywhere!...What if I'm wrong about this?"

"You are right about one thing, Max.…We could search the mountains for many days, and because he is also searching, we would need much good luck to find him,…and should we find him, he would also have found us!...It is better to wait,…he will come to us."

"Wish I could depend on that!...Hell,…he could even come down this hill on top of us!,…we don't know where he is!"

"Again, you must contain yourself, my friend.…My sensor will warn us of his approach!...He is a warrior, and a hunter, he will not sit in wait for us, he does not possess the patience."

"Not like me, right?"

"You have shown extreme patience with me, Max. You did not know me, yet you feared me.…You saw my ship, my strange appearance and knew I was not from Earth,…yet you helped me when I was helpless. That is patience beyond compare, Max. You are only afraid of the unknown, which is a human trait,…and is not one of impatience."

"Sometimes you confuse th' hell out a me, man!"

"One of my traits, Max."

"Then how long do you think we should be patient here, till dark, all night, or what?...Because you're right, this scares th' shit out a me!"

"Again, I am sorry, my friend....But I think we should wait until he comes. Besides, I like the concept of this Duck-blind!"

"Me, too, back in camp....I just hope he's blind!...What are ya gonna hit 'im with, th' laser, and what?

"The laser beam will travel at the speed of light, causing instantaneous molecular degeneration of his organs, resulting in an explosion of the cells. Should I miss, and he escapes and runs, I will use the starburst torpedo, it will vaporize all within an area of thirty of your earth yards."

"And if he returns fire?"

"Then we must run!...Relax, My friend, I will follow his flight-path with more torpedoes until he is no longer a threat....We will have time to leave."

"Tell me this,...if that laser beam misses his body and say, hits a leg, will he die?"

"It will sever the leg from his body and render him helpless, after which, I will assist him....The laser will hew anything in its path, and will only become dormant on contact with the soil, or another object to expel it's energy."

Max sighed heavily. "You must be sick of all my dumb questions, man!"

"The questions you ask are expected, Max, because the answers could serve you well in the future. It is your hunger for knowledge that makes you an exceptional human being!...And it is my privilege to be here with you."

"Thanks, Korak....I'm gonna shut up now." He watched the profile of Korak's smooth face for a time before looking back at the Shelby's blood-saturated yard, and was feeling grief, and nausea as he watched the large black birds fight each other over the mutilated animal parts. How could Korak not feel what he was feeling? He was trembling inside as if he was in a blizzard, he thought, and knew it was nothing but fear. He had never been afraid of anything, man or beast before!...But he was determined not to let Korak down, or him-self once this shindig started.

He continued to watch as Korak intently watched the small screen on the rifle, to wonder how he could be so calm in the face of danger?...For a moment then, he wished he could have had some of his training. He knew, however, that it was the alien weapons that made him so afraid. Compared to them, he was as inferior as his own weapons. He knew within reason, that if he had Korak's guns, he would not fear anything!...But he did not."

He breathed deeply of the pine-scented air, and could feel it growing colder in spite of the lowering sun's rays on their side of the tall hill. The house and outbuildings below them were already in shadows, and would be totally dark before the shadows reached them. He tried to see the road, but it, too, was already quite dark under the cover of trees....He had never thought that waiting could be so un-nerving, had in fact waited all night before for a shot at an Elk....He was startled then as Korak spoke.

"Are you sleeping, my friend?"

"No, no,...not tonight!...I was just thinkin',...you see anything on th' scanner yet?"

"Only the usual,...the birds in the yard there, deer on the meadow beyond the structure....Do not worry, Max,...if he does not come tonight, we will try again." He quickly looked back at the scanner then as the low beeping alarm sounded, and with rifle in hand, slowly moved it to cover the dark road below them. "He is here, Max." He whispered. "He is less than one kilometer away and moving slowly, perhaps on the road!" The minutes passed slowly as Korak continued to watch the fiery image grow ever larger on the screen, and three-quarters of an hour later.

"He is here!" Breathed Korak in a whisper. "He is stopped at road's edge, I believe to scan the mountain,...no, he is moving again now. I will fire when he is at the yard of the house."

Max could hardly breathe as he stared down at the dark house, and it was then he saw the dark hulk of the killer. A giant, he thought as he watched the large dark, almost lumbering alien's form as he cautiously approached the cabin. At that moment, the flapping of large wings as the killer's presence caused the vultures to suddenly take flight, and in that same instant, Korak fired. The alien rifle shooting a long, orange streak of pure energy down through the giant trunks of ageless pines with nothing but a whisper, like rushing air as it left the barrel.

The alien killer's screams of pain could be heard loudly, the sounds echoing in the hills. Korak fired the laser again in three quick successions, the beams of light causing small explosions as they struck the ground in pursuit of the fleeing killer.

"He is running!" Said Korak, quickly changing the rifle's settings as he followed the killer's heat signature then fired the star-burst torpedoes, three of them, one after the other, followed by blinding lights as each one struck trees and ground and burning everything to cinders. He fired a fourth time while still watching the screen, and Max followed the missile's path of travel for what seemed like five seconds before the blinding light again lit up the night.

"He is gone, Max." He said, getting to his feet. "We must go now, too!"

Having to use the brush and trees for support, they finally reached the horses, mounted and urged them back up the treacherous incline to finally cross the hill's tall crest and start down the far side.

Another two hours found them back in Webb's valley and once again in the large meadow of waving grass, and here, Max realized that they had put a whole mountain between them and the killer and breathlessly stopped his blowing horse in the darkness.

"That's that, I guess!" He breathed, and tried to see Korak's face in the darkness. "I heard 'im yell, think ya hit 'im?"

"Yes, he is hurt!...It must be an arm as he was able to run. For one so large, he is very fast when he retreats."

"So, what now?"

"We try again tomorrow, or the day after....He will hide for now to field-dress his wound, a day, maybe....But the pet is still at large, if it heard the invader's screams of pain, it could return to the farm."

"Then let's go back to camp, Man,...th' disappointment a this took about everythin' out a me for one day!...Th' road to Golden's only about a mile past th' Webb farm, we stay in th' edge a these trees, we can by-pass his house and hit th' road on th' other side....We don't, th' bastard might take a shot at us!" He clucked the horse into motion again along the edge of the meadow, and just inside the trees. Still finding themselves battling clinging vines and briars, and for the next two hours they were silent until finally leaving the trees south of the farmhouse to ride down onto the hard-packed road.

Waiting for Korak to pull alongside, they headed south toward the Golden City road. The moon was out now, lighting up the road in spots, and along the treetops with its pale yellow glow.

"You still watchin' th' scanner?" He asked as he stared at the dark beneath the trees.

"Yes, my friend, no sign of the creature."

"I was sure hopin' to kill that Bastard!"

"Yes,...he must have turned as I fired, perhaps startled by the large birds in flight....If he is wounded, he no longer has one of his arms,...or he has lost the use of that arm. And if his weapon was attached to that arm, it will be useless now as well. But if not, we are still in danger from it."

"Th' way he screamed, I know he was hit!...He couldn't a screamed that loud from just bein' surprised,...You hit 'im!"

"His screams would indicate severe pain, yes, that is what makes me believe he has lost a limb."

"I hope th' hell you're right, man!...Now I know why I was so scared a th' dark as a kid. Never thought I'd actually meet the Boogie-man some day."

"Boogie-man, Max?"

"Just somethin' my mother used to say to keep me in line,...worked, too,...some!...In my mind, boogie-man was some evil monster waitin' to eat me alive if I didn't behave."

"It seems it is still working, my friend."

"You got that right, man!...My hair'll be gray by th' time this is over."

"Graying hair is synonymous to growing old, Max,...you are not old."

"We don't end this soon, I will be,...that, or dead!"

"Then we will try to end it soon."

"Somehow, I don't think that'll be up to us!...I know one thing, Korak, I'm gonna need one a your magic pills tonight, I'll never go to sleep on my own."

"You will have it....How far is this Golden City road now, my friend?"

"Quarter mile, maybe, what's wrong?"

"Something quite large, and long is approaching us from behind."

"How far away?"

Maybe a half-kilometer."

"Then come on, let's get to th' road ahead of it." They urged the animals to a trot along the badly rutted road, and were soon entering the intersection of the road to Golden where they stopped again to check the sensor.

Max peered at the fluctuating, yellowish orange image on the screen with pounding heart. "What is that,...You think it's that animal?"

"It does not appear large enough, but it is moving on the road toward us."

"Then get that gun a yours ready, and lets get off th' road." He quickly urged the animal into the tall grass and into the dark trees where they sat their saddles and waited, each staring back along the moonlit roadway.

It was several minutes later when they saw the horses coming toward them, and heard the creaking and bumping of the wagon.

"It's a wagon and team." Said Max. "They could be in trouble. Come on, let's stop 'em." He gigged the horse out of the trees and back to the road, along with Korak and together sat there blocking the road until the wagon got near enough to see them,...and holding up his hand, called out to the man and woman on the seat.

"Hold up there, man!" He yelled. "Stop th' horses!"

"Whoa!..." He yelled as he applied the brake, bringing the blowing animals to a stop some ten yards from them. The man on the wagon's seat got to his feet then. "State your business, God damn it, I got a shot gun on ya!"

"Now you just take it easy with that thing!" Said Max loudly. "We ain't outlaws, name's Maxwell Pruett, I live up here!...We thought ya might be in trouble, that's all."

"Trouble?...Hell, I guess you could say that, since a God damn crazy son of a bitch tried to burn us out and kill everybody!"

Max urged his horse up beside the wagon and could see the two children cowering beneath the wagon's seat. "Where did all this happen?"

"Gold camp, couple nights ago,...It was like th' war all over again, men, women, kids, all runnin' and screamin', Gunfire, explosions, tents on fire, buildings, everything! I seen dead people in th' street!...Ours was th' last tent in camp, coming this way,...and we got th' hell out a there!"

"And a crazy man was doin' all this?"

"A god damn lunatic!...Walkin' down the street between houses, throwin' sticks a dynamite at both sides, then killin' people when they ran!"

"Dynamite?"

"What it looked like to me, everything was blowin' up!"

"Anybody else make it out?"

"Damned if I know." He returned breathlessly. "God help me, I don't know....We lost all we had, clothes on our backs is all we got!"

"What's your name, friend?" Asked Max, his heart going out to them.

"Noah Hawkins,...this is my wife, Millie,...she's still scared half to death,...we all are." He lowered his head then and sighed heavily.

"I'm truly sorry for your trouble, Mister Hawkins, but I got a tell ya,... you ain't gonna make it to Golden you keep runnin' your team this way."

"Yes'ir, I know, but ever time I slow down to cool 'em off, I see that son of a bitch a comin', and here I go again."

"Tell 'im about that other thing, Noah." Urged his wife,

"What other thing?"

"About three miles back, Preston place, I think....We heard gunshots and screamin', same as th' gold camp. I don't know what might a happened,...and I was too spooked to go see."

"No, you done right, Noah, and you're right. There is a crazy killer loose in th' mountains. My friend here is a lawman, works for th' Government. He was sent here to catch 'im!"

"Well he ain't doin' his job, if he was!"

"Now, Noah, he had no idea where th' man was, and he don't know these mountains,...that's why 'im with 'im....We been trackin' 'im since yesterday, but th' ground's so dry he leaves no tracks!...We been warnin' th' farmers up here to leave till we catch 'im,...some are already in Golden. That's what you ought a do, too."

"Somebody ought a see about th' Prestons, Mister Pruett. I'd a done it, but I got my family....Jed Preston's a good man."

Max looked back at Korak then nodded. "We'll go see about 'im, Noah, I like 'im, too.!...You go on down to Golden, you see my wife and son, tell 'em I'm okay."

"I doubt I see 'em, we ain't stoppin' too long in Golden, or anywhere else in Colorado, we're leavin' this god forsaken place for good!...I hope you good luck, Mister Pruett." He whipped the team to a gallop again on the dangerously rutted road.

"Guess it was him!" Breathed Max as they watched the careening wagons departure. "Wonder how many died up there?" He sighed and looked at Korak. "I'd like to go check out th' Preston place, Jed Preston's got a wife and ten kids, maybe some of 'em's still alive."

"I agree, my friend, but we must hurry."

"Can you hang on?"

"I will try."

"Use th' stirrups to stand in, hold on to th' horn!" He kicked the horse's flanks, sending it back up the road at a gallop, and with Korak not far behind him covered the few miles to the Preston cut-off where he stopped again to wait for him.

"You okay, man?" He asked as he stopped beside him.

"Yes, Max, I am,...I'm beginning to like riding a horse."

"What's that sensor say?"

"I am detecting no wildlife at all in the area, the beast was here, I think."

"Lord!...Okay, th' Preston farm is only a half-mile up this road, and we best be a little cautious from here on....Keep that scanner workin', will ya?... Might get that rifle a yours ready, too,...he might still be close enough to come back!"

"If it is here, I will see it."

They walked the horses up the twisting, tree-shrouded lane for more than a quarter hour, and as they cleared the forest of trees, could see the destruction in the light of the moon.

"Lord!" Gasped Max. "Look at it,...fence is down here, smokehouse scattered over there....Tore th' place up!" That's when the horses balked and tried to veer away, each snorting nervously and sidestepping away from the stench of death.

"Let's tie 'em up here, man." He said and dismounted to tie the reins to one of the leaning fence-posts, and as Korak followed suit, pulled the Henry from its boot and walked slowly toward the yard.

The smell of death and blood was strong in the cold air as they neared the yard, and that's when the several yards wide area of blood and body parts caused him to suddenly have to turn away and vomit.

Steam was still rising from the freshly mutilated bodies and widespread pools of blood. When there was nothing left, but an occasional dry heave, he pulled the bandana from his neck and wiped his mouth, then with it held against his nose and mouth, straightened to survey the scene.

They were all dead, all twelve of them, but only a couple of the children had been eaten by the beast, their heads and parts of their legs still lay in the blood-pools. But all had been ripped apart, mutilated, and their bodies scattered haphazardly across the bloody yard,…and amidst the blood and guts lay the Winchester Rifle, and that's what he was staring at when Korak placed a hand on his shoulder. "Son of a bitch murdered all of 'em, man!... Jed tried to fight back, though."

"The livestock is also dead." Replied Korak. "Will you be all right, Max?"

"No, man, probably not!...They was good people.…We should a warned 'em, I wanted to!"

"This is not your fault, my friend.…Now come, we must go! The beast has not been gone for long, and in the dark, it can strike swiftly."

"You see anything on that sensor?"

"Only a fleeting image, then it was gone,…but it was too small to identify."

Nodding, he turned away and followed Korak back out to the skittish horses, mounted and rode back down the road at a gallop, and once on the main road continued at that pace until the animals began to tire, forcing them to slow to a fast walk.

"If somebody asked me, I couldn't even start to describe what I saw back there!" He said brokenly. "Poor bastards never had a chance, was in their bed asleep, for God sakes!"

"No, they had no chance at all!...No living creature on Earth can withstand its rage.…Its instincts are to hunt and kill!"

"Yeah,…well, we have to kill it, man!"

"And we will."

"It didn't have time to go very far." He said, looking up over the trees at the mountains. "It could still be up there somewhere watchin' us."

"It could, yes,…but it is not closer than one kilometer!...It is still hunting my scent."

"Might find it, too,…wind's out a th' South."

"Then we must hurry, perhaps create one more Duck-blind at our campsite."

"Yeah, th' first one really worked!"

"It did work, my friend, he did not detect us! Had he not turned away, he would be dead now!...We must set the trap again."

"Works for me, let's go home!" They spurred the animals to a gallop again, not stopping, except to cool them down until reaching another of his shortcuts back to the ranch, some six miles and three and a half hours away,...and it was here they stopped to rest the horses again.

"My ranch house is six miles due North a here, our campsite another ten from there. We'll cut across from here,...anything on your scanner yet?"

"Only wildlife, Max, no sign of the creature."

"That's good news, at least, come on." He reined the horse off the road and up an embankment into the forest of pines.

* * *

It was well past midnight when they stopped in the trees to look over the silent house and barn. One of the three horses in the corral saw them and came to extend its head over the top rail and snort.

"That's old Blue." He said as he looked at Korak's dark features. "I was ridin' 'im when I found ya....Good horse!...This is my home, what do ya think of it?"

"I like it very much, Max."

"Me, too!" He sighed. "Wait for me at th' house, man." He rode out into the moonlight and opened the corral gate, then rode in to drive the horses out before going to dismount at the barn's open doors,...and in a few seconds was ushering the three milk cows out ahead of him.

He mounted again and rode in beside Korak.

"Why did you do that, my friend?"

"Maybe they'll have a chance if that creature comes this way, they won't go far....Hold on, got a get one more thing." He dismounted and went into the house, returning with a cloth sack in his hand. "More coffee." He said and mounted to lead the way through the front gates, then across a large, grass-covered meadow to once again enter the trees on the far side.

They were on a constant, yet slight uphill climb now, and were in very broken terrain, consisting of mostly rocks, brush, crevices, monstrous pines and tall grass,...and though the darkness made their progress a slow one, Max urged the horse on through and across the treacherous landscape.

It was close to mid-day when they rode out of the trees in front of the bluff and here, Max stopped again while Korak used his scanner.

"It is safe to continue, Max."

"Good, I need some coffee....What about behind us?"

"No, nothing but wildlife."

He led the way through the rock-strewn grass and dismounted at the campsite, then went to assist Korak when he grunted with his leg. "Go sit down, man, and rest....I'll unsaddle th' horses."

"Thank you, Max." He went into the rocks, removed the rifle from his back and eased himself down against one of the large stones before propping the weapon beside him,...and several minutes later was trying to ease the pain when Max returned.

"How's th' rear-end, man,...I noticed you poundin' that saddle with it pretty good back there?"

"Yes, I am glad to be here,...I will be quite sore tomorrow, I think."

"You can bet on it!" He dropped the saddles on the ground then unrolled Korak's bedroll and spread the blankets. "Move over on this, man, get off th' dirt." He grabbed the canteen then and filled the pot before untying the coffee sack and putting in the grounds. He closed the lid and placed it in the cold ashes before retying the sack and placing fresh wood down. He then struck a match to a handful of dry grass to light it before looking back at Korak.

"If that creature was watchin' us back there,...how long will it take it to get here?"

"It will be wary of the daylight, not because it fears detection, but because there is no darkness to hide his approach....It is the way of the predator....It will be very late in the day, most probably tonight before it strikes....And perhaps not at all, it may not have detected our presence there at all."

"I'll be disappointed if it didn't!" He shook his head then. "Yeah, right!" He sighed then and unrolled his own bedroll to sit down and watch the circling crows overhead for a minute before turning to look at the deep hole in the bluff. "Your ship's still there, ain't it?...I mean, just because I don't see it, don't mean it ain't there, right?"

"If you walk toward it far enough, you will know, my friend."

"Yeah, th' ladder, right?...That's okay, I believe ya."

"When activated, the machine inside the star-fighter bends the light in such a way that it is reflected back onto it's self, much like a mirror. The result is transparency,...and there is much, much more to it than that, I tell you only what Idak told to me....The rest, I would not, myself understand."

"It's unbelievable, I know that!"

"Yes, it is a scientific marvel....Should the machine somehow be wired to every building, such as in your Golden, and was then activated, the town would seem to disappear,...it would become transparent."

Max grinned then. "I bet if them steps weren't down, a man could ride his horse right under it and never know its there."

"Yes, If we had not been trying to restart the gravity engines, we would have thought to cloak the star fighter. You would not have seen us at all."

"I would a heard th' crash, man. It weren't all that loud, but I heard it!...And there was th' shadow on th' ground as ya flew over,...there would a been a shadow, right?" He saw Korak looking at the bluff then and looked himself, only to shake his head. The sun was directly overhead, and there was no shadow at all beneath the cloaked airship. "This gets more confusin' every day, man!"

"As do I at times, Max,...but you are right, of course, and I am relieved you were here.....I flew the star fighter, I fired the weapons, as did Idak of course, and as a team, we were a force to contend with....I had only a working knowledge of all the ship's functions,...but no idea at all of how they worked!"

"Well, I do know when th' coffee's ready, so I think I'll have a cup." Still shaking his head, he used the bandana to pick up the hot pot and pour his coffee before moving back to sit down,...and sighing, he placed the cup on the ground to cool some before looking back at Korak.

"I'm sorry, man, and excuse my ignorance....But it don't make sense,... first, that I can't see that ship, and second, it not givin' off a shadow. Th' first part, you explained,...sort a....But it don't make sense, I can't see th' ship, but it's still there, I can go over and touch it, because it's still there....So, if it's still there, why don't it leave a shadow?" He picked up his cup and drank some of the hot brew before grinning at Korak.

"Guess that's why I'm a dumb rancher....Hell, you done tried to explain all a this once, and I still don't know what ya said!"

"You are a curious man, Max....You search for answers when you do not understand something. I am impressed!"

"Well, don't butter me up too much, we still got a Duck-blind to build."

"Butter you up?"

"Another silly sayin', man, I can't explain it anyway!...What I need is some sleep....So, if you don't mind, I'm gonna build me some shade and take a nap, you ought a do th' same." He got up to drape his cover blanket across the tops of two of the large rocks, moved his saddle and bedding into the shade between them and sat down to look at him again. "That scanner's gonna warn ya, right?" And when Korak nodded reassurance, lay down with his head and shoulders in the shade of the blanket and went to sleep.

CHAPTER SEVEN

"No!" He yelled shrilly, the sound of his own voice waking him to an overwhelming feeling of terror, and he lay for a minute to stare up at the blanket he had stretched over the rocks for shade....But then remembered where he was and reached up remove the blanket and sit up.

He was alone in the campsite, and wondering where Korak might be, looked around to see that the ship was now visible again and curious, got to his feet just as Korak exited the open hatch and rode the steps down to the ground.

"You are awake!" He said as he walked back to join him. "I knew you would awaken soon, so I kindled the fire and warmed up your coffee."

"Hey, thanks, man." He nodded and looked back at the fire. "I need it, too."

"More nightmares, Max?"

"Th' Prestons." He nodded then squatted and poured his coffee. "How do ya keep something like that out a your mind, man?"

"Time, my friend, it's the only way,...and soon you will push it aside."

He took a swallow of the hot coffee and looked back at the ship. "Got another problem with your ship?"

"No, I was recording my report on what has taken place away from the ship so far....And because of what has happened, I thought it best to transmit the report on a very weak wave length for the Cryorans to receive when they arrive."

"Won't that mother ship detect it?"

"The signal is far too weak. It will only reach Earth's atmosphere before it dies, but the ship will continue sending the message until it is received.... The Cryorans will deliver it to the Elders."

"Sounds like you're suddenly havin' doubts, man,...you worried?"

"Yes,...and because I am worried, I must tell you something as well.... If I am gone, and you are left, you must take my star burst rifle and fire it at the clay bluff just below the star fighter." He retrieved the weapon and pointed to a row of lights along the side. "Run your finger along the lights from front to back one time....The missile will only be powerful enough to explode the soil away from below the ship, allowing it to fall to the ground."

"Then you must fire again, this time into the hole left by the ship, it will bring the clay down and should bury the ship completely....Will you do this for me?"

"You know I will, man....But why not just vaporize it, like th' other one?"

"Because it must continue to send my signal to the Cryorans, and though it is buried, it will continue to do so."

"For how long?"

"Until it is received. The Cryorans may not return for many years,...and they could possibly return today....The ship will continue to transmit until they do."

"Then what?...They won't know th' rest of it, cause if we are dead, nobody can tell 'em!"

"Once they receive transmission, they will download the ship's database, they will know the entire story. The ship is constantly recording all that takes place inside, and outside of its perimeter. It is recording us as we speak, and will record our success or demise."

"What then, will they destroy the ship to remove th' evidence?"

"Should the Elders order it, Perhaps, or they could just retrieve it,...you will not know....My other reason for burial is that over extended periods of time, the crystals will eventually erode, maybe not for hundreds of years, but they will!...When they do, they will emit a deadly radiation, so strong it will contaminate the trees and grass for half a kilometer around, killing all vegetation!...It will also be air-born,...it will poison both human and animal alike for many years to come, and there is no cure!...However, the radiation will be contained once the ship is buried."

"I don't mind tellin' ya, man,...that scares hell out a me, too!"

"It was meant to, Max, radiation poisoning is not a pretty sight!...Can you do all this?"

"If I'm alive, you got my word on it."

"Thank you, my friend." He held up the rifle again. "To destroy the invader, or his beast, run your finger along the lights from back to front, all the way for full power, like I used on the invader's ship....Stop midway, and the laser will vaporize anything the beam touches."

"Korak," He said hoarsely, then had to clear his throat. "I don't know what to say, man,...but you got my word on it!...I will do what's necessary!...

But nothin's gonna happen to you, man, we're gonna kill these bastards, and you're gonna have some a Helen's fried chicken!"

"And I look forward to it!"

"Yeah." Max looked at the ship again "You tellin' me all this, makes me think you believe they'll be comin' pretty quick now!...You think that creature was watchin' us, too, don't ya?"

"I am not sure, Max....I did see a fleeting image at the farm while scanning, but it vanished almost as quickly!...It appeared to be large, but I am not sure....If it was the beast, it could have crouched behind a mound of soil, or it could have continued down the other side of the mountain,...or there was nothing there at all. I am not sure."

"But you do believe it, don't ya?"

"Yes, Max, I do....And it is not because I believe it has a brain to think with, but that I am the prey, and all predators crouch while stalking their prey."

"Think it'll be tonight?"

"Perhaps, or tomorrow night. My scent is mingled with that of the horses. It may confuse it enough to delay its coming,...but I think it will come."

"From where, ya think?"

"From where we came....It cannot stalk us, it is too open here,...we will see its approach. It will come from the trees there, and we must be ready, because it will cover the distance quickly."

"Okay then, what'll we do?"

"Remain alert, my friend. He looked around at the campsite then. "This will be our Duck-blind, Max."

*　　　*　　　*

The rest of the afternoon was spent with Korak teaching him the basic fundamentals of the starburst weapons, how they should be safely held when firing, and once he became familiar with the different settings, and what each of them would do, he was allowed to fire both the rifle, and the side arm, finding them both to be awesome, if not devastating weapons.

"All I can say, man, is,...Man!" He gave him back the side arm, and still shaking his head, squatted by the fire and poured more coffee. "But they're still better in your hands than mine!...How do ya put that much power in one ball a fire, and in a gun that small?"

"That is one of my questions as well, Max. But it has to do with atoms and molecules. In the star fighter, we keep them charged by placing them in the energy-rack, where you found them. But here, Earth's sun supplies all the energy necessary, all it needs do is touch the weapons for a few seconds to fully charge them."

""So damn much to think about, man!"

"Your descendants will know all this one day, and even now, I think that will be a pity....The thought that one day all the natural, raw beauty that is here could one day look like Promas does today is,...unthinkable! But very much probable."

"Tell ya what then....When we're done here, send 'em a message, tell 'em you're stayin'!"

"That is a thought, Max." He reached to his belt and brought out the wafers. "Mealtime, my friend. It will be dark soon, and we must be ready." He used the small control then to close the hatch and dematerialize the ship, and they both sat down to eat their food and wait.

"You ever regret not havin' a wife and family, Korak?"

"I would not say that I regret it,...but I have wondered what it would be like? My Mother and Father seemed happy before I was sent to the space academy....I did not see them often after that."

"How did that come about,...you must a been awful young?"

"Yes, I was only six when I took the intelligence examination....I was sent to live in a dormitory with other children afterward."

"It's a lonesome life by yourself, man, nobody to talk to most a th' time,...except yourself. I even talked to my horse a lot. It didn't talk much, but I got no sass from it!...Yeah, a lonesome life,...unless ya happen to meet a woman like my Helen!"

"And if she is able to fry chicken, right, Max?"

"Oh, that's th' first question out a your mouth, Korak, after hello, of course!...She says no, get on your horse and leave."

"I like your humor, Max....There is no wit, or humor among my fellow star-fighters....And I will miss it!"

"I been wonderin' about something else, man?...When this is done, what if some day another alien bein' from another one a them million worlds comes to Earth?...If he's like this one, can we expect help from Promas?"

"Once we learn of his presence, of course!...We are of one people, Max."

"That's damn good to know!...Okay,...if th' Cryorans come here a lot, have they ever detected other aliens bein' here? You know, before this?"

"Max,...If they did, it would have been reported to the Council. We would not know until orders were received to come here....If it has ever happened, I do not know. But if the threat to Earth is deemed vital, the star fighters would come!...Do not worry, Max, though there are many species of life on other worlds, only a few are humanoid,...and a great many of those, that are humanoid, live on a world as primitive as Earth....Those that have evolved to master space travel would know that Earth is also a primitive world, and would go to great lengths not to be detected, just as we did."

"Could some a them have also set up colonies here without you knowin' it?...You know, millions a years ago?"

"There is always that possibility....At the time, however, we might not have known of their presence,...but it is unlikely we would not have detected them. But also, a few thousand years before our arrival, the earth was going through great changes, continents were dividing, landmasses separating until, by the time we arrived, the earth was much the same as now....It is very possible that if other alien colonists had been here, their cities would have been under the great water masses."

"Are there more worlds out there with Dinosaurs on 'em?"

"According to the archives, there are worlds with very large reptiles, yes, many as large as your dinosaur,...but these are not otherwise inhabited. I only know these things by studying the Council Archives, which is mandatory....I have never been to any other world until now."

"Sorry for all th' questions, man, I'm just nervous today."

"Do not apologize, my friend. I am honored to answer your questions.... In fact, I have wondered why you wear your sidearm in that position?

"Yeah?...Well, it's easy to get out when ya need to make a fast draw."

"A fast draw?...I do not understand."

"I wish I didn't....Okay,...when a man is challenged, or his life is threatened by another man, or his family's lives are threatened,...they will sometimes settle the dispute with a gun....They'll face each other in the street, and draw. Th' one who draws first and shoots straightest wins th' fight!...Problem is, th' loser is usually dead!"

"Show me, Max."

Shrugging, he got to his feet and lowered his hands to his side. "Count slowly to three, Korak." And as he counted, Max tried to relax, and when he heard the three, the gun came into his hand in a whisper, cocked and ready to fire.

"You are very adept with your sidearm, Max, I am impressed,...and very aware of how quickly death could occur."

Max holstered the weapon and nodded. "For anybody but an alien killer!...Makes me feel helpless as hell, too!"

"You must not feel that way, this alien invader would not be here if not for us. And it is not for you to destroy him, unless I fail."

"Who's to say they wouldn't a come here next anyway, would have, too, you hadn't whipped 'em!...We could never beat 'em!...You shouldn't think that way, neither, you whipped their ass in space, and likely saved a hundred other worlds by doin' it....What's one alien killer compared to several million?"

"I bow to your wisdom, Max, and I thank you."

"I'd feel a lot better if that animal would go ahead and show itself,...I ain't much on sittin' and waitin'!"

"Nor I, but it may not show up tonight, nor the invader....And he will be in pain, and very dangerous."

"I can't get over how good you make me feel!"

"I try, Max....Hey, my friend, I am learning to be humorous."

"It was a good come-back!" He grinned and reached to pour the remaining coffee into his cup. "You got that scanner's alarm turned on?" He asked as he sank to his knees and sat down again.

"It is, yes. We are ready!...Should the creature come within one kilometer, the ship's sensors, as well as this one will detect its presence. The alarm will warn us."

"Which one will warn us?"

"The ship's sensors will sound through this one. It is always scanning."

Max nodded and sipped at the hot coffee while he studied the cattle grazing in the meadow below them. Life had been so simple before all this, he thought. Hard, but simple, and he loved it! Helen never complained about any of it, and Lance, he thought, he always wanted to come with him to work the cattle, and sometimes did. But he was glad this was not one of those times.

He thought back to the night he left them in Golden, remembered the fear in her eyes at not knowing where he was going, and why. But he couldn't tell her the truth, she would never believe him, nobody would. He was not sure yet that he did? It still might be a problem if the Shelbys talked too much about it, especially to Sheriff Tate. But then again, they might not believe Shelby, the shape he was in. But if another survivor should wind up in Golden, one who had seen the creature, or the invader, it might be another story,...and fifty vigilantes riding hell-bent into the mountains might just cause more bloody massacres. Be nice to have one a them force fields, Korak talked about. He turned then to look at the bluff.

"Does your ship have a force-field?"

Korak also looked at the bluff. "No,...a Force-field takes much more power than a star fighter can produce, and there is no room inside for that size generator."

"Makes sense, I guess....What about th' weapons, they still work?"

"Not without the gravity engines, no....You must calm yourself, Max,... we are ready for this creature, should he come. We will succeed."

"I know that, I do!...I just can't convince my nerves!...I'll be okay."

"I know you will."

He leaned back to look at the sky. "Is it scannin' th' sky in th' same way?...I mean, It will tell us if another ship is comin', right?"

"Yes, Max." He grinned. "Do not worry!"

"It's still hard to imagine you comin' from up there. We learned about Mars, Jupiter, Venus and others out there in school,…what time I went!... Even learned about shootin' stars, comets, meteors and such, but I weren't interested in none of it!...Weren't interested in history much at all. But I always loved to watch th' stars at night. Lookin' at 'em always made me want a see what was out there, but now that I know, I don't much feel that way no more.…It's sort of a letdown, too!...But I'd still like to see th' Milky way up close."

"It would not look the same, Max. The stars that appear so close from here, are actually millions of kilometers apart."

"Are they planets?"

"Many of them are, but most are dead, orbiting space rocks the size of planets, the same as your Venus, and Pluto. They only shine at night because of your sun and moon's reflections on icy surfaces. Space has no gravity, no oxygen, and is thousands of degrees colder than Earth's coldest winters.… If my star fighter did not have equal pressure inside the cabin to compensate the pressure of space on the outside, it would crush the ship.…Space is cold, and harsh, Max, and very unforgiving! Believe me, you are better off here."

"I believe you're right."

"Yes,…most of my time is spent in space, it is a lonely place."

"Well." He said and drained his cup. "Guess I'll make some more coffee,…gonna be a long night." He got up to grab the canteen and pour water into the pot, opened the coffee sack and dumped grounds in. "What about Mars, man?' He asked as he placed the pot in the flames and sat down again. "I had a teacher my last week in school, that believed Mars was th' only planet out there that might have life on it?"

"According to the archives, it once did, yes. The world became unable to sustain life almost a billion years ago, this from the Cryorans!...The planet had drifted so far away from the sun that it became very cold, water evaporated, soil contaminated and lifeless. By the time the planet settled into its present orbit, the inhabitants had left."

"Were they human beings?"

"No,…they were humanoid, very unlike you or I. They were very tall, I think, and a gentle race.…The planet is still a dead one, its soil turned almost red in color, no oxygen or water exists.…And the planet is now directly in the path of meteor storms, and constantly bombarded."

"I think he believed they came here,…that was th' gist of his conversations on it anyway."

"According to the Cryoran archives, they did not come here, but into deep space."

"How could a planet commit suicide that way, what happened to it?"

"Perhaps the same as Our home planet, Max,…an explosion in space. One so powerful the shock waves pushed it out of its orbit….It is unknown, however."

"Sort a makes Earth a dangerous place to live!"

"It is a fragile planet, yes, but one with all the right ingredients….It is a beautiful world."

"Yeah,…sort a makes wakin' up tomorrow a question mark!" He looked at Korak then. "That same thing could happen here, couldn't it?"

"It could, yes. It could happen to any planet,…and has to many."

"Only we wouldn't be able to leave."

"If it should ever occur, you will be able to leave, Max. Someday space will be your descendant's playground, like it is ours."

"Th' way you describe it out there, who'd want a play in it?"

"With the right survival tools, as we have, it can be quite pleasant."

"That same teacher said he had a rock that came from Mars?"

"That is also possible, Mars has no gravity….Once a meteor strikes the planet, debris from the crater will be thrown into space. It is quite common that it would come to Earth."

Max was silent then as he rolled and lit another cigarette before looking back at the hole in the bluff. "You said the Cryorans have been comin' here for thousands a years, ever been one a them crash, like you did?"

"Of course,…no airship is infallible, there have been several crashes on earth. One such was when a Cryoran was nursed back to health by another of your tribes of Indians,…I believe in one of your far-western states. But there were several others who did not survive the crash….It does not happen often, however."

"What happened to the one who lived?"

"According to the archives, I believe he eventually died without being rescued, and with his ship so damaged, he had no way to send for help…. The Indians held him in such high esteem that they drew pictographs of him on the walls of caves, and on rocks in the arid sand….we know this because a century later, another Cryoran visited there after seeing the reflection of metal from his airship."

"Man!...That teacher a mine would fall out after hearin' about all this!"

"Yes, Our colonists left many monuments and images on earth, the origins of which are now long forgotten by the ancestors here. But they will be studied for many years to come before your scientists and explorers finally discover the answers to things that you now know."

"Knowin' and rememberin' are two whole different things, Korak. I only wish I could!"

"You will remember the important ones, Max, I am confident of that!"

"I just hope I'm alive to remember this one!...I've waited all day before for one shot at an Elk, and that didn't bother me a bit....But this, man!... Waitin' to see if we're both gonna live or die?...Man!"

"We will both live, my friend. Do not worry."

"Yeah, well like I said a couple dozen times already....That's easy for you to say!" He poured fresh coffee in his cup and leaned back again to sip at it.

"Got a slight chill in th' air today." He commented. "Another fifteen or twenty days, we'll have snow in th' mountains....Sure hope we're done with this by then, got a hundred head a cattle to bring in to winter pasture."

"I am sorry for all this, my friend."

"Stop sayin' that, man,...it ain't your fault! I'm just runnin' my mouth here. Helps th' nerves."

"I understand."

"If you do, ya understand a lot more'n I do." He grinned and drained his cup. "Near-bout dark, my friend....Gonna be a long night!"

* * *

He awoke to the shrill cawing of circling crows and yawning, sat up to throw the blanket aside and stare blurry-eyed at the wafer and steaming cup of coffee on the flat stone next to him.

"Good morning, Max!" Greeted Korak as he came through the rocks and sat down. "I knew you were waking up by the way you were moving around,...so I poured your coffee for you."

"I can see that." He muttered sleepily. "Thanks,...I don't remember even closin' my eyes, man!" He picked up the wafer and ate it. "Thanks for this, too."

"We both needed the rest." Returned Korak. "I, too, fell asleep, until a short time ago, when the sensor alarmed."

Max looked at him quickly. "The alarm went off?"

"Do not be alarmed,...one of your cattle became curious. I watched the creature come all the way into camp. A fascinating animal!...Why do you raise them?"

"I sell 'em, that's why it's called a Cattle Ranch!...People eat beef all over th' world. They didn't, I couldn't make a livin'....You had me goin' for a minute, I was hopin' th' beast had shown up, and you killed it while I slept!"

"I wish that as well, my friend....But it will come soon enough,...and it will be better to fight here in the open, than where it is more comfortable."

"Yeah, it can't get away from us here!" He said curtly, and then got to his feet.

"I will kill the creature, Max."

"I sure hope so, man!...I'm gonna go take a dump somewhere. He shows up while I'm gone, save me a piece!" He grinned as he picked up the Henry, half expecting, and a bit surprised that Korak had not asked for an explanation, and walked off past the cloaked ship toward the large rocks where Idak was buried.

It was on his way back that he saw Korak stand and begin looking off down the valley, and looking that way also, soon saw the group of riders as they scattered the dozen or so cows in passing and curious, came on to join Korak and watch their approach.

"Do you know these men, Max?"

"Guess I'm about to find out." They watched the horsemen's approach and as they drew closer, he recognized the man in front.

"That's Cory Tate in front there!...Sheriff down in Golden....Rest of 'em are men from town, a posse, I guess."

"A posse?" Inquired Korak, looking at him curiously.

"Sheriff gets men together when he's chasin' a bad guy, it's called a posse!...Wonder who he's after?"

"Hold up, men!" Yelled Tate as he held up his hand to stop them, their horses kicking tufts of dry grass and dust as the men formed a line in front of them.

"What brings you to my range, Sheriff,...who ya lookin' for?"

"Mister Pruett." He nodded at them both, his eyes lingering on Korak for a minute before coming back to him. "Man by th' name of Noah Hawkins got me out a bed early this morning and told me a damn strange story! Said he came from that gold camp, thirty or so miles west a here,... talked about a madman bein' loose up here! Said he burned out th' gold camp a day or so back, blowin' up everything with dynamite and killin' folks....He also said he told you all about it!" He stood in his stirrups to look the camp over then.

"He said it was you told 'im about th' killer loose up here,...and that you was huntin' 'im,...that right?" He brought his gaze back on them then. "Well, is it?"

"Well, yeah,...he is." He nodded his head at Korak. "I'm just helpin' 'im, he don't know th' mountains."

Tate looked at Korak then. "You must be that Government man, Hawkins spoke about....What's your name?"

"I am called Korak." He nodded.

Tate stared at him a moment. "That all, just Korak?"

"Nobody's supposed to know he's here, Sheriff,...He ain't allowed to give out his last name, you can understand why!...Look, sheriff, you bringin' a posse a men up here ain't gonna do nothin' but scare th' bastard off!...Mister Korak's been on his tail across three states, nobody knows more about th' son of a bitch than he does!...You need to let us catch 'im, Cory. We're tryin' not to scare hell out a everybody in th' mountains!"

Tate stared down at them for several long moments. Can you do it, Mister Korak."

"Yes." He nodded.

"You ain't very friendly, are ye, sir?" He remarked then shifted his weight in the saddle.

"Ya can't blame 'im, Cory!" Said Max quickly. "He's workin' in secret here, and it ain't gonna be one no more, once these men start talkin'!...Now, we have got a trap set for this killer already, and you could be ruinin' our only chance a catchin' 'im by bein' here!"

"What about th' Werewolf, Sheriff?" Yelled one of the men behind him. "Ask 'im about that!"

"A Werewolf?" Asked Max, trying to look surprised.

"Yeah." Sighed Tate. "Homesteader name of Shelby was ravin' about a wild animal killin' all his livestock. Said it was a giant wolf that stood on two legs!...Said they hid in th' root cellar to get away from it."

"It was a God damn Werewolf!" Yelled the man again.

"Settle down, Kirby!" He yelled back at him, and shaking his head, looked back at Max. "Shelby woman said you was there, too, said you made 'em come in to town, that true?"

"It is,...We were followin' th' trail a this bastard,...we got there too late!"

"Shelby said it ate his stock."

"We saw no evidence a that, Cory!...He butchered all of 'em, them in th' corral and yard, bastard's a lunatic!...If anything ate 'em, it was wild animals come in later. Ain't no such thing as a Werewolf, Cory, you know that!"

"He did say he saw it!"

"What he saw was a very large, ugly man!...Shelby was on th' edge a lunacy his self when we found 'em."

Tate sighed heavily and finally nodded. "He was out of it all right,...wife was upset, too!...Okay, Mister Pruett, if you know more'n I do about all this, I'd sure appreciate you tellin' me?"

"At this point, Cory, that's all we know, too!...But you bein' here could scare this killer out a these mountains. If he leaves, Mister Korak might never catch 'im....That's why we been warnin' folks to leave till we find 'im."

"What about th' Preston's, you check on them?"

"We was too late there as well." He nodded. "Blood and carcasses layin' everywhere in th' yard, don't know about th' Prestons themselves, house was dark, couldn't raise nobody….It's possible he could a killed them, too, if they was there. We just don't know!"

"Guess we'll keep lookin' a bit,…if you'll tell me how to find th' Preston place?"

"I wish ya wouldn't, Cory,…if he gets away from us again, he could go down to Golden. You're gonna need all th' help you can get if he does!... Whatever happened to th' Prestons will wait, they can't be helped anyway if they're dead. If they're not, they'll be comin' to town"

"Never thought a that, sure enough!" He mused, raising himself in the stirrups again to look over the terrain. "Golden would be th' likely place for a man to hide!...Sure don't want no lunatic loose in town." He nodded again. "You sure we can't help ya none?"

"Right now, Cory, I don't think so!...We can't chance scarin' 'im off."

"All right then, for now, Mister Pruett!...But I got ten men on their way to that gold camp, I can't account for what they'll do." He reined his horse around. "Let's go home, men!" He shouted, but then turned back and rode in closer to peer down at them.

"Mister Pruett,…I'm gonna give ya time for this trap a yours to work…. But I know there's more to this than just some crazy man on th' loose. I want ya to know that!" He picked up the reins again.

"If you ain't in my office two days from now with this maniac in chains, or his body draped across your saddle while you tell me all about what went on up here, I'm gonna bring every man I can find up here and flush 'im out myself!...That sound fair to you, Sir?"

"Fair enough, Cory."

"Good!" He nodded. "By th' way,…we came by your place before daylight today, weren't nobody there, no stock neither."

"I turned 'em out, Cory, for obvious reasons….My wife and son are in Golden till this is over."

"Good enough….See you in a couple a days." He turned back and rode through the posse's ranks with them closing in behind him.

"This was bound to happen, Korak." He said as they watched them cross Carbon Creek and enter the trees.

"Yes." He agreed. "You are quite the diplomat, my friend."

"I'm th' world's biggest liar, man,…been lyin' through my teeth for three days now!"

"What will you tell him when we kill them?"

"I'll think a somethin'!" He turned then to look at the deep hole in the bluff. "We're just lucky that ship was cloaked,…couldn't lie myself out a that!"

"Yes,…we must end this soon, or many more people will die."

"If that beast don't attack tonight, we got no choice but to go huntin' again."

"I concur, Max." Korak looked around the small enclosure of rocks then. "When the creature attacks, he uses both sight, and scent. I suggest we take his sight away, leaving only my scent to guide him."

"Yeah." Said Max, also looking around. "I see what ya mean….We got plenty a rocks, so let's do it!"

They were finished with the small barricade of stones by early afternoon, and were once again sitting against one of them to look it over. But the longer Max looked at it, he was not as sure of the plan as when Korak suggested it,…and believed that he knew why.

"Tell me if I'm wrong here, man." He said, looking at Korak again. "But it seems to me this idea of yours was to keep that creature from seein' me, am I right?"

"Yes, my friend, you are right!...The beast must come for me, not be distracted if it sees you. As quick as this creature is, he could veer away as I fire, causing me to miss….I will have only one opportunity to destroy it."

"I guess you're right, but I don't like it! I'm in this as deep as you are."

"You are a brave, and good man, Max Pruett, and I know very well you would stand with me and fight this creature. But my friend, you must live to be with your family. I have no family, but I do have a mission to complete…. You will have your turn should I fail."

Max sighed then reluctantly nodded. "What do ya think's takin' it so long,…seems to me it should a come last night?"

"I can only make a guess, Max. Perhaps it ate its fill, and like all predators after a meal it rested all day and last night….Or perhaps it is waiting for the invader first, there can be any number of reasons!...But I believe it will come, the creature alone, or both at once."

"You really think that?"

"It is a possibility, yes."

"Shit, man!" He breathed. "Then you'd better let me hold on to that sidearm a yours, okay?"

"Of course." He gave him the weapon. "It is on the most powerful setting, should the laser strike the beast, it will vaporize it."

"That's what I'm thinkin' about!...Thanks, man." Holding the lethal weapon gingerly, he got to his knees and carefully placed it atop the rock beside the one he would be hiding behind. "Easy to get to." He said when he caught Korak watching. "I don't know about you, man, but I think if they're gonna come at all tonight, it'll be between just after dark, or about nine o'clock."

"How did you arrive at that time?"

"Ain't got an answer to that, but if that was him you scanned last night, like you said, he would a been stuffed!...He would a slept all day, and maybe last night. But he's hungry again today, and unless he found more food on th' way here, he'll be here pretty damn quick now!...He'll travel faster'n we did, too!" He looked at Korak's unreadable expression and shrugged.

"I might not be makin' much sense, I know, but I think if it ain't here by that time, we'll be goin' huntin' again come mornin', what do ya think?"

"It is quite possible, Max, and I would never disagree with you, because I know he will come!...However, should it have attacked your Sheriff's ten men on that road today, it would have eaten again."

"I completely forgot about that!...Them poor bastards won't have a chance."

"We must remain patient, Max, and calm, because he will come!" He used the scanner again then, slowly moving it in a wide arc to take in everything. "For now, however, he is nowhere to be seen." He said, placing the sensor on the ground between them. "But the alarm is activated, we will know when he comes."

"Where do you plan to be?"

"Where he can see me, and I, him!...I will use the laser to stop him, and the starburst to remove him from the earth."

"And if th' killer's with 'im?"

"The sensor will show his presence as well. Perhaps I can fire a second starburst as he attempts to fire, or, if they are close enough together, all the better."

"We ain't that lucky!...Man, I don't understand your logic!...But if they're both here together, I can fire the laser pistol at him!...Hit or miss, I'll draw his attention away from you long enough for you to kill 'im!...I'll be th' duck-blind here, man,...you said yourself, he could dodge th' starburs!"

Puzzled, Korak peered at him for a moment before finally nodding. "All right, my friend,...I can see where that tactic could work, you the decoy, me the hunter....I think I like this duck-blind of yours!...But remember, should we do this, and you fire at him and miss, you must move quickly to another position, as he will detect your laser's signature....Also, yours will lose power beyond the trees."

"I remember all that!...Don't worry, I'll run like a scared rabbit."

"Rabbit?"

"A small, long-eared animal that's hard to catch!"

"Yes,...I have seen such an animal on the sensor, several times."

"They're also good to eat this time a year, we eat 'em quite often."

"You also eat the Elk, correct?"

"Yeah, Elk, White tail deer, cattle,...we're meat eaters, too!"

"What I have learned from you, Max, and from my being here,...the Elders will hold a special place open for you in the Council Archives, and for my report."

"What if you're not able to send th' rest a your report?"

"The Star fighter will send it for me....It is recording everything as we speak, and storing it in memory-banks. The Cryorans will retrieve all data from the ship when my signal is received. They will present it to the council."

"Will I be on it?"

"You, my friend, will be the pride of Promas, I assure you, and when they see me riding my horse, they will send a special envoy to Earth just to retrieve one."

"They'll need one of each to start a herd."

"Once they see the beauty here in these mountains, they will be envious as well, I know I am!" He looked up at the trees then. "The scent from these tall trees, the wildflowers, I will find it hard to leave here, Max. We have trees on Promas, but they are nothing like this. We have trees with blossoms, too, but they lack the aroma of these. And these mountains, Max,...I have never even imagined trekking through trees and brush the way we have done,...I will never forget it!"

"I'll never forget you bein' here, man, I'll miss you when ya leave."

"Thank you for that, Max. I will miss you as well, and I will view the archives regularly to refresh the memory....As will thousands of others."

"I can't imagine that happenin' man!"

"Yet it will, my friend." He looked up at the trees again. The shadows are getting longer, it will grow dark soon, I think. Perhaps you should make your coffee now as well, we will need to be alert and prepared for our creature tonight."

"Think I'll move th' horses down in th' trees there by th' creek, th' creature could attack them before comin' for us."

"A very good idea, my friend."

"That's what I'll do,...as soon as I go take that dump, I spoke of!" He grinned and walked off into the rocks.

* * *

It was already quite dark in the shadow of the bluff as they sat behind their man-made barricade of boulders and watched the setting sun's last rays on the trees and hills to the East of them. The fire had been replenished with fresh wood and was burning fairly high and already starting to brighten up that area of the bluff behind them….And then it gradually became dark, and the bluff shone even brighter in the fire's flickering light.

Max pulled his watch to check the time, as he still believed the pet would attack before nine o'clock. It was only six o'clock however, and with pounding heart replaced the watch in his shirt pocket and sat down behind his rock barricade to watch the expectant area of trees to the south of them. The laser pistol lay in easy access atop the rock by his head, and the Henry Rifle was leaning against the rock on his right….He was ready, he thought nervously.

"You must relax, my friend, remain calm." Said Korak, from where he was seated atop a smaller rock some twenty feet away.

"That's easier said, than done, man!...I ain't happy you sittin' there in th' open like that!"

"It is me the creature wants, Max,…but it will kill anything in its path. I must have its full attention!...It must come for me so I can kill it! If it is diverted in any way, I could fail, you saw how fast the beast is."

"I saw it!" He nodded, remembering the video.

"It may not come at all tonight, but if it should, I am ready!...My weapon is here, my scanner is here, and the alarm is active. You must remain calm, and remain hidden."

He nodded again and positioned himself even lower behind the rocks, but was still able to see the trees between the gap in them, and by leaning his head slightly to the side, could see all the area in between. He glanced at Korak again, in awe of his courage. The man was calm when all he could muster was the image of those monsters killing those people on Promas.

How could anybody hope to destroy a beast like that, he wondered? He had no doubt what Korak's gun could do, but to stand up in the face of danger, with a creature that big and deadly charging straight at you, with intent to murder?...That takes guts, he thought as he stared back between the rocks,…a hell of a lot more than he had! The thought of that made him wonder if that might have been what made him sit out the war, but he did not think so, he thought seriously,…that damn war was totally stupid, an unnecessary waste of life and in fact, he showed more courage sitting it out than those did who went to fight! No, he thought then, he wasn't a coward, just cautious, the strength of a man was knowing when to fight,…and that war was not the time!...This was, because his life was being threatened, his family's lives were being threatened. Earth was being threatened!...He shook his head then in disgust, thinking of the video again. That creature was one scary son of a bitch!

What if it didn't come at all tonight, what if the image Korak saw at the Preston place was not the beast at all? If that were the case, it likely wouldn't show! No, he thought angrily, it had to come tonight! He wanted it over and done with! Sighing, he suddenly decided he needed a smoke to calm his nerves and took tobacco and papers from his shirt to nervously roll and light the slightly lumpy cigarette, taking the acrid smoke deep into his lungs, and exhaling it thankfully into the crisp mountain air before catching Korak watching him.

"Helps calm th' nerves." He said, holding it up in front of him. "Coffee and a smoke, man, they go together,…and it's not a drug neither!"

"Has it calmed your nerves?"

Max peered at him for a moment then shrugged. "It will,…takes a few minutes."

"I have not seen you do this before today."

"You're right,…guess ya didn't!...Come to think about it, I ain't had one in a couple a days now, and that's strange."

"With air such as this to breathe, why would you, Max?"

"Don't know, habit, I guess!" He shrugged and pulled out his watch again." Seven-thirty, he thought with a sigh and replaced it. "Anything on that scanner yet?"

"No, nothing."

"Aint that strange?...Woods ought a be full a wildlife this early."

"Perhaps,…but the sensor shows nothing. If the beast was there, I would see it.…Relax, my friend. We are ready."

Nodding, he finished the smoke in silence, thinking it strange that not even the birds were singing, there was always night birds singing, and crickets, those irritating insects usually drove him crazy at night, especially around a fire.…That thing is coming, he thought nervously. Korak might not see it, might not think anything of it, there being nothing on that scanner. But something was in those woods, maybe a mile away yet, but it was there, he was sure of it! He looked at Korak again, seeing him watching the scanner intently.

What th' hell, he thought tiredly, and got to his knees to flip the spent smoke into the fire and then to use his bandana to pick up the coffee pot and pour his cup full of the steaming liquid. Then sighing, moved back against the rock to sip at it while watching the trees. If they survived that beast tonight, the killer should be a breeze, he thought,…because he could not be more afraid than he was right now. Damn it anyway,…he had faced men with guns and didn't feel this way, had almost lost a time or two, and never felt this way. So, what was wrong with him now, he wondered?...But he knew why, none of those were men from outer space!...And he was in a war-zone with one right now, possibly a close relative of his. He sighed and pulled out his watch again. Only eight-twenty, he thought sadly and put it away again to sip at the coffee and watch the trees.

His mother had always told him that a watched pot never boils, and he now knew what she meant! So he decided not to look at the watch again and instead leaned his head against the rock to drink his coffee and watch the trees,…and for the next several long minutes continued his vigil, with a glance at Korak from time to time to watch his body language. Until at last, he could stand it no longer and pulled out the watch again.

"It appears you're right, man." He said with a sigh. "Five minutes of nine, and no sign of our guest!...Maybe it didn't see us after all!"

"Perhaps not." Returned Korak. "However, I think we must remain alert and ready."

"Goes without sayin', man." He said as he watched Korak touch his face to bring up the mask. They had been alert for four days, he thought as he looked back through the rocks. He was sure the creature had not seen them now, and they missed their chance at the alien killer….They would have no choice but to hunt them down now, and with no advantage would likely be dead themselves when it was over!...The alien and his pet would have free rein then, unless they were killed, too! He just could not see having any success in this war,…the alien hunters had the advantage of time on their side.

He looked up then as Korak got off his seat to stare at the distant trees before looking around at the rest of the campsite. And looking at Max then, he raised his hands to tap his face again to retract the mask before walking the twenty feet between them to place the sensor on the ground.

"I will return, Max,…please listen for the alarm." He straightened to look over Max's head at the grazing cattle in the valley, and then back at the trees.

"Me watch it, why,…Where ya goin"?"

"I am feeling an urgent need to relieve myself. Do not worry, should the alarm sound, I will have ample time to return."

"What'll I do?"

"Call me loudly, I will come." With rifle in hand, he turned and walked back to his rock, leaned the weapon against it and walked past the cloaked ship into the rocks beyond.

He watched him leave, and at that moment never felt more alone, and the quickly forming bubble of air in his chest just added to his dilemma. He couldn't figure out why Korak would leave the only weapon that could possibly kill that creature behind, and go off to take a piss? The gun was bulky, he thought, but not so heavy he couldn't handle it!

"Shit!" He said aloud then looked back through the rocks. To now, Korak had taken every precaution needed to insure their safety, but this, he couldn't understand at all. As the minutes ticked by, the bubble in his chest continued to grow making those minutes seem like hours. He reached out then and turned the sensor so he could see the screen. There was nothing on it, not even an animal. Damn it!" He said with frustration, and went back to watching the trees.

He must be right, he thought, he usually was! That thing was not going to show up tonight. He thought of Helen then, and wondered what they must be going through?...Tate would have talked with her by now to check on his story. He would have also wired the authorities in Denver to inquire about the supposed killer. But he would not have been able to get a wire through to the Government he thought smugly, too much rigamarow to go through! He chuckled then,...what kind a damn word was rigamarow anyway, just a word his mother used to explain red tape!

People in Washington probably had no idea who was on their payroll anyway. Helen and Lance must be scared to death, especially if Tate decided to bring another posse into the mountains....She would think the worst had happened! He heard the beeping then and at first, could not figure out what it was, being so deep in thought, and began looking around the campsite in search of the source. But when his eyes fell on the scanner's screen, he saw the orange image, and heard the signal. He had no idea how long it had been beeping. He stared at the sensor dumbfounded for a moment, and then it hit him. The image on the screen was large, and moving! He quickly looked back through the gap in the rocks and almost stopped breathing as the monstrous beast walked out of the trees to stop and shake its tremendously large head a time or two before raising it high in the air, as if sniffing it for the scent of its prey.... And then it slowly began walking toward the fire's light.

He let his breath gush from his aching lungs and worked his mouth, but no sound would come out. He cleared his throat and tried to yell. "Korak!" He croaked. And then. "KORAK!" He yelled shrilly.

The creature heard him and with a roar lunged forward in a mad rush at the rocks, and gasping, he yelled again and quickly grabbed for the laser pistol, but in his haste, knocked the weapon from the rock to fall on the other side. The beast was closing on him fast when in a panic, he grabbed the Henry Rifle, stood up and began firing, the sudden bursts of gunfire shattering the stillness as he levered and fired again and again, but still it came. He fired the sixth round at the charging animal to no avail then levered the seventh and last round, aimed at its massive head and fired again.

To his disbelief, the creature's right eye exploded outward, followed by a dark fluid that he took to be blood.

The creature seemed to stumble then and stopped to swing its great head from side to side as it tried to claw at the eye, and then suddenly reared on its rear legs and screamed with roars so loud, the ground beneath his feet seemed to tremble. Awestruck, he held his breath again and at that point, caught movement from a corner of his eye and turned to see Korak sweep up the starburst rifle and fire. He numbly watched the orange burst of light from the weapon's barrel then heard the beast's roar abruptly end as the blinding light forced him to turn away. And when he looked back, all that was left was a thirty-yard circle of smoldering, charred ground, and burning grass.

He was still numb as he watched the rising smoke from burnt earth with open-mouthed amazement, and when he focused on the burning grass, quickly leaned the Henry against a rock, bent to retrieve the bedroll blanket and run the several yards to begin stamping and beating out the flames before they became out of control,...and when the flames were out, he slung the blanket over his shoulder and stepped onto the hot, still steaming area of blackened earth to stare down at it in disbelief,...and with a great feeling of relief.

Before turning to return to the campfire, he stared hard at the forest of trees and felt his pulse quicken again when he remembered that the alien killer might still be lurking there. It was not until he started back to camp that he felt the rush of icy air at the front of his pants and looked down.

"Pissed my damn pants!" He said in disgust. "Of all th' cowardly things to do!" Shaking his head, he walked on back to the rocks to find Korak holding the Henry Rifle and looking it over.

"My friend." He said as Max approached. "I was mistaken to think your weapons were primitive. He watched as Max bent and retrieved the fallen sidearm. "I have no doubt that another of your projectiles through the creature's eye would have felled it!" He accepted the sidearm and returned it to his belt.

"I knocked that off th' rock when I reached for it!" He shrugged.

"Yet you stopped the beast anyway,...I am greatly impressed!"

"I thought you weren't gonna make it back in time, man!" He looked down at himself again. "Scared th' piss out a me!"

"I am sorry, Max,...I was caught in the act of progression, and in truth,...I did not expect the beast so soon."

"I didn't expect it at all there for a while!" He breathed a deep sigh of relief then came around the rocks to the fire, squatted and poured more coffee into his cup before taking the partially charred blanket from his neck and tossing it back on the bedding. "Think th' killer'll show tonight, too?"

Korak placed the Henry back against the rock then bent to retrieve the scanner and look at the screen before closing it. "No, I do not!...If he has indeed lost his arm, he will take the time needed to field-dress the open wound....But he will come, Max! Maybe tomorrow, when he has calmed the pain, maybe the day after, it is uncertain."

"Another day like this, I'll be white headed!" He drank some of the hot coffee and placed the cup on a rock to go get the Henry. "That's one killer rifle you got, Korak!" He said as he took cartridges from his back pocket and reloaded.

"I can now say the same for yours, my friend....It is you who saved our lives this day. You alone will be the hero on Promas....They will show this video on vision screens for many years."

"You sayin' all this was recorded?"

"On the ship's sensors, yes!" He nodded. "It records even now."

"I forgot, you told me that already." He propped the rifle against the rock again and looked down at his pants. "This right here will prove I ain't no hero, man!...I was just too scared to run." He grabbed the cup again and drained it. "I got a sit down before I fall down!" He moved to his bedroll and sat down heavily before lying back on the saddle.

Korak came to sit on the opposite bedroll and place the sensor between them. "It has been a tiring day, Max, you must rest."

"Yeah, right!...I didn't hear that alarm, Korak....I was thinkin' about other things!...Damn thing must a been beepin' for a while before I heard it, cause when I did, th' thing was already here!...I ain't no hero, man, I damn near got us killed!"

"Yet, you did not!" Argued Korak as he reached in his belt and brought out another pill. "Take this, my friend, and rest." He gave him the pill. "Tomorrow will be a much better day."

"It couldn't be any worse." He said, taking the pill and putting it in his shirt pocket. "But first." He said, sitting up to tug the boots from his feet. "I got a get out a these wet socks and pants. Sitting the boots aside, he lay back and unbuckled the gun-belt to pull it from under his body, then came the soiled pants, tossing them across the top of a rock to dry. He sat up again and removed the socks, placing them there as well.

"Thanks, man." He breathed, taking the pill from his pocket and eating it. "I'm gonna miss these things, too!...Hey, man,...if that son of a bitch shows up tonight, don't wake me, okay?" He pulled the slightly charred blanket over his lower body, wet unions and all and lay down again.

"I weren't shootin' at th' bastard's eye, man." He said, looking up at Korak. "Hardly realized I was shootin' at all. Th' sight a that thing charging at me was enough to stop my heart from beatin'!...It was a lucky shot, that's all, my last one, too!. It's a wonder, pissin' my pants was all I done!" He chuckled then at his own mirth.

"Beats hell out a me, how you never get scared a anything." He yawned then. "I'll see that son of a bitch in my sleep for th' next twenty ye,..." He was asleep.

CHAPTER EIGHT

Max opened his eyes as Korak shook him, having to stare groggily at him for several seconds until he remembered where he was. "What's wrong?" He asked as he sat up. "Is he here?"

"No, Max!" Said Korak quickly. "Someone else is coming."

He threw off the blanket and grabbed his socks. "Who is it?" He asked as he pulled them on. "That posse again?"

"I do not believe so." He replied, showing Max the scanner's screen. "Only four men riding horses this time....They are less than one kilometer away, and appear to be coming this way."

He got up and grabbed his pants, pulling them on as he looked down the valley toward Carbon Creek. "Could be riders from Semple's Ranch." He said absently then sitting down to pull on his boots. "Double s ranch, next to mine." He grabbed up the gun-belt and got to his feet again to buckle it on, looking down at the screen again before looking back at the valley. The riders were not in sight as yet.

"I replenished the fire and made your coffee again, my friend."

"Thanks, man,...but right now, I got a go!" He moved from between the rocks as he spoke. "I'll be back before they get here." He continued on past the cloaked ship into the rocks, leaving Korak to scan the rest of the bluff's area of trees.

The horsemen were just rounding the trees at the valley's far end when he returned to squat and pour his morning coffee, and then stood with Korak to watch their approach.

"What will you tell them?" Asked Korak, closing the sensor and placing it on the ground.

"Another lie." He said, casting a glance back at the circle of charred ground. "I'm gettin' damn good at it!" He took a swallow of the hot coffee and continued to watch the riders. "Wonder what brings 'em over this way?"

They were still standing at the fire when the four men stopped their horses and walked them toward them. "That's Ben Semple, all right, th' others work for 'im....Light on down here, Ben!" He said loudly as they stopped beside the rocks. "What brings you callin'?"

"Maxwell." Acknowledged Semple as he dismounted and came around his horse.

"Coffee's hot, you brought cups?"

"We didn't." Said Semple as he walked in beside them to look over Korak's strange attire. "Sam there was puttin' out some block salt last night on my south range." He looked back at Max then. "Said he heard rifle shots in this direction, a number of them....He was worried you might be in trouble, so he came and told me."

"He heard shots all right, Ben,...had a few cows grazin' up here and, ah,...along about ten last night, a few hungry grays decided they'd have supper."

"That would about do it all right!" Nodded Semple. "Glad that's all it was." He looked toward the charred ground then. "Had a fire up here, too, I see."

"Bullet hit a rock'r somethin', caused a spark!...Took a while to put out."

"Bet it did!" He said, looking back at him. "Maxwell,...what's this I hear about a killer bein' loose up here?"

"Where'd ya hear that?"

"Ernie was in Golden yesterday, story is all over town."

"It's all true, Ben." Sighed Max, with a furtive look at Korak. "Ben, I'd like you to meet, Mister Korak." And when they shook hands. "He works for th' Government, been trackin' this man for a while,...till his horse throwed 'im and hurt his leg."

"Government man, huh?" Nodded Semple as he looked Korak over again. "Never seen clothes like them before, Mister Korak,...never heard a name like yours before, neither,...is it foreign?"

"Yes." Nodded Korak, "I am not from here." He touched his arm then. "This is my uniform."

"Uniform, is that so?" Mused Semple. "Just who is this killer you're after?"

"We, ah,...we don't know his name, Ben, all Mister Korak has is a description. Seems he's a lunatic, left a trail a killin's from here to, ah, Arkansas....He's a bad one, butchered all a Shelby's barnyard stock a day or so back. Would a killed them, too, they hadn't hid out."

"That's what Ernie heard." He looked down at Korak's wrapped leg then. "You break the leg, Sir?" And when Korak nodded. "What kind of splints you using, never seen the likes of it?"

"Well." Said Max quickly, after Korak silently looked at him for help. "We knew we'd be huntin' th' killer in th' mountains, so he insisted on wrappin' th' splints with his slicker to keep it dry,...it's wrapped pretty tight with it!"

"And you can stand on it already!" He looked at the cast a moment longer then nodded. "Well, what do I know about it, anyway!" He shook his head and turned back to Max. "This killer the one who attacked the gold camp?"

"We think so, yeah....Preston place, too."

"How close are you to catching him?"

"We found 'im a day and a half ago, Ben. Mister Korak wounded 'im in th' arm, but he managed to escape again."

"You know where he is, though,...is that a good assumption?"

Max nodded. "We think he's hid out in one a th' caves around Shelby's homestead. It was near there we found 'im."

"You helping him, are you?"

Max shrugged. "I know th' mountains, he don't!"

"Anyway I can help,...I can spare a couple of men?"

"I appreciate it, Ben,...but like he explained to me. Aside from hirin' a guide, th' Government won't allow any outside interference....I'm helpin' track th' man, that's all!"

Semple stared back at Korak then. "You are a strange looking man, Mister Korak,...not all that talkative neither. But I can understand, I reckon, everything's a secret with the Government,...all that need to know, crap!... One thing about that uniform though,...all it does is make a hell of a good target for a man with a rifle!" He turned and went back to his horse, turned it around and mounted to sit and look down at them.

"Luck with getting your man, Maxwell." He tipped his hat at Korak. "Maxwell,...you take care, I'd hate to have to buy this place from your widow."

"I'm sure you would, Ben."

"My offer to help still stands, you need it!" He reined the horse around, then stopped. "I'm a bit curious, Maxwell." He nodded at the valley. "Them your horses staked out there in the trees?"

"Yeah,...wolves, and that fire spooked 'em a bit."

Nodding, he tipped his hat again. "You take care now." All four of them galloped their horses back down the slope and rode away.

"Did he believe you, Max?" Asked Korak, still watching them.

"Damn if I know,...Ben Semple's a suspicious man. He was a Union General in th' war."

"Union?"

"Union and Confederate, North against South!...Stupid war pitted fathers against sons, brothers against brothers, Korak. Damn near tore this country apart!

"Yet it survived." He sighed. "War of any kind is never good, my friend. It only creates sadness and destruction."

"Yeah, it does." Sighing himself, he turned to look around the camp again. "What's our plan for today, man,...our killer didn't show?"

"I do not know, Max. However, I still believe he will come!"

"I don't think my nerves'll stand any more a this waitin' for somethin' to happen!...I think we ought a go back to Shelby's place and track 'im, or try to."

"Then we will go."

"I'll get th' horses." He looked down at the coffee pot then. "After I have some more coffee." He took the cup from atop the rock and squatted to pour the hot liquid.

"And here is your morning meal, my friend." Said Korak, giving him the wafer.

* * *

Coming off the mountain, they stopped long enough for Korak to check his sensor before descending down to the road and walking the animals toward the gruesome scene at the homestead.

"Vultures are back to pick th' bones." He commented as they neared the blood-soaked yard,...and once again the giant birds took to the air as they stopped their horses. "Are we still in th' clear?" He asked, staring past the cabin at the large circles of charred ground along the roadway ahead.

"Yes, we are clear."

Nodding, he looked along the road at the tall-weeds, and grass and then spotted something. He looked around at the trees and house then dismounted to walk into the grass along the burned area where he bent to pick up the killer's heavily armored left arm and held it for Korak to see.

"Took it off at the shoulder. Man!" He said with a grin. "Heavy son of a bitch, too!" He watched as Korak dismounted and came to take it from him. "Look at th' size a them muscles on it."

"Yes." He said in response then looked closely at the burnt end of the severed limb. "He is in much pain now."

"Ain't it possible he bled to death,...ain't no man could live after a wound like that?"

"He is not a man, Max, nor a human,...only a humanoid!...And see this." He showed him the arm's severed end. "The laser sealed the wound as it was severed,...he would have lost very little of his life's fluid. The weapon, however, was attached to his right arm, and this means he is still a threat, and very dangerous."

"You always try to make my day, man!" He sighed, his eyes following the trail of burnt earth along the winding road. "He was damn sure fast on his feet,...cause them missiles was after his ugly ass!"

Korak dropped the arm to the grass again. "What do you suggest now, Max?"

"See if we can find his trail, I guess, man that size is bound to leave broken twigs and tracks somewhere....There's a couple a caves along th' hills up there, he could be in one of 'em."

"I agree." Nodded Korak. "But we must be alert...If he is in a hole, my sensor may not detect his presence."

"Set it for underground then."

"Yes, but even so, we must be close to see him, as the soil's natural minerals disrupt the scan."

"Is that a problem?"

"His sensor will show our presence long before we detect his."

"That's a problem!" He breathed. "That scanner can't see through rocks and ground debris, what about trees?"

"Trees have no heat signature, Max. None of these things give off heat....It will see between them if the heat source is behind them, and will see him if he moves away."

"This just keeps gettin' better, don't it?"

"So it seems, my friend. But would that not make the hunt too easy?"

"You're becomin' human, man, you just made a funny!" He chuckled then and when done, grinned at him. "Guess it would at that."

"Did I say something humorous?"

"To me, it was....Okay." He said, looking back at the discarded arm. "Damn, I can't get over th' size a that arm,...big as my leg!...Must be one strong son of a bitch!. Well, Korak,...we can hunt for 'im, or go back and wait, what do ya think?"

Korak looked up the road as far as the trees would allow. "The invader's signature faded one kilometer away. Perhaps we should follow his retreat for that distance, he may have left a trail to follow from there."

"Sounds good to me." They mounted and slowly continued up the winding lane, past the burnt circles of charred ground to finally come to the last one, some thousand yards distant, and at least fifty yards to one side away from the road.

"That last shot took th' tops out a several trees before it hit!...That's one powerful gun you got, man!" He stopped to view the missile's burning path.

"Yes." He nodded. "But they all missed the invader."

"Maybe so." Said Max, getting off his horse to walk around it and pick up an almost small, square, flat piece of light metal. "Could he have dropped this, whatever it is?" He asked, reaching up to give it to Korak.

Taking the item, he studied the square shape for a moment then touched the front of its flat surface. "This is his sensor, Max!" Said Korak, turning it for him to view his own orange image on the screen.

"That means he can't see us comin'!"

"Unless he has another on his weapon, such as mine, no, he will not!"

"Like you said before, man, that one only scans a short distance."

"This is true, but I do not know this technology, the one he has may detect farther."

"Well, it's good enough for me, man, what about you?"

"Yes, we will go on."

"Give me that scanner, you keep yours, together we can't miss 'im!" He took the alien scanner and remounted to continue on up the road, each scanning their own side of the road and timbered hillside, and once Korak had decided they had gone one kilometer, stopped in the road again to use the sensor more thoroughly.

"Deer, couple a wolves, wild hogs,...that's about all I can see, man. Not a man of any size in sight."

"Mine as well....Where are these caves you spoke of?"

Max stood in his stirrups to look through the giant pines. "I think there's an old mine-shaft at the base a th' mountain on your side, about a hundred yards off th' road. The old overgrown trail ought a be just up ahead there, let's check it out." He led the way, and thirty or so yards up the lane came to the barely visible, yet recognizable old wagon trail and stopped. "I'll check it out, man." He dismounted and walked a few yards into the thicket of trees and came back.

"Not a broken twig, or blade a grass out a shape." He said. "Unless he left th' road somewhere and went through th' woods to get there, he ain't there!...Want a check it out anyway?"

"No need, I think." Returned Korak thoughtfully. "He would not know of this mine-shaft, nor of any other cave, I think....He would be in much pain, and would only think of escape!...But, I do not know, Max. He is humanoid, and a hunter, and how his mind might work is a question the Cryorans have pondered for ten years."

"In other words, he could be anywhere!" He nodded. "Well, it's been two days since he lost his arm, man....Seems to me, he would a come back to find this thing." He looked at the smaller sensor again. "He must a thought we were behind 'im and continued to run,...but where?...If he knows what a scanner will, or won't do, and I'm sure he does!...Then with any brain at all, he'll hide behind a Duck-blind of his own and wait for us!... And if he knows th' last position of his pet?...We'd best go back, Korak!"

"Perhaps so." He turned in the saddle to look behind them.

"He's not behind us, man." Breathed Max. "We're still breathin'!...That means he's still ahead of us somewhere, and if he's dug in, we won't know till he fires at us."

"That is true, Max."

"Then let's get out a here, it's already late. For all we know, he could be waitin' on us at our own campsite."

*   *   *

"Well,...this alien sensor don't show nothin' but my cows, Korak."

"Nor does mine....But we must be cautious, he could be, as you say, dug in and waiting."

"I did say that, didn't I?...Okay, I'll ride down a ways and then ride in, you keep that rifle ready...He fires at me, you take 'im out!"

"I cannot allow you to do that, Max."

"Don't worry, man, if he fires at me, I'll leave this saddle like a scared rabbit!...At best, he'll kill my horse!...I'll be okay!" He reined the horse back through the trees to finally descend the slope before turning back toward the dark campsite. I must be out a my mind, he thought nervously, and was able to feel his heart in his throat as he urged the animal in closer, even loosened his feet in the stirrups in anticipation of being shot at. But nothing happened and he rode into the dark barricade of stones and dismounted to watch Korak ride in.

"You should not take a chance like that, my friend." He said as he dismounted. "It would be my dishonor should you die in my place."

"I don't intend for that to happen, man, besides,...nothin' happened! If he'd killed you, us ridin' in together, I'd die anyway. Besides, if he got you, he'd destroy your gun, too, and I'd have nothin' to kill 'im with."

"I realize that, Max....Thank you, my friend."

"Then how about puttin' some fire on them sticks while I fix me some coffee?"

"It would be my pleasure."

Max placed the pot in the flames as Korak gave him the food wafer. "Ya know, man." He said, looking at the large pill. "I just might get so used to these things that I'll starve to death when you leave!" He ate the wafer and watched Korak eat his. "You do plan on leavin', don't you?"

"You have asked me this before, my friend, why would I not?...My presence here would someday be known, and that must not happen!...Should I be forced to stay for a while, my visit with you and your family would be pleasurable....Of course, Max, I shall leave!...Once my signal is received, they will come for me."

"Yeah, sorry, Korak." He sighed heavily. "Deep inside a me, I keep getting' th' feelin' that....Aw, hell, forget it, man! Anyway,...this stuff'll all be gone before they get here."

"Then I will eat Helen's fried chicken."

"Yes, by God, you will!" He grinned. "You sure will." He sat back against the rock then to pick up the alien scanner, and running his hand along the side of it, suddenly caught his breath when the deep space image of the huge alien ship appeared on the screen.

"Look at this, Korak." He gave him the sensor. "That ship is a monster,...is it th' Mother ship?"

"Yes, Max, it is!" He continued to use his fingers along the sensor's edges to bring up even more images of the planet-sized vessel's enormous interior. Along with a strange series of markings resembling hieroglyphics that appeared over each piece of machinery and electronic device. Trillions of lights, levers and knobs adorned the machinery as well. Another set of pictures showed the alien's warship, the engines, the electronics, control panels,...and all with the same hieroglyphics adorning each. After a while, Korak looked up at Max and nodded.

"My friend," He said, looking at it again. "I believe this to be the Mother ship's control center,...and somewhere along one of these panels is what possibly controls their force-field. This could be what the Cryorans need to penetrate the ship's defenses. It also shows complete schematics of his warship, engines, weapons, it's control-panels!...I believe the schematics simulates repairs to his ship should it fail....If I could only decipher the written language?...He was using this to repair his ship, Max. We destroyed it in time!...This could be all the information the cryorans need."

"How would you send it to 'em without warnin' th' Mother ship?"

"I have been thinking of that as well!...If I recall the archives exactly, ten thousand years ago, the Cryorans explored your Moon's surface with deep-probing radio waves in search of useable resources. What they left behind were only those structures too large to bring back, and one of those structures was a tower, I think....I will bounce the transmission off that tower, using the Cryoran wave-length. Perhaps the invaders will pay it no thought."

"Why wouldn't they?"

"Because the Council, and the Cryorans believe that Cryor was destined to be their next invasion, and will not know that we are allies."

"But if they do,...what?...Couldn't that bring 'em here instead?"

Korak looked at him for a moment, then nodded. "You are right, of course. Forgive me, my friend, I cannot take that chance!"

"What about that thing, will it send a signal?"

"What are your thoughts?"

"I ain't got a clue, man....But if your scientists, and the Cryorans are all listenin' to th' signals comin' in, I thought ya might send all them pictures and writings back to th' mother ship with that scanner, your people might see 'em, too, and decipher th' language!...The invaders wouldn't know what was goin' on!"

"If they could possibly do that." He nodded thoughtfully. "They may be able to use electronic waves to disarm the force-field." He thought about that for a minute before sighing.. "All they would need is the codes."

"But would it work,...maybe th' codes are on there?...Would it?"

"We would be assuming a lot, Max, and the risk would still be great!... And they may still not be able to decipher the language."

"Maybe they can recognize the machinery....Once they see it, they might know where it came from?...I still think th' bastards stole everything they got!"

Korak thought long and hard for another minute before shaking his head. "They would still need the frequency codes, Max, and they may not be on here."

"It was just a thought, man!" He shrugged.

"And a very good one, Max!...Thank you....However, what I can do is connect this sensor to my ship's power supply and data base, and then face the screen forward while sending the signal wave....When they see their warrior die, they will know that all is lost!"

"You forgot about th' big weapon they're building!"

"Nothing will change that, Max. It is out of our hands!...And yes, they may try to fire their new weapon, but when they lower their shields to fire, a thousand star fighters will fire their entire arsenal in return, as will every starburst cannon on Promas....They will not survive, my friend."

"I'd like to see that!"

"Perhaps you will, Max." He nodded and took the small control from his belt, opened the ship's hatch, then made the ship materialize before looking at Max again. "Please watch the scanner while I send our message?"

"Sure,...will it take long?"

"Not long at all." He walked across to the escalating steps then up to the hatch and went inside, leaving him to once again listen for the alarm on the sensor,...and to think,...his mind going back to when they found the invader's arm and still not believing the size of it. A man that size, and that strong wouldn't need a weapon to commit murder when he could do it barehanded!

Could he have really lost that scanner, he wondered, or could he have thrown it away?...No, he thought, he lost it, he only had one arm and hand. It would have been in his good hand, or on his body somewhere while he ran, and it bounced out!...With that much pain, he wouldn't have noticed it. He lost it, he decided!...Lost his advantage when he did, too. One thing was going to be for certain, he thought sadly,...whoever won when this thing was over, in one way or another, they would all lose! Because his life would never be the same!...If Korak survived, it would just be another mission accomplished to him, that's what his training required.

'I ain't had no training for this kind of shit!' He thought drearily. He was the one that would have to live with it, when Korak was gone! He had already pissed all over his self when that creature attacked,...he would probably shit his pants next time! Was he a coward, he wondered?...He didn't think so, it had to be the unknown he was afraid of. He was fighting aliens, for God sakes,...monsters from another world!...It is a God damn nightmare, is what it is, he thought then. He would wake up any minute now and go about the business of ranching.

"Yeah, right!" He said aloud and looked down at the scanner,...and not wanting to miss the alarm again, lifted it to his lap as he watched the trees again. He was sure that all they had was another day or two before Tate brought his posse back, and that would be a disaster. Because if they should encounter the invader, they would all be dead,...and should even one of them escape to tell about it?...He pushed the thought from his mind and thought of Helen and Lance alone in that hotel room, not knowing if he was alive or dead?...The stories they have already heard would be terrifying enough!...He looked up then as Korak returned.

"It is done, Max." He said as he cloaked the ship again and sat down. "My on-board computer found the alien communication link, it is now sending everything in its memory banks back to the alien ship on an open channel. It will all be seen by Promas, and Cryor, as well as any other world that happens to be listening."

"Will that Mother ship know all that?"

Perhaps so, perhaps not, only that messages are being sent from the invader's own sensor. They will not know why he is sending it, and should not understand its meaning, because there will be no message."

"Hope they don't decide to send another warship to check it out!"

"Do not worry, if we detected this one leaving, they will have detected me in pursuit!...And their forces are almost depleted now,...I do not think they will chance losing another warship."

"Hope you're right."

"As do I, Max." He reached to take back the scanner. "I have also instructed the on-board computer to transfer the data from the invader's sensor to this one. If you like, you can view it?"

"Don't know if I want to, man, to tell ya th' truth!"

"I understand."

Max got up then and went to pour himself some coffee before sitting down again.

"Our killer will know his pet's dead by now, won't he?"

"If he has another sensor, yes. If not, no,...he lost his sensor before the creature died."

Max put his cup down then rolled and lit a cigarette before picking it up again.

"You do not look well, Max. Your face is drawn, the brow creased with worry,...perhaps you need to rest?"

"And be asleep when th' fun starts?"

"I will be alert, my friend....It is only a few hours until morning." He leaned forward to give Max the pill. "You need rest, my friend."

CHAPTER NINE

Lance Pruett opened his eyes and blinked in the morning sun several times before suddenly remembering, and quickly looked around for his father,... seeing him sitting on a nearby rock behind him smoking and staring at the tall mound of clay beneath the once tall bluff.

"What are ya doing, Pop?"

"Hey there,...mornin', son!" He grinned, getting up to come back and pour more coffee in his cup. "You took some kind a nap." He pulled his pocket watch from his vest and looked at it. "It's nigh on to eight o'clock in th' mornin'!"

"Gosh, I'm sorry, Pop, I never meant to fall asleep, didn't even know I did?"

"Oh, I understand!...My story was borin', I guess,...that, or you thought it was a yarn, like your mother did?"

"No, Daddy, that ain't it, I swear!"

"I know, Son." He chuckled. "I was half asleep myself....Hell, it was two in th' mornin'!...Got more beans in th' skillet there, eat your breakfast."

"Then will you finish th' story?"

"That depends,...you know where I left off?"

"I sure do, Korak gave you a sleeping pill!"

"And before that?"

"He finished sendin' that message to the alien ship."

"Guess you were listenin'....Okay, eat your breakfast and I'll finish it,... and don't wolf it down, got plenty a time!"

"Mama's probably worried about us already." He said as he dipped beans into his tin. "Mad, too!"

"She knows we're together, son. She was too worried, she'd saddle up and come lookin',...now eat!"

"Okay, daddy." He began eating. "I can't believe you stopped that monster with your rifle, sure wish I'd a seen it!"

"I pissed my pants, boy, think I'd want you to embarrass me by bein' there?...Bad enough, Korak seen it!"

"What did Mister Semple say later?"

"Didn't see 'im again for six months, told 'im th' killer got away!... Seemed to satisfy 'im."

"Hey, Pop,…how come we didn't camp out over there where you and Mister Korak did?"

"Full a ghosts over there, it's where he died!"

"Sorry, pop, I understand."

"I know ya do, ya got your mother's heart."

"I'm done, Daddy." He said, wiping his mouth on his bandana.

"All right then,…where was I?"

"Th' sleepin' pill."

"Oh, yeah,…well, I woke th' next mornin' and…."

* * *

Max opened his eyes and had to blink in the bright sunlight, and putting on his hat sat up and looked around for Korak, finally seeing him exiting the star fighter,…and when he looked down, saw the wafer on the small stone beside him and grinning, ate it.

"Good morning, Max." He nodded as he placed the scanner on the ground and sat down,…and once he used the control again to cloak the ship. "Your coffee is ready."

"You're becomin' a regular cook, man." He chuckled, and got to his knees to pour his coffee. "What was you doin' up there?"

"My commander was trying to contact me….Seems they are receiving the video signals from the alien scanner….The messages are coded, but it seems the invaders are still there, and they as yet are still unable to decipher the writing on the videos. However, they have detected increased activity aboard the Mother ship. Rather the Cryorans did, from their listening probes on the ship's outer hull….They still believe they are modifying their primary weapon."

"What did you tell 'em?"

"I did not acknowledge, Max. Should the invaders think I am still alive, they could send another warship, even though they cannot spare it!...It is possible they will anyway, in fact, the Cryorans are saying the invaders will send another ship."

"Shit, man!...When Promas don't hear back from you, won't they send somebody else?"

"Not unless the invaders do."

"I'm thinkin' that sending them video things weren't such a good idea."

"I am thinking that as well, Max....But war is won by trial and error, or lost accordingly. Perhaps no damage has been done."

"Yeah, maybe!" He watched Korak's expression for a minute before sighing. "You expect our killer tonight, don't ya?"

"Somehow, I do, yes." He nodded. "I have learned to anticipate my enemy's moves and act accordingly. He has only one arm, and he has no sensor....He will know that I do have mine, and that I will be warned of his arrival. He will need to find a way to get close without detection....We do not know the pain he is in, or if he feels pain at all,...but assuming he does, it will be severe enough by now to hinder his tactical judgment, somewhat.... That, and the fact that he knows he will need to be close to kill me, might lead him to make a mistake."

"Maybe not, too!" Breathed Max. "What do you think he might do to get in close?...Hell, them trees ain't that far away, you know. He could shoot us from there."

"He will need a Duck-blind, too, Max, to keep us from seeing his approach!"

"Max looked at him in confusion then finally nodded. "I don't know what it would be!" He looked at the barricade of rocks they had assembled. "We still have ours though,....Worked once, maybe it will again. Hell there's two of us, Korak, and only one a him....That gives us th' edge!"

"Edge, Max?...What is this word?"

"Tell ya what,...you tell me what a computer is, I'll tell you what edge means?"

"Computer?"

"Yeah, you mentioned it twice, yesterday....You said, on-board computer."

"It means that the computer is on board my vessel....A computer is a data-base, Max, it stores trillions of bits of information, that we call data. It knows the answer to any question that anyone could possibly ask it."

"How?"

"Because the answers to every known question, was programmed into the data-base beforehand by the most intelligent people on Promas, and Cryor. It can map distances between stars, the time it takes to get there, the planets' positions in space, unheard of mathematical equations concerning a planet's size and atmosphere....And Max, it will do many, many more things!"

"Except decipher th' invader's language." Grinned Max.

"Yes,...but as we speak, it is working on that question as well."

"Well, now that I know about it, I'm as confused as ever!" He grinned again and swallowed some coffee. "Okay,...when a man wants to fight with you, and only has a knife for a weapon,...but when he gets there, you have a gun for a weapon,...that gives you the edge!"

"I see....Edge actually is a short meaning for, advantage."

"There ya go." He looked back at the barricade again, then at the trees. "Believe I'll move th' horses again. He don't see them, or us, he might make that mistake you talked about."

"Once again, you speak with wisdom, Max."

"Yeah?...Well I wonder about that, too!" He drank his coffee then, as he stared across the grass at the tall pines. "How far will that gun a his shoot, you told me already, I think, but,...tell me again, will ya?"

"I have no way to actually know that, Max, but I would think, as far as my own starburst, which is within one kilometer. The energy wanes after that!

"That means it gets weak, right?"

"Yes, it will dissipate with minor damage."

"Then I'd say his will, too!" He shook his head then rolled and lit another makeshift cigarette.

"What were your thoughts, Max?" He asked curiously.

"I ain't thinkin' anything much, man,...but it seems to me he could come through them trees yonder before that sensor would even know he was here!...You said it couldn't see through things that ain't got any body heat."

"That is true, but it will see movement between the trees. We will know of his arrival."

"Unless he does come up with a duck-blind of his own!...But I got no idea what it would be, my mind don't work like a soldiers!...I'd sure like to know where he was yesterday, too?...He could a been in that mine shaft."

Korak watched him for a moment. "Speculation is a waste of time, my friend. The art of war is to outmaneuver your enemy, and I have no experience with that on the ground."

"Didn't you say you could anticipate an enemy's next move?"

"His next move is to kill me!" Said Korak with a sigh.

"Don't you mean, try?"

"Yes, as I will try, Max....And it will be tonight!...I have no experience on the ground otherwise."

"Makes two of us, man....I thought about askin' Ben Semple to come in with us yesterday, but he wouldn't a believed none a this. You, our alien killer, none of it!"

"Yes, it would have been a mistake."

"Throwing the spent smoke in the fire, Max got to his feet. "Guess I'll move th' horses now, be back in a bit."

* * *

The rest of the day was spent with more conversations, and even more speculations, coffee and cigarettes,...and by dark, they were still no closer to a plan of action than they were before,...nor of what sort of tactic the alien might use to fool the sensor. They did, however agree that whatever he might try would be his own version of a duck blind. They also had a laugh at the many uses of the words, duck blind, and of how many times they had used it over the last two days....But between them, had yet to think of a way he might come within a kilometer of them without being detected. Korak was convinced there was no possible way, However, Max thought otherwise,...he just couldn't put a finger on it!

Korak did, however, deem it a good idea to stop sending the signals from the alien scanner for fear that the invaders might send another envoy to earth, and should that occur, another star fighter would surely be sent.... But the biggest fear was that the Mother ship might relocate to earth, and with their powerful force-field intact, those thousand star fighters could not prevent it.

Korak brought the alien's scanner back and gave it to Max as he cloaked the ship again and sat down.

"Think it was the right thing to do, man?"

"I now believe it was the wrong thing, by sending the signals, Max,...I do not know,...I am no tactician....I do know that they now have all of the data the scanner has sent, and that is enough for them to work with.

"Makes us a good team, don't it? Grinned Max reaching up then to scratch through his ten days worth of beard. "I need a shave bad, Korak, and you don't need one at all,...Don't people shave on Promas?"

"No, Max, we do not!...But I think facial hair looks well on you."

"Well, I ain't give it a thought till now." He sighed then. "Not that it matters none....Okay, my friend, it's dark now, how do we do this, same as before?"

"I am sorry for your frustration, Max." Said Korak with feeling. "But I believe he will not come until he believes we are not expecting him to come....And you are right, I think, when he comes, he will have found a way to blind the sensor."

"I believe that, I'm just not sure of th' rest of it!"

"Then what are your thoughts?"

"I don't really know,...but if I wanted to kill you that bad, and I was as mad, and hurtin' the way he does,...I'd already be here....Then again, he might not even know where we are?"

"But you are not a soldier, Max, and he is. His training will prevent him from carelessness."

"I know you're right, man,...I just want this over with!"

"As do I,...we must be patient, the sensor will warn us."

"I guess you're right,....I can't think of any way he could get by it....But I'm still gonna watch them trees!" He got to his knees and reached to pour more coffee in his cup before sitting back behind the barricade of rocks to once again look through the gap.

"Do you wish my sidearm again, Max?"

"I'd likely drop it again,...or vaporize myself. I got my Henry here."

"Yes, and it has proven effective!...And my friend." He said, getting to his feet. "I will take the invader's sensor and take my previous seat....I will see if the scanner might reveal more useful information."

Max nodded and gave him the sensor then watched as he walked away to sit on the ground behind another large stone, several feet away from him. Sighing, he sipped at the strong coffee then turned to stare back through the gap in the rocks.

He didn't know why he felt so sure the killer would come so soon, but he did. He glanced back at Korak then, who was intently searching the alien sensor. But at least, the starburst rifle was there beside him, as was his own sensor. And satisfied that Korak was indeed in a position to return fire, he returned to his vigil and continued to sip his coffee. The trees were beginning to all run together out there, he thought as he stared up at their towering heights in the moon's light. He was never so tired of looking at anything though, but then again, that was where the beast had come from! He sighed again then and drained his cup before looking back, and once again found himself counting the tree trunks with their swaying branches.

Chuckling, he had not thought about it, but remembered that he had counted every one of them before the beast had attacked and here, he was unconsciously counting them again. Disgusted with himself, he had just achieved putting them out of his mind when he thought of something,...and thinking back, he was sure there had been only thirty-one trees above the slope, and he had just counted thirty-two!

Staring hard at them, he began counting them again, and it was not until he had counted twenty-three, that one of them seemed to move,...and he stared at that one intently until he saw the one lone branch begin to move upward. He instantly recognized the alien's duck blind.

"Korak!...Watch out!" He yelled, but the invader had already fired, the blast of pure energy striking the boulder just as Korak was getting to his feet. The Rock blew apart with tremendous force, the shock so loud it shook the earth as debris and rock fragments struck Korak's face and torso with such intensity that he was lifted and thrown bodily over and beyond the rocks he had been sitting against to fall broken and lifeless in a heap on the other side.

It had all happened in a heartbeat, and as the echoes died, he heard the loud, guttural victory roar as he pushed himself up off the ground, seemingly without daring to breathe. He raised himself enough to peer through the gap in the rocks, and his breath caught in his throat, making room for the bubble to form in his chest as he watched the giant of a man stop, and then with his one good hand, began discarding the sections of tree-bark that was tied somehow to his enormous body. That's how he did it, he thought breathlessly.

He was still in disbelief as he watched the alien disrobe, only coming to reality again when the giant had removed all the bark from his body and head and had began casually walking toward the campsite. The Alien had not seen him at all, he thought nervously, but he would, and breathlessly reached for the Henry Rifle as he continued to watch the killer's slow approach. His body was completely covered with snake-like armor, body, legs and all, he noticed, and looking at the head, could see that the only part of him that was truly visible, was his eyes, which were very large as he laughed hoarsely and gloated over his obvious success.

Remembering how he had stopped the other creature, he raised the rifle, inserted the barrel through the gap in the rocks and took careful aim at the invader's right eye,...and realizing that he would have only one chance to save his own life, held his breath and pulled the trigger.

The rifle's explosion was loud, and also echoed down the valley, but he saw the giant's eye explode outward, causing the lumbering invader to suddenly stop and emit a tremendous roar of pain as he raised his arm to his head. His legs seemed to buckle then and he fell backward onto the very charred ground where his pet had died....He lay there in obvious pain, his screams impossibly loud as he turned his large head from side to side with every scream of pain.

Still in disbelief, Max got to his feet and quickly scanned the area of explosion, and could see Korak's broken, lifeless body beyond the rocks where he had fallen and had to swallow the lump in his throat. He looked back at the alien, who was still alive and thrashing about as he held his injured head,...and as he watched, he was suddenly filled with pure, murderous rage. He saw the starburst rifle then and quickly went to grab it before walking around the rocks toward the killer,...and approaching the giant with caution, he stood to stare down at him with a sudden and overwhelming hatred.

"Look at me, you son of a bitch!" He shouted, transferring the starburst rifle to his left hand,...and when the alien's left eye looked at him. "That's right, a primitive man from the planet Earth just killed your sorry ass!" He drew the Colt Peacemaker and shot him six times through the eye, bringing another lingering roar of pain from him before he finally shuddered and lay still.

Max stared at him with tears of joy, and sadness on his face as the echoes of gunfire slowly faded into the distance,...and then turning to look where Korak lay, nodded as he backed away a few yards.

"This is for you, my friend!" He raised the starburst rifle, ran his finger along the lights to almost full power, pointed it at the invader and fired. The ball of pure, blinding energy forced him to cover his face, and when he looked back, there was nothing there but smoldering, smoking ground.

Swinging the gun onto his back, he sighed and forced back a sob as he slowly walked back to where his friend lay, but then to cry as he stared down at him. Finally, he stood the rifle against a rock and bent to remove the sidearm and utility belt from Korak's waist to place them down beside the rifle.

"Well, my friend." He choked. "We did it!...It's a pleasure to have known you, and if there truly is a good Lord above there somewhere, I know that's where you'll be." He looked up at the stars then and removed his hat.

"Lord, if you're there, and listenin' to me, this man here was a good man, from your neck a th' woods, too!...He was my very good friend, and brother....Watch over 'im for me....Amen!"

Sighing heavily, he donned his hat, stooped and picked up the broken body to carry it into the rocks and place it down beside the grave of Idak,... and then spent the next longest hour of his life covering Korak in a tomb of stones. When done, he removed his hat to say goodbye again then went back to retrieve belt and weapons before going back to pick up the scanners and return to the fire.

Placing it all on the ground beside his Henry Rifle, he found his cup and refilled it before picking up the utility belt and sitting down. Tears came to his eyes again as he ran his hand over it, and then sighing, opened the pockets until he found the wafers and ate one,...suddenly feeling more alone than he could ever remember.

He sat there and chewed the multi-flavored wafer for a minute, and stared at the blinking yellow light in the sensor's upper right hand corner for several minutes before realizing, and then hearing the beeping noise coming from the machine. What he had dreaded most had happened. They did send another ship! He stared out over the rocks in the general direction of Korak's grave for a time, and then for what seemed like hours, just stared at the fire's leaping flames.

After a time, he sighed deeply, drained his cup and stared up at the brilliantly lit heavens as he recalled every minute of the last seven days, every conversation they had, and everything Korak had told him about his life on Promas, and all he had said about how to fight the invader because now, it was going to be up to him alone to defeat the devil. He had the weapons to do it, he thought,…but did he have the know-how? He missed Korak, at that moment, more than anything ever in his entire life!...He would never forget the man, nor the experience,…nor the sadness at losing him. Finally, he took a deep breath and raised the cup. "Mission not completed yet, my friend." And threw it against the tall rock! "I'll do my best!"

Remembering his promise then, he turned to look at the deep hole in the bluff for a minute before reaching for the scanner,…and touching the screen, it came on, showing the yellow blip at the corner with even more prominence,…and wondering how long it would take for the other ship to reach there, stood up to slowly scan all around the entire area. The only images on the screen were the two horses, still staked out on Carbon Creek. There was not a bird, nor any other creature appearing on the sensor at all.

"Don't know all that much about heaven, Korak, or even if there is one now….Or even if you are capable of seeing, or hearing anything after death. But somehow, I know you heard the alarm go off. You know he's comin', don't ya, my friend? Wish you could help me with this new problem, but wishin' don't amount to much in th' real world, does it?"

He closed the sensor's lid and set it aside before taking the small control from the utility belt, pointed it and touched one of the lights on its face to watch the ship's hatch open. Looking as if it was a doorway into some other world, the hatch appeared to open a hole in the air itself. Shaking his head, he touched it again to close it then touched another one, seeing the star fighter slowly materialize….Another light retracted the escalating steps back into the ship's underbelly.

Putting the control back on the belt, he breathed deeply of the cold mountain air and leaned against the rock, stared at the starburst rifle for a moment, and then picked it up and walked out of the rocks, ran his finger along the lights from the top down to stop about mid-way, looked at the clay bluff and aimed the rifle at it just beneath the ship and fired. The ball of energy exploded the clay wall away from the ship, allowing it to tilt backward, and then completely crash to the ground.

"He waited a minute to admire the vessel's sleek, glossy appearance one last time and then, following Korak's instructions, looked up at the stars again,...and unable to detect anything moving, aimed the weapon at the deep depression and fired again,...this time, bringing the entire northern portion down, covering the ship with tons of red and blue clay.

* * *

Returning to the fire, he placed the starburst rifle and smaller handheld weapon on the ground, picked up the utility belt and buckled it around his own waist, surprised that it had no buckle, but joined itself together, as if by a strong magnet. That was all he had to fight the coming alien invasion, the weapons, the food, and the two scanners, of which he had almost come to understand and operate on his own. He picked up the scanner again and turned it skyward, still able to see the blinking yellow blip in its upper corner. It appeared closer now, and he wondered just how close it was, and how much time he might have before it found him. How was he going to fight a flying machine that powerful? The starburst rifle would destroy it, he had seen Korak do it!...But that alien ship would detect his presence before he could fire at it, he was sure of that!...It likely had already pinpointed his camp, all it had to do now was follow the heat signature of the Starburst rifle! But then again, it may not have detected it. The Alien was not close enough to be detected by the sensor until after he had buried the starship. His heart was beating rapidly in his chest as he stared skyward again.

"Okay!" He said aloud. "I'll just have to create another duck blind!... It worked before, maybe it'll work again." First thing, he thought, was to get the horses and get away from this place. Then, he would have to find a way to confine the invader to these mountains, because if he were to go to Golden first?...He refused to think about that, it gave him goose-bumps. He gathered up the weapons, slung the rifle across his back, stuck the side arm inside the utility belt....Grabbing his blankets, he poured coffee on the fire, wrapped pot and cup in the blanket, placed the alien sensor in the blanket and rolled it all up.

Sighing, he looked around the campsite, and then kicked sand and dirt onto the smoldering embers before picking up the Henry rifle, Korak's sensor and walking down the hill into the tall prairie grass toward Carbon Creek and the horses.

Both animals uttered a low grunt as he entered the trees and after patting both their necks affectionately, he saddled them and untied Helen's horse before slapping her on the rump. "Go home, girl." He said as she left the protection of trees and galloped across Carbon Creek.

"Hope you're up to this, old gal!" He said as he placed Korak's scanner in the saddlebag, and placed the blanket, containing the confiscated gear behind the cantle and securing it. "We got us a damn scary job to do." He led the horse out of the trees then retrieved the scanner, turned it on and pointed it upward. The blip was still there, and much closer than before,... but it seemed to be moving across the screen, and not down!

"What's it doin'?" he muttered aloud. "The Alien sensor!" He yelled, and quickly untied the blanket from his saddle to remove the smaller scanner. He looked skyward again as he held it, 'Could he have been following this sensor's signal', He wondered? Of course, he thought then, that had to be it! He touched the small screen to turn the signal on again before placing it back in the blanket and retying it behind the cantle.

"I hope to hell that's it!" He said, pulling himself into the saddle. "But what now?" He said, reining the horse back toward the campsite. He had to steer the bastard away from where the starship was buried, and he had to find a way to lure him into his trap,...once he had one! Funny, he thought, his mind was full of ideas when Korak was alive and now, it was all up to him to build his duck blind, and trap the monster.

It would have to be someplace too small for the alien ship to maneuver in. It would have to be someplace only accessible by a man on foot,...he would have to make him leave his ship to find the sensor. He knew within reason that this Alien did not know, well, he believed he didn't know that his counterpart was dead, therefore, he would possibly think that the deceased alien was still in possession of his sensor....That sensor would be the key to defeating the killer, and he must not suspect anything!...But how,...he would need to find the perfect spot for his duck blind, but where was that perfect spot, he wondered?

He reined the horse around the campsite, and continued down into the deep arroyo he and Korak had taken a few days ago. He would know the right spot when he saw it, he decided and as he rode, tried to retrace his steps on every hunting trip he had taken, even those with Lance. He had been all over this section of the Rocky Mountains at one time or another. He would remember a place, he decided, he had to.....He opened the sensor again to check the sky. The blip had moved back, and seemed to be a little larger than before. Well, he thought, that was the signal he was following and now, question is, how far away is he? He urged the horse at a faster pace down the deep gulley with fear and anxiety like a wild animal clawing at his backside, and the feeling was enough to make him want to turn tail and run.

He continued to watch the brilliant star-filled sky as he maneuvered the horse in the dark, rocky, brush-filled gulley, and could tell that it was becoming darker as the moon descended beyond the mountains. Well hell, what difference does it make, he thought ruefully, there was better than a seventy-five percent chance that he would be dead tomorrow anyway!

He had been in the arroyo for some time now, his thoughts going from the alien to his wife and son. What would they do if he were killed, how would they survive, Helen couldn't hope to run a ranch with a ten year old son to raise, she couldn't do it alone, there was just no way!...But that wouldn't matter anyway, if he failed to kill this alien Bastard, he thought. He would be unstoppable! He turned his head to listen to the steady audio signal from the alien sensor, a sound so steady that it had become like a rasp continually filing at the sharp edges of his already shattered nerves.

Stopping in the arroyo, he opened the scanner again, the yellow blip was pulsating on, and off the screen, and because of the lines depicting the landscape, he was almost sure the invader's ship was already in the mountains somewhere. Because according to the lines on the screen, it would show the ship to be behind a mountain, or in a valley. If that was the case, he thought quickly, he would be right on top of him shortly, and he was not ready to be found yet. He quickly untied the blanket and removed the smaller sensor and touching the screen, turned the machine off. He also knew that the alien would continue the search in the vicinity of the last signal, even though he could no longer detect it....'At least, I hope so', he thought.

He clucked the horse into motion again, and a hundred yards further on, climbed out of the steep gully and into the heavily wooded foliage of the mountainside, and had just made the safety of the trees when he was visibly startled to see the large, almost black alien ship suddenly appear not ten feet below him, nor twenty feet away from him. Almost afraid to breathe, he stopped to watch as the craft stopped in midair, hovering silently just above the gully. His heart had almost stopped at sight of the war machine, but at the same time felt a thrill at seeing a space ship so close up. this was a sight that no other man would ever see.

He studied its long, metallic fuselage and at the same time, still wondered why he had not been detected? This ship was similar to that of Korak's, but larger, bulkier, and it was unbelievably fast, as it suddenly moved farther along the twisting arroyo, doing it in the blink of an eye,... only to hover once again some distance away.

He felt the presence of the starburst rifle on his back, and could not believe that he had already forgotten he had the weapon. He had been close enough to that ship to destroy the thing, monster and all!...But now, he had to get away from this arroyo, he decided, and reined the horse higher into the trees, making his way up the side of the mountain. The ship was not in sight now and relieved, he continued up and along the mountainside until dawn began to turn the darkness into light again.

He had watched for, and seen the almost grotesque alien ship several more times during the upward climb, but only from a distance as it darted from arroyo to arroyo, hovering for long minutes while he tried to locate the alien sensor's signal again, only to move again. He wondered once again why he and his horse had not been detected. But as intent as the invader seemed to be at finding his counterpart, Max finally decided that all the ship's scanners must be trained on the ground, and not at the tall mountains.

He silently cursed himself again for losing the opportunity to destroy the alien ship, and he vowed not to let a similar opportunity pass him by again. It was coming on to full light now as he reined the horse along an old animal trail near the mountain's crest, and there, was startled once again when he rode into the middle of a silent group of Ute Indians all squatting on their haunches and staring down the mountainside.

He quickly raised his hands in friendship when several of them raised their rifles and pointed them at him,...and was relieved when another Indian grabbed their guns by the barrels and pushed them downward to point at the ground. Recognizing him as the one whose wife, and mother were murdered by the Alien's pet, he dismounted and walked to meet him.

"It's good to see you have survived your grief!" He said, shaking the Ute's hand in friendship. "What are you doing up here?"

"You kill Diablo for killing my family?" He asked without smiling.

"Yes, we killed the Devil Dog, and his master." He said, nodding at the others.

"If you kill Diablo, why is great iron bird here?"

"Iron Bird?...I don't understand?"

"Iron Bird with no wings!" He said, turning to look down the mountain at a distant valley. "See!"

"It is hunting for Diablo, and its master. It does not know they are dead!" He looked at the distant ship again. "Now, I must kill this one, too."

"How you do this?"

He reached up and touched the starburst rifle. "With this,...It's th' most powerful weapon you'll ever see....But I can not kill it because the ship moves too quickly, does not remain still long enough. I will need to wait until the Devil inside the iron bird comes out!"

"Diablo is inside?"

"Yes,...and I need to find a place to kill him....Maybe you know a place?"

"What place?"

"A narrow place, a deep place, a place where only a man can walk to get there. A place where his bird can not go."

"I know of such a place, we will take you."

"Where?"

"Not far,…a cave is there."

"We have got to hurry,…if he sees us, he can kill us. If he leaves, he can attack your homes, our cities."

Nodding, the Ute roused the others, they all mounted, and he followed them along the old trail as it wound down the side of the heavily timbered mountain.

He kept the scanner on, watching the alien ship's movements on the screen until mid-afternoon, when he was finally lead out of the trees to stop on the lip of a very steep ravine, one that didn't appear to be more than a couple of yards wide at the bottom.

"This will do, it'll work!" He thought, dismounting to retrieve the alien sensor from the blanket. "How far down is the bottom?" He asked, taking the rope from his saddle.

"Many feet." Replied the older Ute.

He nodded and tied the rope around his waist. "Will you lower me to the bottom?"

"Yes, we will do this."

He gave them the end of the rope, and placed his hand on the Indian's shoulder. "Now hear me!...That Diablo is very bad, a warrior from another world."

"Like the Gods of long ago? They came from the stars."

"No, not like them, this one is evil. Your arrows cannot kill him. Only I can!...Now, when I get to the bottom, I will turn this machine on. It will send a signal to the iron bird, and it will come….When I turn it on, I will leave it there, and you must pull me up very fast, I will need time to hide. When you pull me up, you must leave quickly, go over the mountain so he cant see you. You understand?"

"No, but we will do as you say."

"Good!" He moved to the lip of the ravine, dropped to his knees, and lowered himself over the side, but had been lowered only a few feet when he stopped them. He took a deep breath and raised the alien sensor, touched the screen and turned it on. He waited for a few seconds and turned it off again, hoping that it was the right thing to do. He motioned for them to lower him down again.

He knew that the ground itself would not allow the signal to reach the alien ship. Nor would wood, or thick brush. So, if those few seconds allowed the signal to reach the ship, the invader would be curious enough to search the area of the crevice,…he hoped! He was on the rocky floor of the steep ravine now, and quickly placed the sensor on the ground in front of the large cave the Ute spoke of then, breathing deeply, yanked on the rope and began climbing as they pulled him up. Once on the crest of the deep crack, he untied the rope, and sent the Indians scurrying back up the tall mountain.

He watched them disappear in the trees then pulled the starburst rifle over his shoulder while he looked for a suitable duck blind, choosing a thick tangle of brush at the base of a towering, ancient Pine Tree,...and after first checking the area for snakes, he dropped to his knees and wormed his way inside the thicket to wait.

It was hot in the brushy enclosure, but he found an opening where he could see the crest of the ravine, and the sky above it, and waited. Fifteen long minutes later, he was watching the trees across the way, when the fleeting movement crossed his vision from the corner of his eye. He watched the portion of sky above the tall trees then as the alien ship crisscrossed the area a few times before hovering above the deep crevice. He watched the ship for several minutes, and then it suddenly zipped away over the trees.

'Come on now, you son of a bitch!', He whispered. There was no way that he could see the upper end of the crevice, or know when the alien might reach that part of the ditch and start down it on foot,...so he began to listen intently as he watched.

Close to a half hour had passed, and his entire body wet with sweat before he heard the rocks fall. He listened even harder then, and in a couple of minutes heard more pebbles fall. "He's in the crevice!" He whispered, and taking another deep breath began working his way quietly out of the tangle of brush. Once out, he scanned the area by sight, and seeing nothing, painstakingly picked his way through the brush and broken branches to peer over the edge of the ravine. His breath caught in his throat when he spotted the giant, still some twenty feet away from the beeping sensor, but slowly working his way toward it.

He worked the starburst rifle into position, still watching the monster of a man move slowly down the narrow ravine until he was standing above the sensor on the ground. The alien began looking around at that point, then up at the crest of the ravine, causing Max to quickly lower himself out of sight.

The alien invader began uttering loud growl-like bursts of sound from deep in its throat, that Max took to be some sort of language and thinking that the beast was calling to his counterpart. Then it stopped, and this caused Max to edge his way back to the rim of the ravine for another look, and was surprised to find that the monster had obviously gone into the cave in search of the alien. He looked both ways up the ravine, but saw nothing,...and sure that the alien had in fact gone into the cave, he ran his finger down the row of lights on the rifle, pointed it down at the wall of the ravine just above the entrance and pulled the trigger.

The explosion of rock and dirt as the fireball of energy struck the earth was tremendously loud, causing the entire cave, and the wall to crumble and cave in on itself. Dust and rock particles filled the air for a thousand feet above the trees, and caused the ground to shake beneath his feet.

He got to his feet to stare down at the rubble as the dust cleared. The entire crevice had been filled completely. And the relief he felt was nothing like anything he had ever felt before. But then, the longer he waited, the more he was worried that maybe the bastard would be able to claw its way out before it died. It was buried alive, but somehow that didn't seem to be good enough.

He whirled then, and almost fired the rifle again, but stopped when he recognized the Ute Indians.

"You kill the Diablo?" Asked the older Ute.

"I buried 'im." He nodded at the protruding branches and trunks of several pine trees in the avalanche of rock and dirt. "He's under several tons of dirt and rock!...I just don't know if th' son of a bitch can get out before it dies?"

"It will die there!" Confirmed the Indian. "Mother Mountain will embracc the evil forever."

"I still have to destroy that iron bird, too." He said. "But I don't know where it is, and I'm afraid to leave here." He looked both ways along the area where the ravine used to be. "Can you help me one more time?"

"We will help."

"That thing came in from that direction." He pointed West. "And the bird's got a be that way somewhere....Can you send a couple of warriors to find it?" He watched as the Ute issued the orders, sending two braves to search for the craft.

"Thank you." He said. "Now, could you send another to watch the far end of the ravine, that way, I still don't trust that bastard to stay dead?" He watched the other one leave and nodded. "Now,...We wait to see." He said, and both of them squatted at the previous edge of the once deep ravine.

A slow four hours passed before the two Indians returned and told them where to find the alien ship, and that had to be enough time to be sure the alien was dead. He looked at the older Ute then. "That cave down there,... was there another way out?"

"Cave was buried, no way out!"

"You been in it before?"

"Yes,...no way out but in gully."

"Okay then,...let's go find that Iron Bird!"

Still watching the landfilled jumble of rock, dirt and shredded debris, he got to his feet and looped the Starburst rifle over his head and nestled it onto his back.

"How you get weapon with so much power?" Asked the old Ute, coming to gingerly touch the rifle. "I never see such a gun before."

"Well, if it makes you feel any better," He said, turning to look at him. "Neither have I!"

"Where you get gun?" He insisted..

"From the man, I was with th' first time you saw me." He watched the old man's dark eyes for a moment and knew that with the tragedy the tribe had gone through, and the family the old Ute had lost in the last few days, anything could happen. What he was afraid might happen, was that the old man might have a mind to take the Starburst rifle from him for some reason.

Clearing his throat, he squared himself around to face him. "That man was a law man!" He said sternly. "He was after this alien killer,...and I was helping him."

"Where is this law man now?"

"He's dead,...that thing down there killed 'im!"

"He give you this gun?"

"Yes,...This gun is th' only thing that can kill somebody like him."

The Ute nodded his head. "Gun has much power,...will it destroy iron bird?"

"Yes, it will!" He continued watching the old Ute, as well as the other braves as he turned and walked on into the trees to his horse.

"Horse no good where iron bird is." Said the old man as he stopped behind him. "Must go on foot!"

"Where is it?" He watched as the Indian pointed southward.

"Two mountains, two valleys, iron bird there....Horse no good!"

Max nodded at the other warriors. "Can they show me?"

"They will take us." He turned to go join the others and as they conversed, Max pushed the Starburst pistol into his belt and went to stand beside the old man.

"They lead, we follow!" He said, turning to stare at Max, and then they both followed the buckskinned warriors at a half trot through the tangle of giant pines.

An hour passed, and still they continued at that pace, up one tree-studded mountain side, and down another and all the while, Max marveled at the old Ute's stamina as he matched the younger Indian's step for step.

Almost two hours later, they stopped on the crest of another mountaintop, where the two braves pointed down at the valley below them.

"Iron bird is there." Said the old man, also pointing downward.

"Tell 'em to show me!" He said, still looking down through the maze of mountain forest.

"They can not, they no see iron bird!...They see only lights in the trees far below....They afraid to go see, they come say they find iron bird."

"That's just great!" He nodded. "Okay, you tell 'em to take me to where they saw th' lights." He pointed down. "In th' valley there....Tell 'em they don't have to be afraid,...tell 'em this rifle will protect us,...they saw what it did to that cave back there!"

Nodding, the old Ute conversed with the others for a few seconds then sent them down the side of the mountain, with him and Max in pursuit.

They continued down the broken, uneven slope at a half run, half sliding, and stumbling gait, having to use the trees for support at times and dodging large boulders and shifting shale at others. But after three quarters of an hour, they were finally on the floor of the forested valley.

"Which way now?" Asked Max between labored breaths.

The two braves pointed, and once again led the way through giant fir and Pine trees until at last they stopped again, pointing at the heavy foliage.

He saw the blinking lights then, barely visible through gaps in the heavy briars and brush. There were mostly white lights, but occasionally some reds and blues could be seen, but that definitely had to be the alien ship. Remembering what Korak's ship was capable of, he was sure the alien must have arranged for his ship to protect it's self from intruders. However, he did wonder why he had not cloaked the craft, as Korak had? But that really did not matter, they had found it.

"Okay!" He said finally, and turned to the old Ute. "We can go back now,...in a straight line from here."

"No,...you destroy iron bird first, then we go!"

"Ohhh, no!" He laughed. "If I shoot it from here, we all die!...I'll shoot it from top a th' mountain we crossed."

Nodding somewhat reluctantly, the old Indian ushered the braves back through the trees to the base of the mountain, some several hundred yards away, where they stopped once again.

"No, no!" Said Max. "Send them on to th' top a th' mountain!" He took the rifle from his back as he spoke and watched as the old Ute ordered them on up the mountainside, and as they left, turned back and stare at him.

"No, no, man, we got a go, too!"

"I stay with you, you go, I go!...I see iron bird destroyed!"

"Well, I can't shoot it from here!" He argued. "They're almost to th' top already, man, go on, I'll be right behind ya'."

They had just started the climb when the fiery explosion shattered the stillness, the concussion of which shook the ground beneath their feet, and threw them both back down into the trees on the valley's floor. They quickly rolled to their knees in the rocks and covered their heads with their arms.

Cautiously peering upward through the swaying, cracking timber of the mountainside, all he could see was black smoke and fiery debris. Dirt and rock was so thick, the sky above them had turned almost black as the sun's rays were blocked out.

The thunderous explosion had been tremendous in the stillness, it's heat burning living trees and animals to a cinder as it rolled away into the distance, and then it was over!

Max, and the elder Ute remained behind large boulders in the cover of trees until the falling debris had all but crashed back to earth. Dread was causing his heart to work overtime as he stood and helped the old Indian to his feet, and then they both stared in awe up the devastated side of the now treeless mountain.

"What has happened?" Groaned the old man. "My warriors are gone,… the Great Spirit is angry!"

"That might be!" Said Max. "But he didn't do this!" Nothing but an alien weapon could have caused what just happened, and that being the case, he thought, it could only mean one thing!…The alien killer had somehow found a way out of his would-be grave. 'Damn it!', he thought worriedly, knowing he should have used the weapon on the giant, instead of trying to bury him!

"Then what has happened?' Insisted the Indian. "My warriors are gone, they are dead!" He raised his arms in futility, letting them fall back to his side in despair.

"Get hold of yourself, old man!" Urged Max breathlessly, his eyes straining to search the mountain tops west of them. "They're dead, we're not!…Not yet….Our alien killer is alive, he's west of us somewhere. See if you can spot 'im!"

They both searched the hillsides around them for several long minutes, but the giant alien was nowhere to be seen, but Max knew he was there. He knew he must have spotted the retreating Indians and fired at them,…and that being the case, he may not have seen him and the old man. He didn't know they were there!

It also meant that the monster was on his way back to his ship and if he made it, his efforts to kill him could be lost forever. Once in his ship, he would surely detect their presence, and they could not survive that kind of fire power!

'No!', he thought then, and bent to retrieve the Starburst rifle. They may not be able to see him, but he would have to have been at least three quarters of a mile away, maybe less, to chance firing his weapon. At any rate, it would take him some time to get back to his ship, so he had time,...for what?, he thought. They couldn't climb the now treeless expanse of mountain, he would see them,...and to shoot the alien ship from this distance was dangerous, he thought worriedly. But what choice did he have?

Holding the rifle in front of him, he turned to the Ute. "Get th' hell out a here, old man!...Head off up th' valley there and climb out a here somewhere, that killer is still alive, his weapon did all this, killed your warriors,...go!"

"No!" Returned the Indian angrily. "I stay,...I see you destroy iron bird, and then the Diablo!...I stay."

"At least take some cover!" He said, and quickly ran his finger along the rifle's row of lights to the maximum setting,...and as the Ute dropped behind the large boulder again, he pointed the Starburst rifle in the alien craft's general direction and pulled the trigger.

A sound akin to an electrified crackling of a lightening strike emitted from the weapon as pure plasmic energy exploded it's way through the forest of trees, turning the magnificent, ageless Pines into splinters. It was a deafening noise from exploding trees as Max quickly threw himself behind the rocks also, and at that very moment, the alien space craft exploded in a blinding flash of pure energy, followed by an atomic-like nuclear explosion of such magnitude that it sent debris mushrooming in a hail of black, billowing smoke a thousand feet into the clear rocky mountain sky, the concussion flattening and splintering trees like match sticks. The tremendous generated heat starting fires so hot that anything in it path was instantly vaporized.

Luckily, the direct force of the explosion had spread more forward and outward, away from where they had taken shelter, obviously losing momentum after having cleared a half mile swath of bare earth surrounding the spot where the space craft had been.

As reality slowly returned to him, Max opened his eyes to quickly look around at the more than a mile expanse of treeless, debris saturated valley floor, and then at the large pine branch that lay across his legs and stared at it until he fully regained his faculties. Once fully aware of what had taken place, he urgently began checking his own body for any wounds or damage. He was fully intact, and breathing a sigh of relief, and utter disbelief at surviving such a devastating blast of raw power, he inched his way from beneath the heavy branch and got to his feet. Looking around, he was surprised to find that he was several yards from the rocks he had hidden behind, and realized that he must have been thrown into the trees by the force of the blast.

The Starburst rifle was gone, and so was his own handgun. Neither was anywhere in sight. But when he touched his midsection, he felt the smaller alien pistol there and pulled it free. 'This will have to do.', he thought, and moved the setting to maximum before making his way back to the rocks. He saw the old Ute Indian then, a long, sharp splinter from an exploding pine protruding from his ribcage.

"God damn it, old man!" He cursed. "I told you to stay down!" He shook his head then. "Well,...you had a little of your revenge, I reckon!" Sighing, he began searching the debris for any sight of his missing weapons, but saw nothing and looked back at the far end of the valley's still smoldering expanse of cleared ground to shake his head again. It was then that he heard the loud, obviously angry, guttural roar, and spotted the very large beast of alien invader as he walked down onto the treeless expanse of valley floor and again, the roar of anger emitting from that animal of a man was like nothing he had ever imagined.

Fear was a living thing in his gut as he felt himself began to tremble violently. However it only lasted a short time, as urgency of the situation forced him to calm himself to some degree, realizing that he had to kill the alien. There was no one else to do it, he was alone. If he didn't kill him?... He didn't want to think about what would happen! He pushed the thoughts from his mind and began to frantically search the rocks and debris again for the Starburst rifle, to no avail, and breathing deeply, placed Korak's hand gun in the empty holster.

The beast of a man was too far away for the smaller weapon to be effective and so, taking several large breaths of cool air, he made his way through the tree rubble and onto the cleared landscape to slowly walk toward the invader, hoping breathlessly that the killer would be curious enough to wonder who he was, or even how he could have survived the devastation? He didn't care as long as curiosity was enough to allow him to come into range of the laser pistol.

He had no doubt that he would be killed, and silently prayed that he would be allowed to return the favor and if not, that someone else would be lucky enough to find a way to kill him before he murdered too many people! He only regretted that he would not be able to see his family again, to tell them that he loved them....At least, he thought,...by killing the animal, they could live a happy life!

'All I need is a couple dozen yards, and I'll have a chance.', he thought, but then saw the alien stop and stare at him, and his heart about stopped. He was still a good hundred or so yards away from him, and expected the killer to raise his weapon and fire at him at any second. But when it didn't happen, he continued to walk toward the giant, his feet threatening to snag and trip him on the debris field left by the starburst rifle's destructive power. Debris that was so deep in places that he had to almost crawl over it. Ragged tree stumps were numerous jutting up through the mess. He dared not fall, or lose his balance, for fear the giant might take advantage of it and fire. He could see that the invader's upper torso, like the one before, was covered in armor. A metal cap covered it's head and nose with nothing but his large eyes visible. The massive legs were encased in armor, from knees to feet, with only his thighs being visible.

The giant continued to watch his approach, making no effort to raise his weapon.

"Hold your fire, asshole!" He breathed aloud, continuing to watch the creature's long, dangling arms as he unsteadily made his way toward him on legs that were threatening to buckle on him at any second and still, the alien watched him, his long, muscular arms still dangling loosely at his sides. The giant's right arm had the powerful weapon strapped to it between the claw-like hand, and the elbow.

He continued to walk toward him, with each minute seeming like a lifetime but at last. he was some thirty yards from the monster when he stopped, unable to make his legs carry him any closer. Somewhat unsteady, and after taking a deep breath, he let it out and heard himself say,..."Draw, you son of a bitch!"

The alien suddenly raised his arm, and with his left hand, reached across his body to activate the weapon just as Max drew the Starburst pistol and fired. The killer roared loudly, only to have it snuffed out as he was vaporized,...and then he was gone!

"Thank you, Lord!" He gasped, and then sank to his knees on the charred valley's decimated floor. He looked up at the clear Colorado sky. "I got a believe you're up there somewhere, Lord,...but even if you're not,... thank you!"

After several minutes, he pushed to his feet, turned and walked back to where the old Indian lay, and after another long, arduous hour of upturning and tossing the debris aside, and searching the ash covered valley floor for the weapons, he found both the peacemaker, and the starburst rifle.

"Lord, another favor, if you don't mind. Make a place for this old warrior up there, he lost his whole family, his entire life trying to atone for their deaths. He was a good man.

CHAPTER TEN

"That's it, son, that's th' whole story,...might a left a few things out, but that's about it!"

"Gosh, Daddy," He exclaimed with a smile. "I can't believe you really told 'im to draw....What made you do that?"

"If I'd a walked up to 'im with a gun in my hand, he'd a seen it and likely killed me before I got in range....Besides, I was so damn scared, I couldn't think a nothing else to say!"

"Sure wish I could a seen that!"

"No ya don't, son." Sighed Max, shaking his head. "No, ya don't....I hardly slept at all for a while and when I did, I lived th' whole thing over again!"

"Sorry, Pop, guess I really know how you must a felt." He stared down at the fire then. "Nothing's happened since, has it?...I mean, they haven't come back,...have they?"

"If they did, it weren't in th' rockies, Lance....Th' world's a big place though....But I believe they might one day,...that's why we have to be ready!...I more than half expected another Promasian starfighter to show up in pursuit of that Alien, but if it did, it didn't show up on the scanner....Yep, I believe they might one day."

"I hope you're wrong, Daddy." He turned on the bedroll to stare across at the large mound of clay. "You sure that star fighter is still there, under all that clay, after all this time?"

"Far as I know, It's still there, clay's just as I left it, not a clod out a place!...Don't ever try to uncover it, though, Lance, Remember what I said."

"The radiation. I remember, Pop....I never will!"

"And keep th' secret?"

"My word as a Pruett, Pop....Unless I have a son one day."

"Good boy!" He grunted to his feet then. "Let's take a walk."

"Take a walk,...where?" He followed him into the trees for about twenty yards to a brush-covered spot on the southern edge of the clay bluff where Max stooped and began moving debris and dead branches aside enough to reach into a wide hole and remove the large bundle of blanket and rain-slicker.

"What's that, Pop?"

"You'll see, let's get back to th' fire."

Once back in camp he placed the bundle on the ground, sat down and unwrapped it, hearing Lance gasp at sight of the weapons.

"Jesus, Daddy,!" He breathed. "Is that his guns?"

"Sure enough, both of 'em!...Found th' rifle and pistol when I buried th' old Ute, just became fully charged, too,...th' sun did it!" He picked up the alien sidearm and ran his finger along the row of lights, the way he remembered then pointed to a large rock down the slope from them, aimed the pistol and fired. The long streak of orange laser erupted from the barrel,...and the large stone shone brightly for a fleeting moment then vanished.

"Hot damn, daddy, that's...."

"Unbelievable!" Interrupted Max as they walked back to camp. "I know, Lance." He said as they walked back into the group of rocks and sat down again to lay the weapon down beside him.. "It did th' same thing to that alien son of a bitch!" He leaned to pick up the scanner then. "Son, some a th' things you're about to see here'll give ya nightmares....But you need to know what ya might be up against someday!" He touched the screen to turn it on then touched several of the lights along the side of it to finally bring up the videos Korak had shown him.

"You can stop watchin' when ya want to....But by watchin' it all, you'll know what has to be done, if it happens again." He gave Lance the sensor as he spoke.

"God," Exclaimed Lance. "How can pictures move like that?"

"You heard th' story, son, just watch it!" He sat back to reach a wafer from the utility belt, surprised that they were still intact after ten years in that hole, and ate one before leaning back to watch his son's reactions.

It was mid-morning when he heard Lance gag, and looked up to see him lean over and vomit,...he got to his feet and went to take the scanner from him.

"You okay, son?"

"I,...I don't think so, Pop!" He stammered then heaved again. "Wa,... was th' animal here that big?"

"Th' creature?...It was bigger, I think!...Never seen nothin' like it, never imagined nothin' like it!...All that's left of it though, is a black spot on th' ground!"

"What about th' space war, was that real, too?"

"Recorded as it happened, by Korak's own ship....Yeah, Lance, it's all true!...Now keep watchin', you'll see it all." He helped him to sit up again and gave him the scanner,...and an hour later, heard him yell.

"I seen it, Pop....I seen you shoot th' thing, seen Korak kill it!" He laughed then and continued to watch. "Hey, Pop, you just killed that alien,...my God, Daddy!" He closed the scanner's lid and gave it back to Max. "I don't need to see any more, Pop....But I promise you, I'll be ready when it happens, my son, too, if I ever have one!...We'll be ready, Pop!"

"That's good, son, I hope so!" He pulled lance to him in a hug before sitting back down beside him.

"I didn't see anything on there about your gunfight, Pop,...is it on there?"

"No, The starship couldn't record it, and th' scanner was a mile away in my saddlebag."

"Well, now I know what you meant by not tellin' anybody,...about religion, too!...If everything Korak told you is truth, then we got kin on a planet called Promas."

"And some little gray friends on Cryor."

"Yeah,...how about that, Pop?...Back when you came for us in Golden, I remember you goin' to the Sheriff''s office....What did you tell 'im?"

"Told 'im th' killer escaped to Wyomin', and Korak went after 'im!... Tate was just happy to be rid a th' problem!...And I was happy to hear that only a couple dozen people died in that gold camp, could a been a lot worse."

"Yeah,...do ya think anybody else will remember seein' 'im?"

"I wish I knew, son, I don't know!" He sighed and looked up at the clear sky then. "It's been ten years now, and they ain't been here yet, that I know of....If somethin' like this happened anywhere else in th' world, I wouldn't think we'd a heard about it, do you?...I want a believe they did though." He reached into the utility belt then and gave Lance a wafer. "Eat this, son."

"What is it?"

"Lunch." He grinned and watched him eat the wafer with wide-eyed relish. "You lost your breakfast.".

"Hey, Pop, this is great!...I'm full as a tick."

"I lived on 'em for ten days."

"There's somethin' I don't understand, Pop,...after listenin' to your story, then seeing Korak die, and you killing that alien that way,...How is it that Mister Korak left himself open to be killed like that?"

"You noticed that, too, did ya?...I don't know, Lance, thought about it a lot over th' years. Only thing I can figure, is that he wanted to erase any proof a his bein' here,…since he wouldn't be able to leave on his own, that was the only way he could see."

"He must a had a lot a faith in you though, leavin' you to kill that guy all alone."

"I believe he did, yeah. He was infatuated with that old Henry Rifle, too, after seein' me stop that beast with it!...Yeah, I think he knew I'd kill th' bastard.…A smarter, wiser man never lived, Lance, wish you could a talked with 'im.…He didn't know about that other alien ship though.…I was one lucky man that day!...I just wish he was still here."

"Me, too, Pop. He must a been some kind a man!"

"Next to you, he's the only man I ever met that I would call my best friend! He never smiled, never laughed, always talked above me, with all that technical jargon, usin' words I never heard of.…But he never got tired a my questions, always answered 'em, no matter how stupid they sounded, or how many times I'd ask th' same one."

"It was a long while before I'd believe where he came from, even when I saw his ship crash and him get out of it!...It was a hell of a shock.…Accordin' to him, your great, great, great, great Grandchildren might be usin' them stars up yonder to play in one day!...And Earth,…well, I just can't picture all this lookin' like Promas some day!"

"Don't worry, Daddy, we won't live to see it!"

"Thank God for that anyway!"

"Yeah,…wonder if them gray aliens ever did receive his signal?...If they did already, it's a shame Korak done himself in when he did, he could a been home by now."

"I think he is home, Lance. He wanted to stay here, I know that!...But I think he didn't want a chance changin' th' future."

"Why,...His ship's still here?"

"It's on our land, son, he knows it's safe."

"It won't be safe always, pop, it'll be uncovered someday. Twisters, earthquake, prospector or something, somebody will see all that shining metal and know where it came from."

"Be bad news if they do."

"The Radiation, yeah." Nodded Lance. "Pop, all this stuff here needs to be at home, not left up here where it could be found."

"It's been in that hole for ten years."

"Still, if we have to fight aliens someday, be a long way to come get a weapon!"

"Reason I ain't brought 'em home is cause a your Mother."

"She needs to know about all this, daddy. Needs to know how to fire one a these guns, too!...She's stronger than she looks."

"All right, we'll take 'em home,…and she'll listen this time, if I have to gag 'er and tie 'er to a chair! After she hears th' whole story, and she wants to see th' videos, she can."

"I agree, daddy." He turned to look toward the clay mound again. "I want a see your campsite, Pop."

Max looked at the distant grouping of rocks and sighed. "Been more'n a year since I was over there,…but sure, let's saddle and stow all this stuff first." He went to pick up his saddle and blanket and carry it to his horse. "I got a tell ya though." He said as he hefted the saddle onto the animal's back. "That spot has an emotional place in my heart, Lance,…it's haunted ta-boot!"

"Don't worry, Pop, the spirit's a good one." Grinned Lance as he tightened his own cinches and dropped the stirrup.

"Yes, it is.…Put th' scanner in your saddlebags, son, I'll take th' rest."

When they were ready, Max scattered the fire and poured the rest of the coffee on the embers, and after hanging the supply sack on the saddle and stowing the alien weaponry and other items in his bedroll, they led the horses through the grass to the original campsite.

"This is it, huh, Pop?" Asked Lance as he stood over the old scorched area of fire remnants. "I can just see you and Korak here right now talking,…this is great!"

"It does bring back memories!" Sighed Max as he eyed the mound of clay.

"Where was you hiding when you shot th' alien?"

"Behind ya over yonder, I watched 'im through a gap in th' rocks."

"Man, this is great, Daddy!...I'm proud of ya.…Let's check out th' grave, see if any animal's bothered it?"

"When's th' last time you was up here, son?"

"With you, three weeks ago."

"No, I mean alone, to see th' graves?"

"I ain't seen th' grave in months, pop."

"Well, I ain't seen 'em in more than a year now."

"Why not?"

"Too emotional, I guess, don't know!...Well, come on, let's go see." He led the way past the mound and was about to enter the rock field when he stopped to look around.

"What is it, pop?"

"Somebody's been here,…it looks different."

"Looks th' same as when I was here."

"Idak's grave is gone, at least th' rocks I buried 'im under, and where is th' body?"

"I wondered what you meant, Daddy?...But when you said you buried Idak here, too, I thought you might a dug a grave for 'im,...because this is the only one I saw....You think animals might a drug 'im away?"

"They must a took 'im....Animals wouldn't a moved all th' rocks like that!"

"Who took 'im?"

"Th' Cryorans!...They were here, Lance, they took his body home."

"Wouldn't they have taken Korak, too?"

"Damned if I know!" He walked past the spot where the small alien was laid to rest and shook his head as he looked over the display of stones,...and was about to turn back when noticing something out of place atop one of the stones that covered Korak's remains.

"What is it, Pop?" Asked Lance, seeing the expression on Max's face.

Max reached to pick up the circular piece of metal and stare at it. "It's an amulet a some kind,...and quite heavy."

"Wonder where it came from?" Asked Lance as he looked over the well-placed stones, but then suddenly looked up at Max. "You think......?"

"Yeah, son, I'm sure of it, They came to show their respects....Got his name on it here." He gave Lance the amulet,...could be gold, I think."

"It is gold,...hold on, Pop." He rubbed the accumulated dirt and grime away from the amulet's outer edges. "It's a medal of honor, Pop, and, oh, man!" He breathed suddenly.

"What,...what's wrong, son?"

"Your name's on it, too, Pop!"

"So it is." He said, taking the amulet back. He looked at it for a few seconds then took the kerchief from a hip pocket and blew his nose before wiping his eyes. "Ah,...sorry, Lance."

"It's okay, Pop,...I'm proud for both of ya,...this thing speaks for itself."

"Yes it does." He took his bandana from around his neck and cleaned the amulet before placing it atop one of the flatter grave stones, and looking around gathered up a few more to completely cover it.

"My God, Pop!" Gasped Lance. "You're a hero! They had to have left this here since you was here last, and before I came."

"Could a been here all along, Lance, we just didn't see it."

"Wonder why they didn't take his body back, too?"

"He didn't want a go back, he loved these mountains....anyway, It makes no difference when they came, son....Even if you had been here, you wouldn't have seen 'em!...Th' Cryorans took their own hero home, and left this for me to find....I'd like to think, it also means th' war's over up there!...

At any rate, my emotions won't keep me away from here anymore. Gonna put 'im up a nice marker, too!"

"We can do that, Pop, you and me!...We'll find a real nice flat stone up here somewhere, polish it up, and I'll chisel whatever you want to say on it."

"That'll be damn nice, son, he would a liked that a lot!...I know I do!" Swallowing the lump in his throat, he looked back at the grave and nodded. "Your Mother's bound to be a little worried now, let's go home, we got a lot to tell 'er!" He took Lance by the arm and together walked back to the horses.

"Tomorrow's Sunday, Daddy,...after we tell her all this, think she'll want a go to Church anymore?" He mounted as he spoke, and once in the saddle. "I don't know if I do....I don't know what to believe in anymore?"

Max pulled himself into the saddle and looked at him. "Son," He began, looking from Lance, back at the grave again. "I have my doubts, too, had 'em for ten years. But I have been takin' your mother and you to Church on Sunday for all that time, knowin' it could all be a lie,...and thinkin' that it surely was!...At times I even wanted to get up in th' middle a th' Reverend Holts sermons and tell 'im so right in front a th' whole congregation, took all I had not to do it!...But I didn't,...know why?"

"I think I do, Pop!"

"Your Mother will, too!...Ain't a hell of a lot in th' world to believe in anymore, really never was!...But I think that without God in our life, it would be a hell of a lot worse!"

"I think so, too, Daddy....It's just gonna be hard, now I know the truth."

"Sure it is,...but truth is what ya make of it, it's hard keepin' it to yourself, too!...But ya got to, Lance, for all th' reasons I told you about."

"But what'll we do about it, Pop?"

"Be alert,...watch th' skies, and be ready, son!...And hope th' rest a th' world never finds out!...Because without God and th' Bible, we are lost."

"I don't know how you did it, Pop, keeping all this to yourself?"

"It ate me alive, Lance....That's why I keep comin' back up here. One, to prove to myself it was true, and two,...so I'd never forget th' truth....It's gonna be easier now that you know."

"And Mama?"

"We'll see, Lance. But no more secrets and lies, not in this family!" He reined the horse around, and with another look back at the grave, said a silent goodbye to Korak and clucked the animal back down the slope through the tall grass."Would a been nice, though, Lance."

"What would?"

Max turned to watch as Lance pulled alongside him. "Havin' Korak get to know you and your Mother. I had bragged on your mother's fried chicken so much that I had him almost tastin' it."

"I wish we could have, too."

"Because a him, I see these tall mountains and sequoias in a whole lot different light now, and you know what?...This place is beautiful, Lance. It's mysterious, dangerous and breathtakin', all at the same time."

"Pop?" Said Lance suddenly as they were crossing Carbon Creek. "We got company comin'." They stopped the horses in the tall grass to wait on the riders to meet them.

"Sheriff Tate." Sighed Max, not at all glad to see them. "Wonder what brings a posse out here?" He nodded at the men as they rode in beside them.

"What brings you out this way, Tate?...Hi ya boys." He nodded at the rest of them.

"You lost any livestock lately, Maxwell?"

"Far as I know, we haven't, why, what's goin' on?"

"Ben Semple sent for us, we're on our way there now....Says he found a half dozen of his best steers slaughtered two days ago."

"More like massacred!" Yelled one of the other men.

"What's he mean?" Asked Max.

"Semple says they was parts a them steers scattered out over twenty yards, what weren't eaten. Whatever done it ate parts a all of 'em."

"Good Lord, Man!" Breathed Max, looking at all of them.

"When he told me about it, I recalled that werewolf thing that was goin' on ten years ago, same kind'a thing was happenin'. You recall all that, don't ya, Maxwell?"

"Well, yeah,...but it weren't no Werewolf, Tate,...it was some deranged killer on th' loose up here."

"Well, maybe he's come back, Maxwell, you did say he escaped."

"Hard to believe Korak didn't catch up to him." He glanced at Lance as he lied. "Even if he didn't, why would 'th man come back here after ten years?"

"Don't know the answer to that one." Returned Tate. "But it's th' same kind a killin'....We was on our way to Semple's south pasture, that's where it happened, we saw you two and decided to see if you might want a go with us to check it out?"

Listening to the conversation with Tate, Max felt the ice cold fingers of gloom closing around his throat. EverythingTate was saying led to the very same way the Alien's pet killed it's victims,...but that beast was dead, vaporized before his very eyes. This just couldn't be happening again, not after ten years....Could it?

"Well, do ya,...it happened almost in your own back yard, Maxwell, I would think you'd want a know?"

Max shifted his position on the saddle and frowning, looked across at Lance before nodding. "Guess it won't hurt to check it out, Lance, you go on home, let your mother know we're okay."

"No way, Pop!" He said with determination. "If,..." He quickly glanced at the Sheriff and the other men. "If,...that killer did come back, I'm not gonna let you face 'im alone, not after what happened last time."

"Your Mother,..."

No, Pop!" He repeated sternly. "Mom may be worried some, but she knows we can take care of ourselves."

"Let's go, Tate." Said Max, and reined his horse toward the patch of Pines between them and Ben Semple's south Pasture and holding pens, some five miles away.

Lance spurred his horse in pursuit of his father and after a few minutes pulled alongside. "I'm sorry, Pop!" He said loudly.

"I know, son....I knew you wouldn't go, let's make th' best of it....If need be, just do as I tell ya!" He saw Lance nod, then brought his attention back to the gopher contaminated, uneven terrain ahead of them and at the same time, wanting more than anything else to turn back and head for home as visions of fields of dismembered, bloody flesh and torn body parts filled his mind.

after winding their way through the thick, wooded area of majestic Pines, maneuvering around and over fallen limbs and gouging vines of sharp needles, they rode out of the tree-line and crossed the several dozen yards of open grass to go through the cattle gate of Ben Semple's south Pasture.

Semple and a dozen of his hands were waiting at the scattered remains of the old corral as they rode up and dismounted.

"Wasn't expectin' you, Maxwell." He said, looking at Max with a worried frown on his face. He nodded at Lance then turned and led the way to the other side of the log corral's remains. Blood and animal parts lay scattered everywhere, The tall, once luscious prairie grass pasted to the ground with dried blood and uneaten cattle entrails. Legs, torn hides, several complete heads of the once high dollar steers, some horns that had been torn away and discarded, and the kill field covered several dozen yards surrounding the old corral.

Hearing Lance suddenly gag, Max turned to place a hand on his shoulder while he heaved. Watching the other men move around the area of death, he watched as several others were also relieving themselves of their noonday meal. "You all right, son?" He asked as Lance straightened up.

"No, Sir,...I'm not." He wiped his mouth with his kerchief and looked back at Semple and the Sheriff. "A man didn't do all this, Pop."

"No,...he didn't!" He breathed, looking back at the other men and then at Ben Semple and Tate as they walked toward them. "Don't say anything, Lance." They turned to wait for Tate and Semple.

"What do you think, Maxwell?" Asked Semple, stopping beside them. "This th' work of your deranged killer, come back to even th' score?"

"A man didn't do this, Ben." Gritted Max, looking back at the ground.

"Then what th' fuck did?...I just lost a half dozen a my best brood cows here!"

Max stared at him a moment before taking a deep breath of the death-filled air and looking up to watch the ever growing number of vultures gliding around them. "An animal did this, Ben."

"What?" shouted Semple, moving to take Max's upper arm in his grip. "What kind a animal could do all this, Maxwell?"

Max reached to forcefully remove the rancher's hand from his arm and then to point at the ground in front of them. There in the blood churned red mud was the largest animal track Max had ever seen, and the sight left Semple staring at it in disbelief.

"A three-legged animal did all this, Ben." Added Max as the Rancher straightened up to stare at him. "Come on, I'll show ya." He led Semple a few yards ahead of the others and pointed at the ground again.

"An animal with three legs left in that direction." He nodded to the northwest of them.

"What th' fuck kind a animal leaves a track that damn big, somebody tell me that?" Yelled Semple. "I could set a gallon bucket down in it!" He looked back at Max then. "Do you know, Maxwell Pruett, huh?"

Max watched his fear stricken face a moment longer before shaking his head. "I only know what I see here on th' ground, Ben....It was an animal,... three large tracks on the ground leavin' here in a hurry."

"What kind a animal only has three fuckin' legs, Maxwell, Huh?"

"Settle down, Ben." He soothed. "Ain't no animal I ever heard of born with only three legs, this one must a lost a leg somewhere, that's all."

"But th' size a these tracks, Maxwell, look at 'em, man, thing's got a weigh a ton to leave tracks that deep."

"I don't know what to tell ya, Ben." Said Max. "We'll just have to track th' bastard down and kill it, it's all we can do."

"Kill it, Maxwell?" He blurted, waving his arm at the killing field. "Look at this, can you see us killing that son of a bitch?"

"You got a better plan, Ben?"

Semple breathed deeply of the rancid air, and then shook his head. "No, I don't, Maxwell, sorry for th' outbursts, man....You're right, that's all we can do."

"Have you heard of anywhere else, of any livestock killins', or mutilations?"

"Not till this, no,...and I don't understand it....Big as this fucker is, we should a heard somethin'."

"What did you two figure out?" Asked Tate, coming on to stand beside them. "Sure looks like animal tracks to me,...big son of a bitch, too!"

"That's exactly what it was." Returned Semple.

"Well, then,...appears you won't be havin' a need for a posse, anymore, huntin' animals ain't in my jurisdiction." He turned away and waved at the other posse members. "Let's pack it in, boys." they all quickly headed toward their horses, mounted and rode away.

"I expected nothin' less from that cowardly son of a bitch." growled Semple.

"Yeah," Breathed Max. "It's up to us, I guess....We'll need supplies for a week or so, Ben. If you have a couple a buffalo guns, ya might want a bring them along, too." He turned to survey the bloody ground again.

"Me and Lance is goin' home,...We'll see you back here at sunup tomorrow. I was you, I wouldn't bring more than a half dozen men to do th' huntin', that thing sees a bunch a hunters, it'll dig in somewhere till we stop lookin'."

"Sounds reasonable, Maxwell, count on it,...see you tomorrow....Lets go home, men." He shouted at the milling cowboys. "I want three of ya to stay here, tonight, brad, go with us and bring back supplies." He went on to his horse and mounted, followed by his hands, and rode off toward the main headquarters.

"What are you thinking, Pop?" Breathed Lance as they watched them leave.

"There's only one possible explanation for what happened here, Lance." He surveyed the scene again and shook his head. "But how can that be,... after ten years?"

"You're talkin' about th' alien beast, right, Pop?"

"Oh yeah,...but it can't be,...unless...." He looked at Lance then and shook his head again. "That other Alien killer had a pet as well, Lance,... that's th' only possible explanation....But he must a left it with th' airship, to guard it, maybe. Yeah, that's what he must a done, he was sure Korak was dead, and thinking that his own counterpart was roamin' around th' countryside alone, thought he wouldn't need th' pet to help 'im."

"But you destroyed that airship, Pop."....

"Th' beast must a been outside th' ship, lookin' for food, maybe, I don't know....That has to be it, Lance,...he was far enough away from th' ship to lose only one of his legs in th' explosion."

"That was ten years ago, Pop!"

"I know, Lance....Thing must a been at a loss not havin' that alien to lead it, tell it what to do. I don't know, maybe without that alien, it was afraid to venture out, maybe it held up somewhere all these years, only goin' out to find food when it got hungry. Maybe it lived off th wildlife it could catch, otherwise, just hid out to wait for his alien master to return,...maybe, maybe, maybe!"

"Then if that was th' case, why, all of a sudden, did it do this?"

"That's another question, Son." He sighed. "Let's get th' hell away from this stench." He led the way back through the strewn carcasses, their boots making suction sounds in th' blood soaked earth and grass, mounted and rode at a gallop back through the barbed wire cattle gate, and once more headed back through the giant Pines toward Carbon Creek.

They hardly spoke on the way home, each left with their own horrible thoughts of the pending job ahead of them, until finally dismounting in the barn's open doorway.

"We still have to tell Mom, ya know."

"Yeah," Nodded Max. "No more secrets,...but I'd still feel better if she was down in Golden for th' duration." He sighed deeply as they walked to the house. "After supper, Lance, we'll do it then....My God, Lance, fried chicken, you smell that?"

"Couldn't help, but smell it!" Laughed Lance as they stepped up to the porch and went inside. "We're home, mom!"

They were met at the front door as Helen went, first, into Max's wide open arms, then Lance's.

"Come on in, Gents,...we don't have much time, my husband and son will be home shortly, so make it quick."

"Awww no, not this time," Grinned Max, hanging his gun belt on the peg at the door...."This time, I think we'll wait on 'em, might even take you away from 'im, he can't be all that deservin' anyway, leavin' a looker like you home alone."

"Suit yourself." She laughed. "Got a warn ya though, he one tough hombre." She giggled again. "wash up, chicken's done, potatoes are about done. I fried yesterday's red beans, Mexican style."

"Great God, honey," Gasped Max. "I love ya!"

* * *

Lance wiped his mouth with the table linen and pushed his plate back, sitting quietly then while Max and Helen finished eating.

"Alright now, Mom," He said, a bit sternly, and was enough to get their attention. "Pop has something very important to tell you, Mom, and I don't think it can wait any longer, it's already been ten years. So you two go to the sitting room and get comfortable, Ill bring your coffee on my way out."

"On your way out?" She asked with a frown. "Where are you going?"

"To the barn,...I have to bring in a few things that we'll be showing you, now go, both of ya. Pop has a story to tell you, Mom, and as God is our witness, you had better listen to him." He ushered them both into the sitting room, and left the house as they sat down.

"Maxwell," She said, staring at him with questioning eyes. "What's this all about?"

Sighing, he moved his body to the edge of the homemade double seated lounge and took her hands in his.

"Helen, got somethin' to tell you, and I want you to listen to me without interruption till I'm done!...Ten years ago, September, there was a killer loose in these mountains, if you'll recall, sometime later, I tried to tell you all about it, but you wouldn't listen....Now, you have got to, because it has started all over again. That day, I went to pick up our cows at Ben Semple's place, remember?...Well that night, I was camped in th' trees across from Carbon Creek, when about an hour later th' cattle woke me up.... I grabbed my Henry and went to see about it, thinkin' it was a puma, or somethin'....I was wrong!"

"You're beginning to scare me, Maxwell."

"It should scare you, Helen, because it scared hell out a me!...I'm scared now, too,...and so's Lance, so listen."

CHAPTER ELEVEN

It was close to midnight when Helen placed the kerchief to her mouth and turned away from the video on Korak's scanner. "I've seen enough, Maxwell, my dear God!"

"No, don't get up yet, Helen." Said Max. "Some of what you just saw is happening again, or about to,...Ben Semple's steers were torn to bits yesterday, six of 'em, all prime brood cows. It was a massacre, somethin' like what you just saw on th' scanner there....And we have to hunt th' thing down again and kill it, me and Lance. We'll be meeting Ben and his hands at daybreak to begin th' hunt."

"Dear God, Maxwell!" She sobbed loudly, her breath catching in her throat. "Is that m,...monstrous beast loose again, is that what you're hunting?"

"Yes,...but it's not th' same one, Helen. I told you of the second alien soldier I killed, this beast had to have belonged to him. I don't know where it's been for ten years, but it's here now, and it's angry."

"Well, why do you have to go, why does Lance, that thing will kill you, both of you?"

"Because we know what we're huntin', Helen,...and we have th' only weapons that'll kill it!...Right there!" He said, nodding at the starburst rifle and it's smaller counterpart. "That beast is an alien, Honey, it's not of this world. Our guns won't stop it."

She stared at the weapons for a few seconds before taking the kerchief and wiping her eyes. "Then go do it, Maxwell." She sniffed. "Get it done, and come home....You let anything happen to my son out there, and you'll rue th' day!"

"Then, will you please go back down to Golden till it's over?"

"I will not!,...and if you're not back here in a week with my son, I'm coming to get you."

"Helen!"

"I've said my piece, Maxwell." She returned, and got up from the lounge. "I'll get your supplies."

"Just coffee, Helen,...that's all we'll need."

"What'll you eat?"

He reached into Korak's large utility belt. "These." he said, holding up one of the large wafers. "It's a condensed meal, complete with meat, and vegetables, and quite good, I'll leave this one here for your lunch, try it, you won't believe it."

"That's true, Mom." Said Lance. "You'll be full as a tick."

She cleared her throat. "I'll get your coffee, then....If you're leaving at dawn, you better get some sleep, now go." She trudged off toward the kitchen.

* * *

The pre-dawn mountain sky was overcast with a thin layer dark clouds as they rode out of the trees toward Ben Semple's south pasture before Maxwell suddenly pulled up to stop Lance in the tall, lush prairie grass.

"Th' Starburst rifle covered enough not to be recognized on my back?"

"Yeah, pop, that Indian rifle boot was just th' thing."

"If anyone asks, it's my old spencer rifle."

"Don't worry, Pop, we're covered."

"Good." He reached inside his jacket and pulled out the white flour sack. "Take th' scanner out a them saddlebags, Lance. Turn it on and put it in this sack." He gave him the bag and waited while Lance accomplished the task. "Hang it on th' horn there, Son, you got better ears than me, so listen intently. Anything shows up within a kilometer of us, it'll make a beeping sound....It'll tell us where that thing is, how close it is?"

"It's done, Pop,...how'll I know it's him?"

"Whatever lifeform shows up on it, it'll show th' animal's shape in an orange color on the screen....Don't let Ben, or his hands see you lookin' at it, we have got to keep this whole thing a secret as best we can, th' world's not ready for it."

"And we are?" He asked with a grin.

"Yeah," He nodded. "Just do your best, son."

"How'll you kill it, when th' time comes, everybody there will see ya do it?"

"We get close to this thing, Ill pull out away from th' group somehow.... Play it by ear, Lance, just watch that scanner, that'll be th' key to it all." He gigged his horse into motion and they galloped on toward the cattle gate to Ben Semple's range.

Semple and six of his best hands were sitting saddles and waiting as they arrived, and after greetings all around, Max urged his mount up alongside that of Semple's.

"I know you're an avid hunter, Ben," nodded Max. "But as prominent anthem tracks are, they'll be easy to follow across this meadow a yours."

"I brought Eli Rhodes, he's half Ute and th' best tracker I ever saw."

"Good, we'll all stay behind him, so as not to mess up any sign, at least till we get to more broken terrain. We might need to spread out then....Well, if you're ready, lets get this show on th' road." With Lance on one side and Semple on the other, they followed some several yards behind the tracker as he followed the retreating beast's tracks in the soft mountain soil.

"Guess you know, that son of a bitch now knows where he can get a good meal at." Said Max. "If not your place, he'll hit mine. If it get's hungry again before we locate it, th' damn thing could double back on us to feed again."

"I know." Returned Semple. "Mine's th' likeliest place, though, got ready to eat hindquarters layin' around....I got men comin' to watch for th' thing."

"Good." Nodded Max.

"You ever hear of an animal like this before?"Asked Semple worriedly.

"No,...but I thought about it last night some. When me and that, Mister Korak was huntin' that fella, we ran into a group a utes back in th' mountains, west a here....They said that some animal, they called it Diablo, had attacked them, killin' th' old Chief's wife and several horses before their rifles scared it away."

"Could be th' same one." Nodded Semple. "Eli told me about that, his grandfather still lives with that bunch....Speakin' of which, he's gettin' a bit too far ahead of us to suit me, let's pull up closer to 'im." they urged their horses in closer to the tracker as they were nearing the treelike of majestic Sequoias that blanketed the crest of a deep canyon bordering Semple's holdings, and that's where the Tracker stopped.

"You lose 'im already, Eli?" Inquired Semple as they stopped beside him.

"No, sir." Replied the tracker, and pointed down some twenty feet out, and below them. "Son of a bitch must a jumped from here to that flat boulder yonder, finished it's meal there."

"No good Son of a Bitch!" Shouted Semple, staring angrily at the remains of shredded meat still hanging to a steer's hip bone and leg. "Any sign of that creature from hell?"

"Won't know till I find a way down there, Boss....Won't be easy, but I'll find it, I was up here a few times last year huntin' them calves, so I think I know a way down."

"We'll be close behind ya, Eli, move out." He watched the tracker ride off down the crest of the ridge before turning back to Max.

Not even a fuckin deer could make that jump, Maxwell, not with fifty pounds a beef in it's mouth."

"You're right about that, Ben....Ben, you know your own range, there any natural caves that you know of?...Caves large enough for that thing to hide in?"

"I can think of one, maybe two,...if they're anywhere close to this thing's trail, we'll check 'em out, come on." They followed the direction of the tracker's exit at a slow walk.

The brush littered ground amid the tall Pines was just barely passable for the horse and rider, and after a half hour of enduring the poking of downed and broken branches, to the piercing of five inch thorns adorning great thickets of briars, they came to a broken branch beside a somewhat treacherous looking trail down the almost precarious slope of the canyon wall.

"Guess he went down here," Breathed Semple. "Best lead th' horses down....Dismount boys, we got a walk down." He shouted, then watched as the men dismounted behind him. "Eli must a led his horse down here, Maxwell, but it looks too damn reckless to do so from here, what do you think?"

"I think there ought a be a better way down than this, Ben,...I say we look for it, Eli's gonna have to backtrack up th' canyon anyway, to find them tracks again."

Semple nodded in agreement. "We best walk th' horses anyway." He led the way afoot through the dense undergrowth and giant Pines until at last, found where part of the canyon wall had caved off creating a partial sliding, downward slope toward the deep canyon's floor.

Without hesitation, He led his horse off the canyon's crest and began the sliding descent atop moving shale and shifting dirt to finally make his way to the canyon's floor.

Max was close behind him, followed by Lance and the other men to at last gather amid a large grouping of boulders and splintered trees. "That was an adventure." sighed Max, turning to Lance. "You okay, son?"

"Yes'ir,...now that I've swallowed my heart back down....Must be fifty, sixty yards to th' top there."

"At least." Nodded Max. "Well, Ben,...it's another fifty yards to th' other side there, do we cross, or wait for Eli to find us, it's logical, he'll be comin' this way, if th' tracks do?"

"Damn if I know, Maxwell,...What do you suggest?"

"Well, was me, I'd spread th' men out along th' bottom here and head back to where Eli last saw th' tracks a that thing....We can help 'im out some by lookin' for th' tracks as we go. We find 'em, send a man to find him."

Nodding, Semple gave the order, and with rifles in the crook of their arms, led their animals across the treacherous, uneven canyon floor until they were about evenly distributed apart from each other, and with rifles in hand began to slowly move back toward where the beast had stopped to finish it's meal.

"Ben," Said Max, as they began to move forward. "Them old Utes told me their bullets had no affect on that thing."

"What are you sayin', Maxwell, that we are fightin' a losing battle?"

"Not exactly, Ben,...but if that's th' case, it means it's hide is too thick for a bullet to penetrate."

"Okay, so?"

"That bein' th' case, the only real vulnerable spot on th' son of a bitch, is it's eyes. A bullet in th' eyes hits th' brain, it's got a die then."

"Shit, man!" Stammered Semple. "What else do you know, that I don't, Maxwell?"

"It's been ten years, Ben, what do you expect?" He replied, a little angry.

"No offense, Maxwell, no offense....I don't know how you handled all that manhunt thing back then?"

"I still dream about it, Ben. I couldn't even begin to tell what we went through."

"I can imagine,...okay," He got the attention of the closest man to them and waved him over. Told him him to pass the word to the other men that if the beast was seen, to shoot for the eyes. "Don't even know if I shoot good enough to hit th' bastard's eyes."

"Makes two of us, Ben,...but we'll do it. We don't, we stand to lose everything we got." He began moving forward again, leaving Semple staring at his back.

"Why did you remind me of all that, Maxwell, I said no offense?"

"Thought you'd want a know."

Semple looked across at Lance and shrugged, bringing a smile from him. He nodded and followed his father through the giant rocks and boulders.

The going was slow, and painstaking as the line of hunters picked their way through the debris and fallen timber, and not discounting the large rocks that literally covered the canyon floor. The giant Sequoias had somehow took hold in the canyon's hard packed floor and flourished, though not yet as tall and majestic looking as those on the crest above them, but working on it.

There was not a man of them that had not had to avoid the large Timber Rattlers as they hid beneath the shady side of the giant rocks to cool off. The men could be seen with sticks tossing them aside. It was miraculous that no man, or horse was bitten.

For the better part of an hour, they walked and toiled at the hunt before finally, one of the other hands called out to them and pointed up along the canyon's opposite wall and looking, Semple saw the tracker, horse in tow waving down at them and pointing up toward the opposite crest above them.

"Guess he found it." Said Semple, seeing Max nod in agreement, and began leading his horse in that direction.

Max looked at Lance then, seeing him open the sack to peer at the scanner. Lance shook his head and they followed Semple to the far side of the canyon to gather around the tracker, who had climbed back down to meet them, and the other men.

"Tracks lead up to th' crest up there, Boss." Said Eli, looking up again. "Either crossed over and down th' other side, or went along th' top there somewhere."

"All right," returned Semple, looking up at the crest again. "Go ahead, Eli, back up th' way you were goin'. Stay with those tracks. We'll go back down th' canyon here, I know an easier way out….Leave us a marker if th' trail takes you elsewhere, we get up there, we'll backtrack in your direction."

"Want me to fire a shot, or somethin'?"

"Fucker would know we were huntin' 'im then, man,…No,…break a branch or somethin'….We'll look for it's tracks down here on our way back."

Nodding, Eli led his horse back to the canyon's tall embankment and began climbing back toward the rim.

"Me might never find th' damn thing, Maxwell." Said Semper, as he turned to look back down the canyon's debris filled floor. "This is a big place up here, a thousand places to hide."

"You're right about that, Ben,…but if need be, we'll find a way to bring th' thing to us."

"How?" asked Semple, peering curiously at him.

"You know, as well as I do, how wolves act when they smell meat….Hell, they'll even come to investigate a gunshot, when they hear it."

"And you think this,…creature will do th' same thing, right?"

"Yeah, I do,…it's a hunter, a wild animal." He glanced back at Lance then, who was just hanging the sack back on his saddle and when their eyes met, Lance, once again, shook his head.

"Okay men," Said Semple. "You heard th' plan, let's us backtrack back th' way we came, and keep your eyes open for any sign a that fucker."

Nodding, Max led his horse back to begin walking down the canyon again, and after straining his eyes for the next twenty or so yards for any sign of the large beast, he cast a furtive glance across at Lance, admiring at how tall and strong he had become.

He had wanted desperately to leave him behind to take care of his mother, but neither one would have any part of it. He didn't know what he would do if anything happened to his only son. He also didn't know what he would do if they failed to find the alien hunter. That beast of an animal was the most dangerous creature anyone could ever imagine. Even on three legs, it was capable of wiping out a man's complete way of life. Right now, maybe for the last ten years, the animal had no direction, relying on nothing other than instinct to survive, and doing that by aimlessly roaming the mountains when it became hungry and then returning to it's place of refuge to sleep it off.

It had to be the only one left on earth, he thought, and that being the case, it could not reproduce. He couldn't help but grin then, thinking that, ' if that thing was to breed with a grizzly?', he shook his head, and after another glance at Lance, continued to look for the creature's huge tracks on the tall, grass covered canyon floor.

The partly cloud covered sky was dotted with hundreds of circling crows, emitting a continuous chorus of the song they loved to sing. A Bald Eagle, and several hawks were seen in the tall trees, and on rocks up the side of the canyon, and it made the going easier just watching the majestic hunters.

Still searching the tall grass, having to move it aside to even see the ground at times, they continued to search for the monstrous tracks, and at regular intervals now, having to deal with the growing number of rattlers. It was in one of these instances that Max glanced across at Lance again, seeing him suddenly lift the sack from the saddle to quickly open the scanner.

Dropping his horse's reins, Max hurriedly walked the few yards to stop beside him. "You hear somethin', son?"

"Yes'ir, but it don't appear large enough to be our animal, it's movin' now, too." Max peered at the scanner, seeing the orange feline looking animal moving on the screen.

"Got a be a Puma, Lance, i,...." It was then that the big cat made it's piercing screech of a growl as it leaped from the lower branch of a Sequoia and disappeared in the rocks ahead of them. It was enough, however, to cause panic in both men and horses, as they were suddenly finding themselves fighting to control the terrified animals.

Max had instantly bolted into a trotting run to intercept his own mount as it suddenly whirled and was about run in the opposite direction. Catching the animal's dangling reins, he quickly subdued it, and after a few seconds finally quieted it down.

Lance quickly put the scanner away and watched as some of the other men were just leading their horses back to resume the search for tracks, and breathing deeply of the Pine scented air, led his horse forward again.

The next hundred or so yards was uneventful, and it was at that moment that Ben Semple called out to them and began leading his horse toward an old cave-in along the canyon's West wall, making it a somewhat easier way to climb out of the canyon for them, and the horses.

Max grunted the last several feet to the crest of the canyon and tugging at the reins, finally urged the horse up and onto semi-level ground again. moving off to the side, he joined Semple to wait for the other men to climb out.

"Any sign of your tracker?" He asked as they watched the others reach the top.

"No,...don't think he made it this far, can't see any broken branches.... All right, let's backtrack a little!" He said loudly, and walking beside Maxwell, led the way to try and intercept the tracker.

"I love these mountains, Maxwell,...but they weren't made to walk in, let along ride."

"I agree, Ben....Which way is this cave you know about?"

"Well,...this here tapers off again about fifty yards through th' timber, off yonder." He nodded to their right. Wall drops off again into this same canyon, it circles around back this way a half mile or so further on. It's up and down situation from then on, canyon after canyon, up one side, down another....Th' biggest cave is just a jagged hole in th' canyon's south wall. About a quarter mile down there. If that fucker went back down in th' canyon again, it could be held up in that one."

"Any cover down there?"

"Cover?"

"Yeah, somethin' to get behind, Ben. These rifles'r gonna be like throwin' rocks at this thing, unless somebody gets lucky and hits it in th' eye. That's the only vulnerable spot on this creature.

"Damned if I know, Maxwell, haven't been down there in years. Besides, your lands starts up down there somewhere, and I wouldn't have much reason."

"Can't raise cattle in mountains like these, Ben....Ain't my land, ain't actually yours, we just claim part of it, good place to hunt."

"Yeah, that's about it, I guess....Fucker might decide to head over your way."

"Might,...that's where th' Ute was attacked. Hell of a lot a good folks live over that way, too, Reverend Holt, for one."

"Hold up here, Maxwell." Said Semple as he walked ahead a few more yards. "Somethin' big, and heavy went through here, look at how th' brush and small trees are broken and pushed over....Eli's been here, too." He said, reaching the trackers red bandana from a broken limb. "Well, let's do it." He led his horse off through the debris and broken shrubbery for a long fifty yards or so before coming to the edge of the canyon wall again.

"Can we make it, Ben?"

"Appears Eli did, there's where his horse went down,...you up to it?"

"No sir," Breathed Max. "But, we ain't got much choice in th' matter, do we?" He turned around to look at Lance then. "Stay close to your horse's head, don't let 'er jump, stay clear of her feet and legs, too, you both go down, your mother will kill me."

"Lead off, Pop." He grinned.

"Guess I'm first, Ben." He led the way to the crest and jumped down the foot or so to solid ground, then urged the horse over the edge to wrap his hand tightly in the animal's bridal, holding it's head down as he forced it to follow him down the almost eighty feet of the Northernmost canyon wall to finally lead the skittish animal off to the side in the tall prairie grass and wait for Lance to make it down.

"You okay, son?"

"Yeah, I think so, Pop,...that's scary thing to do."

"I know." He looked up to watch the others for a second, then. "Back on up a few feet, see what's on th' scanner." He watched Lance as he led the horse away then turned back to watch as Ben Semple made the bottom.

"Would not want a do that more'n a dozen times a day."

"No, sir." Agreed Max. He turned to look at the many trees and scattered rocks that surrounded them and sighing, looked back at Lance to see him motion him over. "Be right back, Ben." He said then dropped the horse's reins and quickly walked to where Lance stood behind his horse.

"Don't know if it was him, Pop,...But look," He held the scanner where Max could see the screen. "There's what I think is that tracker and his horse." He pointed at the two orange blobs on the screen."

"I'd say so, what else do you see/"

"Nothing!...No birds, no animals, no nothin', and there should be, what do you make of that?"

"Th' creature's been here, scared th' wildlife away. Which way?"

Lance turned in a half circle, holding the scanner in front of him. "Damn,...just lost 'em, Pop, they just disappeared behind th' Canyon wall off yonder."

"Okay, put that away quick, here comes Ben." He fumbled with the front of his trousers as Semple came around his horse.

"Everything come out all right, Maxwell?" He grinned as he looked the forest of trees over. "Guess we ought a fan out again here, find th' tracks."

"Might ought a." Agreed Max, and after Semple gave the order, began moving up th' canyon, through the waist high prairie grass.

"That was almost too close." He said. "Keep your ears open for that signal, Lance, son of a bitch is close. That Eli, fella ought a slow is ass down a mite, he's got no idea what we're after."

"Okay, Pop." They both began moving down the debris riddled canyon floor, and the going was quite slow at first, having to be wary of the snake population as well as looking for the animal's huge tracks. but it was not long before Semple, himself, called out that he had found what they were looking for.

They mounted their horses at that point and, keeping their attention focussed on the ground before them, moved on at a faster pace toward the bend in the canyon. It was mostly uneventful, save several skittish horses shying away from the large Rattlers as they got to close to the deadly serpents.

They had just neared the bend in the canyon wall when they heard the six unanswered pistol shots, the sounds echoing down the canyon to die out with distance.

"That's Eli, men,...He's in trouble, let's go!" Yelled Semple as they all spurred their mounts toward the canyon's directional change. The yelling scream that followed the shots sent chills down the spine of every man there as they rounded the canyon wall at full gallop.

Slowing their horses to a cautious walk through the scattering of Sequoia, boulders and tall grass, the rounded the bend and stopped, all staring down the canyon to try and spot the huge animal.

Meanwhile, as everyone strained their eyes at the canyon's tall walls, Lance had pulled out the scanner, and motioned his father back to see what he had found.

"It's here, Pop!" He said anxiously. "Not very far, neither."

Max looked at the scanner. "Got a be a cave along that wall there,... you're right, son, that's where it is. Stay with me, come on." They pulled up alongside Semple.

"Where's that cave, Ben?"

"Bout a mile off there, on th' right side." He looked at Max then," Why?"

"That's where it is,...or was....Any sight of your tracker?"

"No,...I sent Red on ahead to se what he could see, here he comes now."

"What'd ya see, Red?" He asked as the hand reined up beside them.

"There's a wide swath a red grass about a quarter mile ahead of us, Boss,...and forgive me for sayin', but it's got a be blood."

"Eli's blood." Breathed Semple." Removing his hat to run his fingers through his own hair. "You see th' beast?"

"Nary a sign."

"Well let's go see." They all moved forward through the tall trees, and it wasn't long before their fears were known to be true. Parts of the tracker's horse lay strewn about the dozen yards of tall grass, and after urging their horses through the foul smelling death scene, they moved ever closer to the cave's entrance. That's where they stopped again, the scene before them causing almost all of them to lean from their saddles and retch. Eli's half eaten torso lay grotesquely crumpled in the tall grass, and as they moved ahead, each man of them cursed the creature vehemently and held their rifle ready to fire as they rode ahead.

They were almost at the cave's large entrance when they discovered the tracker's head and one of his arms, there was still no trace of his legs or other arm. Semple raised his hand to stop them then sat staring at the cave's opening.

"IT's gettin' late, Maxwell." He said, turning to look at him. "It's already dark as hell in that cave, what do you suggest?"

"I say we move over to th' side a this valley, dig in with th' canyon's wall at our backs,...and wait till mornin'"

"That's sound reasoning, I think. Move over to th' canyon's wall men." He shouted. "We'll build a barricade and wait out th' night....it's gettin' late!"

* * *

Semple placed the men in a line behind large rocks, a good ten feet in front of the tall canyon wall, and while they were pulling up bunches of the tall prairie grass and tossing it aside to make room for them to sit, or lie down behind the boulders, Max, Lance and Semple stood with their backs against the rocky bluff and staring out across the expanse of rocks, grass and trees. Lance and Max had picketed the horse while the other men prepared to wait out the night, giving Lance the time to check the scanner for any sign of the creature, and finding nothing, not even any wildlife. They knew that the creature had left the scene and was more than a kilometer away somewhere.

"Hard to figure that thing sneakin' up on Eli that way." Breathed Semple. "Man was almost full blood Ute Indian."

"I don't think it did," Said Max. "I think, when he saw th' thing, it was already too close to run, so he did the only thing he could, draw and fired his weapon....He warned us, Ben, could a saved our skins."

"He was a good man." Nodded Semple. All right," He called out. "You men stay alert, every other one of you stretch out there and get some shut eye, couple three hours, th' rest of ya, and so forth. Right now though, I'd like a couple a you to go back out there and collect what you can of Eli, I want a bury what's left of "im....Rest a you go along, too, to watch for that thing....And don't tarry, it's gettin' late."

"What about his weapons, Boss?" Asked Red, getting to his feet.

"Yeah, bring 'em in if you find them." He watched them all leave and shook his head. "Maxwell,...these men are all like kin a mine, been with me for years,...I don't want a lose any more of 'em."

"Hopefully, you won't, Ben,...we didn't bring any shovels, though, how do you want to bury 'im?"

"Rocks'll have to do, if we find any small enough to handle."

"Me and Lance'll start lookin' for some."

Nodding, Semple watched them leave then turned back to watch the men as they tied bandanas around their lower faces and began walking toward the area where parts of Eli had been seen. Feeling his eyes begin to dampen, he sniffed, reached for his kerchief, and wiped his eyes before blowing his nose. He fought down any more efforts to break down and bawl by taking deep breaths of the Pine scented air. He would miss the Indian tracker. Now, eight men, instead of nine would have to stop this nightmare of an animal,...if that were possible!"

* * *

"It was nearing full dark when they placed the last stone on top of the Tracker's body parts, and they all walked back to their chosen place to do battle, if need be.

"What about a fire, Maxwell,...do we dare make one?"

"Be easier to see th' thing with one....There's thirty yards a grass between us and any trees out there, and it's too big to hide in th' grass,...we got light, we'll see th' bastard."

"How right, you are, lets build a big one, we need some coffee, anyway."

Once the fire was going, Max put coffee in the pot and filled it with water before placing the pot on the flames. That done, he moved back with Lance to sit with their backs to the canyon wall.

"You bring supplies, Maxwell," Asked Semple, coming to look down at them...If not, we brought biscuits and ham to go around?"

"Thank's Ben, we're okay." They watched Semple nod, and then walk back to talk with his men. "Coffee's done." He called back before squatting to pour the dark liquid into his tin cup.

"Be there in a minute, Ben."

He grinned at Lance and reached inside his shirt to open the flap on Korak's utility belt. "Dinner time, son." He grinned again and gave Lance the wafer, and they ate before getting up to go pour their cups full of coffee.

"What do ya think, Maxwell," Asked Semple, placing his cup on the ground. "Think that Devil's still around here, th' cave, maybe?"

"I sort a doubt it, Ben, it would a been on us already....No, what I think likely happened is, that thing was on Eli so quick, and likely attacked his horse first, that bein' th' animal's food source....When it did, Eli must a run a ways, and drew his pistol, after likely dropping his rifle in surprise....He likely knew he didn't have a chance, Ben, and thinking that we were close behind him, did the only thing he could....He emptied his gun at th' thing.

"But it tore him to pieces, too, even ate 'im."

"Bullets made it angry, had to of hurt it some, likely even scared it....It was likely tryin' to protect itself when it attacked Eli, and bein' hungry,..." He shrugged.

"You seem to know an awful lot about this damn thing, Maxwell!" Said Semple. "How is that?"

"I saw what th' thing could do ten years ago, Ben,...Utes told me th' rest. Th' way it acted, th' way it ripped and tore at it's victims. Yeah,...I feel like I know th' son of a bitch!...I just don't know what th' hell it is, or where th' hell it came from!...Now, if you want a blame me with somethin', somehow, come right out with it!"

"No offense, Maxwell,...I'm just so fuckin' scared, and angry right now, that I'm pickin' at straws."

"None taken, Ben,...I know how you feel, I really do....We will kill this thing, I promise you that."

"I know, Maxwell." He got up and walked to the edge of the firelight to stand and stare off into the oncoming darkness.

"This might be a little rougher than I thought, Son,...gonna be hard keepin' everything from 'im."

"We could tell 'im, Pop, make 'im promise to keep it a secret."

"Wouldn't work,...not havin' gone through what I did, not havin' known Korak, not havin' fought th' aliens....No, he would never be able to keep it, why, because it is too damn farfetched for any of it to have happened, and after a time, he would share the most unheard of story he had ever heard, and those he would relate it to, would laugh right along with him….And then, and then, he would involve us, make us th' laughing stock."

"I admire you, Pop, for knowin' people th' way you do."

"Thanks, Son, but I don't know people that well, I just know what would happen, if I was him….I wouldn't believe it neither….Let's go get some rest, Lance, they'll wake us if need be."

"What'll we do if we can't catch up to th' thing, Pop" He sat down and leaned back against the embankment.

"That ain't an option, Lance,…we can't let that thing get over to our part a th' mountain. Your mother's there alone."

"How would we stop it,…we don't even know where it is?"

"I've been thinkin' on that,…we have to bring it to us, find some way whet it's curiosity and at th' same time, it's appetite."

"Well, good luck with that one."

"We don't have a choice, son,…now get some sleep, and keep that scanner close to your head….We best get our jackets out, too, gonna be cool tonight."

*   *   *

dawn found them both curled up in a fetal position, as the overnight temperature had dropped into the mid forty's. Semple woke them up by lightly kicking them with a booted foot.

"Coffee's on, Gents." He said, and moved back to the fire.

"You were right, Pop," Said Lance, turning the light coat's collar up around his ears. "I liked to have froze."

"As you well know, Son,…it ain't cold at all, yet."

"Don't remind me….I can sure use that coffee about now."

"Let's eat breakfast first." He reached in his shirt for the wafers and gave him one.

"I can't get over how good these taste, Pop,…I'm pretty sure Mom's meatloaf was in this one."

"Let's get that coffee, Son." He grinned as they stretched tired limbs and sidled over to join the others.

"How'd you sleep, Maxwell?"

"A mite cold, Ben." He returned, pouring coffee onto Lance's cup, then his own.

"Should a bedded down here closer to th' fire,…Got any ideas on what wc should do today to catch that thing?"

"Well,...I know within reason th' bastard's still in th' area of this canyon, or th' next one over. But it's still here, it knows where it's next meal is."

"Yeah, my Ranch." growled Semple.

"Or mine, Ben,...we both stand to lose if we don't stop that thing....But what I planned to do today, is split up. Me and Lance find a way out a this canyon and travel along th' top, while you continue down th' valley here."

"Is that wise, th' damn thing could be up there already?"

"Don't think so, it fed yesterday, it'll be sleepin' it off somewhere close by. At least, up there on th' rim, we'll have a clear overview a this canyon. We see th' thing, we'll place a well aimed Spencer shell at it, that'll warn you and th' boys, give ya time to set up a firing line."

"That might work, Maxwell, but I'm not all that sure it's th' thing to do....What if it's on th' rim, and not down here."

"Then we find a way down, or try to....Ben, we don't have a hell of a lot a time to corral this thing before it feeds again."

"Okay," He sighed, draining his cup. "You have a point,...Will you at least take one a my men with ya, he might come in handy?"

"I'm sure he would, but no, you'll have th' firing line, you'll be th' one to take it out if we spot it,...and don't hesitate, you might have a tendency to stare at this thing in awe at it's monstrous size,...just aim everything you got at it's eyes and let go."

"Maxwell," He breathed, standing up to stare off at the distant line of trees. "I don't like it a little bit, I want you to know that....But what you say does make some sense, so go ahead....There's another way out a here, th' other side a that stand a Pines off yonder. You can do that after we check out this cave here."

"If he's in that cave, we won't have much of a chance, Ben."

"Guess you're right,...we'll find it's tracks again, they lead into that cave, we'll go from there. They don't, you do your thing, we'll follow th trail on around th' valley floor here."

Once the fire was out and utensils put away, Max and Lance, followed the rest of them toward the large cave opening, but once there, saw no evidence at all of the beast's being there. No blood trail, no foot prints, no nothing and sighing, Semple led his horse around and mounted before turning the animal to face them as they mounted.

"Maxwell, th' way out a this canyon is a wall cave-in and washout, straight across this valley and forward about a quarter mile, ya can't miss it....You see anything from up there, or on th' way there, try and give us advance warnin'"

"That goes without sayin', Ben, watch yourselves down here." He turned his horse, nodded at Lance, and they both urged their mounts to a trot across the waist high prairie grass.

Semple watched them disappear into the trees and turned to his men. "Okay, we'll follow th' tracks on around th' valley here, and watch what ya do, that thing can be on us before we even know it. Any suspicious lookin' mound in th' tall grass, anything at all, we need to know,...thing could be crouched down in th' grass waitin' on us....Let's go, remember, we see it, we dismount and form a firing line, shoot for th' eyes, remember that, shoot for th' eyes." He led the way back to the animal's retreating tracks and followed them at a slow pace along the grass covered, rock infested, canyon floor, each man with rifle in hand and eyes focussed on the terrain ahead of them.

*   *   *

Maxwell led the way through the briar infested trees, trying to avoid the raking, splintered and rotting branches of fallen trees. Each of them wincing and cursing when pricked by six inch thorns, but finally they were out and on the other side where they continued to follow the canyon wall for a distance, until Max pointed to a slanting washout and turned the animals toward it.

After several long minutes of sliding dirt and broken shale, they made the crest of the canyon wall and rode into the trees.

"You okay, son?" He asked, turning in the saddle to look at him.

"Well, I'm here, Pop," He said in return. "Most of me, left some a me on them damn thorns."

"Know what ya mean,...best take a look at that scanner now." He waited while Lance took it from the sack and placed the strap around his neck. "Anything?"

"Got a couple deer, what looks like wild hogs, even some wolves, but none big enough to be that animal."

"Keep close watch on it."...He led the way off through the Sequoias, staying as close to the rim as possible. "You see Ben and th' others on that thing, Son?"

"Yes'ir, all six of 'em." He followed his father on through the giant trees, having to bend in the saddle at times to dodge low lying limbs and before long, fell into a not so likable routine, but above it all, remained alert, knowing that the lives of all concerned could very well rely on him and his father,...and they had the only weapons that could possibly kill the thing.

"Tell me somethin', Pop,...Exactly why are we up here?"

Maxwell stopped his horse, and moving a low branch aside, turned to look back at him. "Because of th' weapons we have, we couldn't very well kill that thing in front a everybody there, th' secret would be out."

"I understand all that, Pop, but can you kill it from this high up, it's a long shot, and you ain't never even fired that gun, but once."

"I thought of all that, Lance, all th' do's and don't's,...but I just can't take th' chance on them finding out th' truth about all this, I just can't!"

"I know you're right, Pop, th' consequences might be a terrible thing. I just hope we can pull it off."

"Makes two of us, Son, come on, keep an eye on that scanner." He led off once again through the trees and brush, and for the next several hours fought the brush and flying insects to finally come to a clearing in the jungle of Sequoias.

Stopping his horse, he dismounted, as did Lance, and both went through the routine of stretching tired, aching limbs before sitting down atop a couple of rocks to stare down into the canyon below them.

"You see 'em, Pop?"

"No, they on your scanner?"

"Can't tell, trees in th' way,...I can see several, what looks like deer movin' around this side a th' trees." He turned the scanner to view what was in front off them. "Nothin' that big, Pop."

"Wish I knew if Ben and crew was ahead of us, or not....I've been in this end a th' canyon before, it can't be more'n a half mile till they'll have to climb out....If that thing's still down there, it's gonna have to show itself soon, it's got a be hungry, too." He got to his feet, and with one last look down into the canyon, turned back to his horse and remounted.

"How much longer we gonna stay up here, Pop?" Lance mounted and waited for Max to answer him." I don't think it's still here."

"We get around that next curve in th' canyon, yonder, we'll hunt us a way down, or wait for Ben to come up,...won't be any reason for them to stay down there if that animal ain't there....At any rate, that scanner'll tell us for sure in another two, three hundred yards."

"Yes, sir." He sighed deeply and followed Max on back into the trees, and for the next two hours endured the unforgiving wilderness of Majestic Sequoias, but then suddenly, the distinct beeping sound emitted the warning from the scanner.

"Hold up, Pop!" He shouted excitedly. "I got somethin'." He pointed the scanner ahead of them, but saw nothing, but when he pointed it down into the valley below them, the large orange-looking blob appeared in almost the center of the screen. "Is that it, Pop?"

"That's it,...but it don't appear to be on a level plain with Ben and th' others, it's higher than them....Come on." They dismounted, then Max pulled the Henry rifle from the boot and led the way to the crumbling edge of the canyon wall. "See if you can pick up Ben and his boys, Lance,...can't see 'em from here?"

"Yes, sir,...they're just coming out a th' trees yonder." He turned the scanner back to see the large animal again. "Pop, that thing's got a be up on th' canyon wall somewhere ahead of them there."

"Can't see it by lookin'." Breathed Max. "Got a be hid pretty good." He gazed back at the scanner for a few seconds. "But th' son of a bitch is for damn sure there, Lance." He continued to watch the scanner, studying the lines that represented the terrain itself in comparison to where the animal was laying in wait. "Ben's gonna ride right into a trap, Lance."

"What can we do, Pop, we can't see it?"

"Maybe not, but I know where it has to be."

"You gonna use th' Starburst?"

"I knowed for sure it would stay still long enough, I would,...th' Starburst would take out half a th' embankment, but if th' thing survived, it would run headlong into Ben." He breached the lever on the Henry rifle. "Here, Son, take th' Henry,...Midway along the embankment down there at th' end a th' canyon, and about fifty feet up is where th' scanner shows th' thing to be....You can't see it, but when you fire th' Henry at that spot, it'll do two things,...warn Ben, and maybe cause that thing to move out before it wants to. It does, and I see it, I'll use th' Starburst."

Lance took the long rifle, raised the rear sight to adjust the distance. "Here goes, Pop,...keep that thing ready." He fired, the explosion ear-piercing loud as it echoed away, but before it died down completely, Lance had levered another round into the chamber and fired again. It took several long seconds for the echoes to fade away as they watched Ben Semple and his men dismount and form their firing line. Able to see the creature now, it took them all by surprise when it went straight up the embankment, instead of attacking. Max had the Starburst rifle primed and on maximum delivery, but he was watching for the animal to leap down to the valley's floor and attack, he wasn't ready for the beast to climb up and over the canyon's rim, and all the while under assault from Semple and his men.

"Son of a bitch!" He cursed loudly, getting to his feet again. "I should a been prepared for that, I knew better!"

"What now?" Asked Lance nervously.

"I don't know,...we follow it, i reckon....I don't want that devil to head off toward th' house, your mother won't have a chance."

"Lets go get it, Pop." Lance put the scanner back around his neck, shoved the Henry back in his father's gun boot and mounted his horse.

"Right with ya, son." He mounted, and with the powerful alien rifle held at ready, they both headed off through the trees in the direction the large animal had scaled over the canyon's western rim.

It took another major part of an hour to reach the area where the beast had made contact with the crest of the canyon, but once there they stopped to look down the canyon's crumbling embankment at Semple and his men, all searching for an easy way to get up to the top.

Dismounting, Maxwell gave Lance the horse's reins. "See anything on that scanner, Son?"

"Yes, sir." He turned the screen around for Max to see. "It's not that far from here, Pop."

"Sin of a bitch,...it's backtracking." He walked to the edge of the canyon, cupped his hands and yelled down at the other men.

"It's comin' around behind ya, Ben!...Dig in right there!"

"What?" Yelled Semple back at him.

Max stood further out to be seen better and waved his left arm out and around. "It's comin' around behind you, dig in right there!" He saw Semple nod and turn to give his men orders, and they all began pulling up brush, and moving large rocks around, one or two of them even began digging holes behind the rocks, with their bare hands.

"Maybe we should a stayed with 'em, Pop." Suggested Lance. "They won't have a chance if that thing attacks 'em down there, they'll have no way to retreat."

"Lance, it has to be this way,...come on, we'll follow that thing's tracks around th' canyon wall, we see it, I'll take it down."

"I hope so, Pop,...Be hard to live with if we let 'em down."

"We won't, son,...Lance, what will be, will be, Son,...we just can not allow th' whole world to know about this, th' people will panic big-time, remember th' werewolf thing? It'll get out a control damn quick....This way, whatever does happen, it'll be over with, life will go on as before, with nobody th' wiser....That's how it has to be."

"In my gut, I know that, Dad, but after what I've seen lately,...makes it hard to think about, that's all."

He reached up to grip lance's leg. "I know, son, it bothers me, too. Let's do it my way, okay?"

"Okay, Pop, I know you're right."

Nodding, he walked out a ways toward the line of trees, and finding the animal's large tracks, came back to mount up again. "It's headed through th' trees, and I was right, it's stayin' close to th' rim a this canyon....Damn thing's a predator, Lance, a hunter, it stalks it's prey." He led off through the trees in pursuit of the alien monster, and the trail was very easy to follow, they just had to stay in the beaten path of broken shrubbery, small trees and splintered branches.

Urging the horses to a faster pace, they continued in pursuit of the beast, and mid afternoon found them where the animal had made it's way down to the canyon's debris littered floor. Urgency and a feeling of impending doom caused them to quickly dismount and lead the skittish horses down the loose shale rock and sliding dirt, as they had all but thrown caution to the wind in their haste to get back to Semple and his men.

It took them a good fifteen minutes to descend to the valley's floor, and once there, used the scanner to try and locate the animal.

"It's somewhere in front of us, Pop, and movin' slow."

They mounted and urged their mounts to a slow walk in the wake of the large animal, both on edge, with caution a nerve ragged event. They were nearing the forest of ancient Sequoias, and not wanting to chance following the beast into the trees, turned their horses back to proceed along the tall wall of the canyon and continued to move in the direction of Semple and his men.

"You still see it, Lance?" Asked Max in a half-whisper.

"Still in th' trees, Pop, movin' awful slow, too,...you think it knows we're here?"

"It's a hunter, Son, you know it does....It don't know what to make of it, is all....It's just as cautious as we are....But it has determined where th' biggest threat is, and that's Semple and his men. Damn thing has a plan, I guess." He laid the starburst rifle across his lap, the barrel pointed directly at the stand of giant trees. He glanced down at the row of lights on the weapon's side panel, making sure the setting was set to vaporize the Devil on contact.

The giant trees became less and less as they neared the end of the canyon until suddenly, there were no trees at all between them and the distant cowboys against the tall embankment. He stopped and turned to scan the trees.

"What's wrong, Pop?"

"We can't go any closer,...we do, they'll all see me when I use th' starburst. I can't allow that to happen."

"Well, let's stop here, you can shoot it when it leaves th' trees to go after Mister Semple....Or when it comes after us."

Max dismounted in the tall grass, as did Lance, and holding tightly to the animals' reins, squatted down against the hard canyon wall, then finally sitting down to watch the trees over the tall prairie grass.

"I think there's somethin' wrong with' th' scanner, I can't see it anymore."

"Can't be," Breathed Max, taking the scanner from him and trying the other settings. "All's fine, maybe th' thing found a hole to lay in, maybe he dug one,...I don't know, Lance, but he's there."

"I hope it attacks soon, this is scaring th' hell out'a me, Pop."

"Well, I've been scared now for more than ten years, Son, ain't had a good night's sleep in that time, neither. "Don't see any wildlife on this thing, neither, Son of a Bitch scared them off, too." He gave back the scanner, lifted the Starburst cannon, flipped up the screen on it to take a look.

"Don't show up on my screen, neither, Lance, it's definitely burrowed up in a low spot in there somewhere." He pulled his old pocket watch and opened the cover.

"It's after four in th' afternoon,...thing's either waitin' for dark, or not planin' to attack Ben before tomorrow....Comes down to it, Lance,...I'll destroy it, and this whole forest a trees there....Like you, I'm sick a th' waitin'"

"Will it do that?"

"What, destroy th' trees there?...Hell yeah, won't be nothin' left, but scorched ground and grass fires. But, I just can't chance that! Like Korak said, our entire way a life would end, not right away, might take a few years,...but it would end. Nobody would believe in anybody, or anything anymore....No more Churches, no more law, people killin' each other over nothin' at all, Burning, rioting, you name it!"

"I know, Pop." Returned Lance quickly. "We'll get it,...But ya' know what?"... He chuckled aloud. "People are killin' each other over nothin' now, get down to it,...might not be a damn bit a difference."

"Yeah,...I know. But we ain't gonna be th' ones to destroy what faith and good will that is out there."

"I agree, Pop,...But ya know what?...You won't have a choice, it that thing decides to attack us first."

"Been thinkin' about that." He shook head and stared toward the far end of the canyon for a minute. "We'll still be okay, if I do....I'll have to lie like hell, but I'll do it!"

"Like how, Pop?"

"I'll deny ever shootin' at th' thing, tell 'em we heard th' ruckus and came runnin',...Ben'll believe me, cause after seein' that thing chargin' at 'em, he'll believe anything."

"If he don't have a heart attack first."

"You're gettin' to be quite humorous, Son,...you just made a funny."

"There any money in it?"

"What, bein' funny?...Evidently there is,...There's people puttin' on funny stage shows and th' like. They call 'em actors, vaudeville, I think."

"What kind a stage shows?...What do they do?"

"They get on stage and dance, sing songs and tell jokes, hell I don't know, read about it in th' Gazette, showed a tintype, too."

"Well, I ain't that funny."

Max reached into his shirt, raised the flap on the utility belt and brought out two wafers. "We ain't had any breakfast yet." He gave him one, and they both leaned back against the hard dirt wall of the canyon and ate their meal.

"It's hard to believe a full course meal is in this little wafer." Sighed Lance, chewing up the last bite and swallowing it.

"Well, there ain't very many of 'em left,...gonna miss 'em, too." He looked up at the sky and at the quickly encroachment of shadows along the canyon walls. "Gonna get dark pretty quick now,...God, I wish that bastard would do somethin'!"

Lance turned the scanner to point back down the valley. "Well, It's either still here, or it went back down th' canyon, Pop,...I ain't showin' nothin' on here, no birds, animals, nothin'!"

"It's got a be still here." Said Max, still staring at the stand of trees.

"Got somethin', Pop!" Whispered Lance. "Just a glimpse of it, before I lost it again, but you're right, th' thing found a hole or somethin', it must a just turned over, or came up for a look around....Wait, there it is again."

"It's gettin' ready to attack." Breathed Max. "Stay ready.

"It's movin' Pop,...goin' straight toward Mister Semple and his men,... it'll be leaving' th' trees in a couple minutes."

Straining his eyes at the line off trees, he held the Starburst cannon ready to fire the moment the creature showed itself, but at the precise moment it did, the air around them seemed to become very thick and hard to breathe, the light of day turned a weird silvery color with even brighter flashes seeming to explode out from it. They could almost feel the hair on their arms and head stand on end, causing Max to tremble and quickly look around the area of waist high grass for the source, and as he allowed the Starburst rifle to waver in his hand, he looked at the enraged alien beast as it emerged from the trees to charge toward the end of the valley, and Ben Semple. But in that instant, the alien animal, the trees, canyon, nothing seemed real to him and still, he couldn't move.

All of this, everything was happening in an instant, and all at once. Yelling in futility, and with no strength to move, he felt a tingling sensation on his skin, heard the crackling static in the electrified air, and looked skyward in time to see the Starfighter de-cloak and fire it's weapon, a long, narrow yellow and orange streak of energy shot from the airship and suddenly the charging beast screamed out it's death song and disintegrated completely right before their eyes. The air instantly cleared, everything became normal, as if nothing had taken place. Quickly, and in awe of what just happened, he looked skyward again to watch the ship slowly turn around just below the thin coating of clouds, cloak itself again and in the blink of an eye shot through the layer of clouds, leaving an almost perfect circle in them, and then the silence.

"I saw it, Pop." Said Lance, excitedly, causing him to turn and look at him. "I saw a space ship, was that like th' one buried at th' bluff?"

"Exactly th' same." He smiled then, and looked back up at the dissolving hole left by the departing airship in the clouds.

"Why was it here, how did they know when to come?"

"Cryoans must a been back in our neighborhood." He said, looking back at him. "They detected it's presence on their scanners, and sent word to Promas....That's got a be how it was, Lance, th' only possible explanation."

"Yeah,...I can't even start to understand what I saw, Pop. Did you see what happened to the air around us, it changed colors?...And th' static, like a bolt a lightening!"

"Yeah, I did,...now listen, son, we are lucky th' horses didn't break loose and run, so let's put all this stuff away, mount up and run like hell toward Ben and his men, and son, this is very important,...We'll tell 'im about th' air, th' static, th' scream we heard, but nothin' else,....We'll ask him what happened?,...Okay?...We don't know anything."

"I got it, Pop,...I know what has to be done."

"I know ya do." They went about quickly putting the alien weapons and scanner away then mounted and spurred the animals into a hard run toward Semple and his men.

Cutting across the area of rocks and waist high grass, they brought the horses to a sliding stop in front of Semple and the others, who were now searching the exact spot where the animal had vanished. They all looked up as he dismounted.

"What happened, Ben?" Shouted Maxwell as he quickly came to confront the dazed and somewhat disorientated Rancher. "What happened with th' air, we heard th' scream, what th' hell happened?" He asked again, clutching Semple's arm. You okay, man?"

Semple gazed at him for a moment before recognizing him, and then sank to his knees in the dirt. "I don't know what happened, exactly," He looked up at the sky then and shrugged. "Lightening struck it, Maxwell, came right out a them thin clouds and struck th' thing dead, we saw it with our own eyes!"

"Come on, Ben,...where's th' body, lightenin' don't make it disappear?"

"Maxwell,...I am tellin' you like it was, man, ask my men, they saw it, too."

Max glanced up at the others and seeing them nod their head in total agreement, sighed and stared back down at Semple. "All right, Ben," He breathed. "I ain't never knowed you to lie, man,...so if you saw a lightenin' bolt do that thing in, that's fine with me. Th' Good Lord works in mysterious ways, I do know that!...I know, too, that nothin' is impossible."

"Thank's, Maxwell,...I'm not crazy, man, we saw that thing disappear right in front of our eyes, it had to be th' lightenin'!...It screamed so fuckin' loud, it hurt my ears!"

"It's over, Ben, think about that, you won't be losin' any more cows....It's best, I think, that you don't tell anybody about any a this, they likely won't believe you anyway. But we know, man,...we know!"

"Damn right, we do, Maxwell!" He said, getting to his feet to look around the area again. "Funny thing, though,...There's nothin' left a that thing, not even burned grass to tell us it happened, lightening leaves burned grass when it strikes,...but there's nothin'!"

"It happened, Ben." Soothed Max. "We can't question what th' good Lord does, it's what it was meant to be."

Semple nodded his head in agreement. "I ain't never been a Church goin' man, Maxwell,...never seemed to have th' time. It weren't that I don't believe, man, because I do....I think I'll find th' time now, though, yeah, I will." He smiled at Max then. "I'm goin' home, Maxwell, See ya in Church."

Printed in the United States
By Bookmasters